'Which is it you want, M
marriage ritual?'

She drew breath to repl
For the first time in her life
up towards the sky, hoping
but all she saw was Winter
down at her.

His eyes seemed unnaturally bright in the darkness. She watched him blink, once, twice; watched his gaze rove over her face, felt it, like a dragonfly's wing, brushing her skin and her hair. Why could he not encircle her with his arms and draw her into him, hold her as if he never wanted to let her go?

'Well, Moon Hawk . . . Which is it that you want?'

A trembling anxiety rippled through her. Dare she say it? Dare she leave her heart open for his knife again?

'I—I want to be loved . . .'

Linda Acaster lives in a coastal town in the East Riding of Yorkshire, her native county. Ever since she can remember, she has been fascinated by the nomadic plains peoples of North America. Over the years she has accumulated a large library of obscure books relating to every part of their daily lives. It is armed with this knowledge, and a profound empathy with a way of life which no longer exists, that her second novel, *A Wife for Winter Man*, has been written.

Her first novel, *Hostage of the Heart*, won the 1986 Netta Muskett Award for New Writers presented by the Romantic Novelists' Association.

A WIFE FOR WINTER MAN

Linda Acaster

MILLS & BOON LIMITED
ETON HOUSE 18–24 PARADISE ROAD
RICHMOND SURREY TW9 1SR

First published in Great Britain 1987
by Mills & Boon Limited

© Linda Acaster 1987

Australian copyright 1987
Philippine copyright 1987

ISBN 0 263 75811 7

Set in 10 on 10 pt Linotron Times
04–0987–82,500

Photoset by Rowland Phototypesetting Limited
Bury St Edmunds, Suffolk
Made and printed in Great Britain by
Cox & Wyman Limited, Reading

HISTORICAL NOTE

THE NATIVE PEOPLES who lived on the plains of North America during the nineteenth century and before have been depicted as nothing more than primitive, war-whooping savages who daubed their faces with paint and wore feathers stuck in bands round their heads, but this was not so.

They were people who lived in close-knit, highly-structured communities. They had well-defined moral and religious ideals. In a word, they were civilised. They were not red; neither were they 'Indians'. They were people; people with loves, and hates, and ambitions, and sorrows. They were like you and me, but in a different place and at a different time.

There are words, phrases and spellings which may need some explanation. The term 'Crow' is the English-American/European form of 'Apsaroke'. They are one and the same people, but would, naturally, refer to themselves as 'Apsaroke'. 'Tipi': this spelling has been used, and not the more English 'tepee', because the former is the more correct, and is the recognised usage on both sides of the Atlantic. 'Buffalo': strictly speaking the American buffalo is, in fact, a bison, but 'buffalo' is the common usage. 'First Maker' is the nearest relevant translation of the Apsaroke name for 'God', and is less absurd than 'Great Spirit'.

A Wife for Winter Man has its setting in the region which is now known as Montana and Wyoming in the United States of America; the date, the late 1840s. For the people, the Apsaroke, whose story this novel conveys, the place is Apsaroke lands; the time, the good years between the coming of the horse and the arrival of land-hungry settlers. Game was plentiful; the creeks ran clear. A man could prove his worth by his military exploits—and a woman, if she wanted, could snare herself a husband . . .

CHAPTER ONE

'. . . BUT OTHER WOMEN of my age have a lover.'

'No man of standing will bring horses to the lodge of a woman who has had lovers. You know this. So do they.'

Moon Hawk stopped scraping the clinging fat from the pegged buffalo hide and sat back on the heels of her moccasins. She eyed her mother irritably. 'At least they are happy. At least they are not ridiculed for still being a maiden.'

Little Face did not falter in the rhythm of her work, nor did she raise her eyes from the skin. 'Who is it who teases you? Other young women? They are jealous. They know what they have let slip through their hands. Is it the young men who tease you? They are showing interest. They see in you the makings of a wife, a woman for whom they would bring horses to the lodge of your father.'

Moon Hawk slapped down her elk-horn scraper, finally losing grip of her rising annoyance. 'Tease me? I would need a love-charm for them even to notice me!'

Her mother sighed and raised her eyes from her work. 'You exaggerate beyond belief. If you stopped scowling, your true beauty would be seen by all men. Your nose is straight, your eyes bright. Your skin is soft, and unmarked by the spotting sickness which killed many during your childhood.'

'I am *small*.' The girl spoke the word like a judgement.

Little Face straightened her bent shoulders and raised her head proudly. 'My lack of height did not deter your father.'

Moon Hawk was about to point out the dissimilarity of their situations when she stopped herself. Bear On The Flat had never taken horses to her mother's lodge. She was not an Apsaroke, but born of their enemies, the Piegan. He had captured her on a raid and carried her back in triumph as his personal property.

Because her mother rarely spoke of her life before being brought to the Apsaroke village, Moon Hawk did not like to mention it, either. On the few occasions that she had, Little Face had merely smiled and said, 'I was happy there. I am happy here.' At times, it was difficult to know what she truly meant.

Moon Hawk dropped her gaze, embarrassed that she should even think of parading her mother's past before her, but, as always, Little Face seemed naturally attuned to her daughter's thoughts.

'It is true,' she admitted, 'your father did not bring horses to my lodge.' A wry smile crossed her face. 'My father and brothers would have scalped him on the spot if he had! But that does not mean that he thinks any less of me. Bear On The Flat has had me as his wife for nineteen winters, come the snows.' She threw her hands up in the air in a show of mock amazement. 'It is almost unknown for an Apsaroke to have a wife for so long. His joking relatives taunt him about it, I know, but he just smiles in return. I have borne him five children, two healthy sons before you, and none of you has ever lacked for love, or anything that a mother can give.'

She paused a moment, a proud and wistful look filling her eyes. 'Your father is of the Fox society. On eight occasions has he abducted a former lover during the wife-stealing ritual—eight occasions—but how many Lumpwood men have stood singing songs outside our lodge wanting me to go with them? None! Not a single one. I have been faithful to Bear On The Flat. I have never made his heart sad. That is why I am still his wife. That is why he will never divorce me. If, when the time comes, you can say the same about *your* husband . . .' She left the rest unsaid, but her meaning was plain enough.

Moon Hawk worked a little, trying to be convinced, but it was difficult.

'He is not the only eligible young man in this village,' Little Face reminded her.

'No,' Moon Hawk admitted—but Winter Man was the one she wanted.

Tall, slim, handsome in features and in dress, Winter

Man had the courage of the cougar and the cunning of the coyote. He, too, was a member of the esteemed Fox warrior society. He had gained a number of battle honours, counting a minor coup on two occasions, once by being the third to touch a living enemy, and the other by being the second to touch a newly-killed enemy without enraging the dead man's ghost; but his most important coup had been gained the previous year in the taking of a gun from a Lakota warrior during a skirmish outside the village. In recognition of the act he was allowed to wear a shirt with hair-lock pendants ranged along the sleeves.

How he had worn that shirt! As she recalled, the only time he had taken it from his back had been during the communal ablutions performed each morning at the creek. Their families shared the same stretch of water. She had often glanced at him, willing him to look her way, but he never had. His initial flush of triumph had passed some time ago, and he did not flaunt the shirt now, except on festive occasions when all the men wore their war honours and proudly told of the actions in which each had been gained. Moon Hawk had dreamed about that shirt. If she had been a female relative—or Winter Man's lover—she would have donated a lock of her own hair to hang upon its sleeves and walked with him when he had worn it to bask in his glory. Because he was a man with war honours, he carried the title of Good Young Man, and was openly praised by his elders at feasts and celebrations. With more coups to his credit, especially a grand coup, he would become a Good Man and lead his own raids against enemies of the Apsaroke people.

There were other things she liked about him, subtle things. He was generous. He owned many fine mounts, and regularly gave one away as a gift to someone less fortunate than himself. He was well skilled, too, in racing horses, wrestling and the intricate dart-through-the-hoop game. With his handsome face and keen sense of dress, he was, in short, the answer to an Apsaroke maiden's prayer. The problem, Moon Hawk acknowledged with an inward groan, was that he knew it and took good advantage of his fortune. He was hardly ever to be seen without some youthful beauty in his arms. What man needed a wife when he had so many lovers?

She attacked the buffalo-skin with such purpose that her mother threw up her hands in dismay.

'Enough! Enough! I will not have this robe damaged for the wishing of a man.'

Moon Hawk hung her head, her dark eyes misting in spite of her efforts to control her despondency. 'I am sorry, Mother. I am unworthy.'

Little Face gazed at her daughter for several moments before returning her attention to the large hide. She stroked its damp surface with her finger-tips, gripping and re-gripping the fleshing tool in her other hand, but she did not attempt to work the skin.

'I—I have not mentioned this,' she began, 'but two days ago I had an enquiry about you from the mother of Skins The Wolf.'

Moon Hawk felt the small hairs prickle on the nape of her neck. 'Skins The Wolf?'

'Yes. He is a member of the Lumpwood warrior society, I believe. He has coups to his name, is young, of a good family . . .'

Moon Hawk did not need to be told of his background. She knew of Skins The Wolf. Often in the company of Winter Man, he had looked at her on more than one occasion. In her mind she could see him now, his steady charcoal eyes burning into her.

'I do not like him,' she said quickly. 'I do not like his smile.'

It was a childish reply, she realised, one that would be cast aside with a derisive flourish of her mother's hand, but how could she put into words what was only a feeling? It was true that Skins The Wolf was of a good family. He was brave. He had gained honours and the respect of older men. He had lovers, of course, as was expected of a man who had gained a war honour, but he was discreet. He did not parade them as Winter Man did his. There was no specific reason for her to feel the way she did about Skins The Wolf, but a look from him made her flesh crawl. She did not like him and could say no more.

Instead of admonishing her daughter, Little Face seemed positively relieved. 'Hearing you say that takes a great weight from my shoulders, for I took it upon my own judgement to refuse the advance.'

Moon Hawk was astonished. 'You did not discuss this with Bear On The Flat?'

Little Face shook her troubled head. 'Your father already knows, I can sense it, but he has said nothing. He will be waiting for me to broach the subject.'

'Will he not be angry with you?'

'He has every reason. I should have consulted him.'

Moon Hawk let the scraper slip from her fingers and stretched out her hand to comfort her mother. 'Why did you do it?'

'I did not wish you to go to Skins The Wolf.'

Moon Hawk shook her head, unable to perceive her mother's concern. 'But I do not wish to go to Skins The Wolf. Father would never force me to marry someone I did not want.'

'You do not understand, Moon Hawk. Your father and the father of Skins The Wolf have always been close. Once, many years ago, when Bear On The Flat was unhorsed during a fight, Fire Club saved his life by riding back and taking him up behind his saddle. Your father has always felt that debt. I was afraid that he might insist on the marriage. I could not take that chance.'

Moon Hawk held her peace. There was more to this than one man risking his life for a friend.

'When your father took me from my people, I was not alone. I was with a clan-sister. She was taken by Fire Club. He did not treat her well, and the first winter we were here she walked out into a blizzard. She preferred death to being with him. Skins The Wolf was very small then, but he has grown, and he has the look of his father.' Her voice faded to a whisper. 'I did not want you to go to him.'

Moon Hawk gazed at her mother, not knowing what to say. Little Face had never spoken of this clan-sister before.

'Even if Bear On The Flat insists, I will not to go Skins The Wolf,' she declared. She straightened her back, more determined than ever. 'It is Winter Man that I want for my husband, and I will have no other.'

Little Face brushed a tear from her cheek and forced herself to raise her head and smile. 'If that is your final decision, we must see that it is brought about, and as soon as is possible, I think.'

Thankful to be able to draw her mother from her haunting memories, Moon Hawk openly guffawed. 'First Maker has touched you with the sun! Winter Man does not know I exist. If you go making advances to his family on my behalf, he will laugh so loudly that we will die of shame.'

Little Face inclined her head in that manner she used when she knew she was about to win a large cache at dice. 'There are many elk for the hunter to take, yet he invariably concentrates on the one that defies him.'

'Defies him? Winter Man does not even see me!'

'Then we must make him see you.'

Moon Hawk felt a tingling expectation begin to climb her spine. 'How?' she whispered.

'There are ways.'

The song was loud and bawdy and sung with gusto. It finished with a high-pitched cry, such as a warrior might exclaim on the taking of a coup, and the singers playfully laid about each other's horses with the long thonging of their riding quirts in an effort to make the animals unseat their riders. Only Frost looked unsteady on his mount, and his companions laughed and jeered at him, making him blush and bluster and blame an imaginary prairie-dog hole beneath the hooves of his pinto.

'What you need,' Skins The Wolf laughed, 'is a woman to teach you how to ride!'

'What he needs,' countered Hillside, 'is a woman to make a man of him!'

Frost blushed deeper still, almost the colour of the vermilion he wore about his eyes, but he would not rise to that particular bait. His friends jeered him once again, all except the tallest. Winter Man slipped a long-fingered hand behind his neck and drew his unbound, blue-black hair behind his broad shoulders. Finely dressed with the grease of a young fawn and smelling of sweetgrass, it surged down his bronzed back as if water from a breached beaver dam. The tips of each thick lock danced about his waist, reaching for the hip-hugging belt which kept his breechclout and leggings in place. Other men glued hair into their own to gain such a length, but Winter Man needed no red-painted balls of pitch in his hair; it was all his own.

He pursed his lips as his gaze swept over his companions. His raven eyes grew wide and bright, and he grinned broadly.

'Tokens!' he cried. 'Tokens!'

Displaying their lovers' tokens was a favourite pastime for young men away from the village, and they quickly drew their horses to a halt and arranged themselves in a tight circle. Winter Man was the first to pull his from his belt, a tasselled otter-skin bag no bigger than his palm, and press it to his heart.

'Given to me in love, I swear, from the beautiful hand of Kills By The Water.'

His statement was met by wide-eyed astonishment. It was Hillside who broke the silence.

'Kills By The . . . She is Butterfly's wife!'

Winter Man looked at him, his face a mask of innocence. 'I did not seek her. I seek no man's wife, you know that.'

Walking Backwards nodded wistfully, 'Oh, yes, we know you do not seek them, but if any smile at you . . . Word will get back to Butterfly, Winter Man, it always does, and he is not noted for his forgiving ways.'

'You are merely jealous!' Winter Man lifted himself on his pad saddle to over-ride their noisy derision. 'Besides, who will tell him? You four are the only ones who know.' He gazed at each of them in turn and watched their smiles fade. The displaying of lovers' tokens while on the trail was, by custom, cloaked in secrecy. Winter Man was almost insinuating that one of them might disclose the knowledge, that there was among them a man lacking in a warrior's honour.

The humour was wrenched away from the moment, and for a while no one said anything; then Hillside forced a chuckle from his lips to alleviate the strain, and hooked up one of the three bone and bead necklaces he wore about his neck.

'Given to me in love,' he avowed, 'from the hand of my beautiful Jay.'

The others groaned, and shook their heads, and smiled good-naturedly. 'If we hear any more about your wife . . .'

Hillside deflected their disparaging remarks with a flick of his wrist. 'One day . . .' he retorted. 'One day you will all find yourselves wives, and then you will know what you have been missing.'

With a flourish, Skins The Wolf lifted a small beaded pouch into the air. 'Given to me with love, I swear, by Mint, so that I might forever smell of the herb which gave her its name.'

Winter Man was fast with a cutting response. 'Because you stink from never washing, you mean!' The others laughed, but Skins The Wolf did not bear the joke well and scowled at him.

Walking Backwards began to wail, making a great point of brushing aside feigned tears. 'No one loves me!'

There were great hoots of laughter. Hillside pushed him playfully in the shoulder with his quirt. 'So, Cherry has had her eyes cleared at last! I salute her! What she ever saw in your ugly face I cannot imagine!'

'Give Winter Man a horse,' one of them interjected. 'Perhaps he can find a blind cousin for you!'

The banter slowly abated. It was Frost's turn to produce a token. The youngest of the group, he did not lack valour in the face of his people's numerous enemies, and had gained himself a minor coup, but to the knowledge of his friends he had never had the courage to tempt a woman to be his lover.

Frost altered his weight in his saddle and leaned on the antler pommel to draw out the moment. His head was bowed slightly, and from beneath hooded eyebrows he anxiously surveyed his companions. Without warning, his hand darted into the food-bag hanging alongside his mount's neck. As if he had just taken a scalp, he punched the air triumphantly. Caught in his fingers was the most beautiful clipped-feather hair ornament, decorated with red and yellow dyed porcupine quills and strings of blue and white trade beads.

'A token!' he cried. 'From Pine Fire, my lover!'

There was a resounding cheer, and with help from Hillside, the ornament was tied into the back of his hair to show it off to its full effect. Brandishing their quirts as if to strike a grand coup on some imagined enemy, they kicked their horses into a gallop and charged abreast across the rolling grasslands.

Winter Man was the first to draw his mount back to a walk, Hillside following soon after. They rode together a while, calling both encouragement and derision to the racers until they could no longer be heard.

'You knew about Pine Fire,' Hillside taunted.

Winter Man nodded, an indulgent smile pulling at his lips. 'She is very friendly with my youngest sister—and my youngest sister talks.' He opened his arms in an expansive gesture. 'Frost is her first, too. It is a good time for them both. I am happy for them.'

Hillside almost choked on his mirth. 'You—who have had so many women to warm your nights—sit astride that horse with eyes as bright as a maiden's on her first courting!'

'Ah! You are an old married man. You have lost your sense of excitement, your sense of challenge!'

The laughter faded from Hillside's sunburnt features and he gazed at his friend through narrowing eyes. 'And what was that challenge you laid at our feet? You spoke as if we had the honour of Piegan dogs. Your joke was not appreciated, Winter Man.'

'It was no joke. Remember Squirrel?'

Hillside remembered Squirrel. Like so many women, she had been a former lover of Winter Man.

'She came to me only the once, during the berry-picking. She was unhappy. Marks The Trail and she were not sitting well together. She wanted a little understanding.' He shrugged. 'She was not looking for my embraces, neither was I for hers: it simply happened.'

His voice took on a harder edge. 'But someone told Marks The Trail—told him that I had been her constant lover since the day of their marriage. He took her out of the village where her family could not see and interfere, and he beat her until she could hardly stand!' His anger whistled free between his clenched teeth. 'I heard of it later from one of her clan-sisters who thought I had been boasting of my seduction. I went to Marks The Trail and gave him the truth.'

'Did he believe you?'

'Not until I offered him one of my best horses and swore upon his pipe.'

Hillside shook his head. 'I cannot say I am surprised. You do have a reputation with women. I wondered why Marks The Trail had left the village to join another band. Is Squirrel still with him?'

'She considered her punishment deserved and would not return to her father's lodge.'

'It has left you with a sick taste, I can see.'

Winter Man turned hard, uncompromising eyes on him. 'It was done for spite, pure and simple.'

'But to whom? Not necessarily you, my friend. It could have been done to spite Marks The Trail, even Squirrel herself. You cannot be sure.'

Winter Man did not reply. He gazed out across the grasslands towards the dark band of trees which marked the foothills of the Shining Mountains.

'What I cannot understand,' Hillside continued, 'is this pain that still rages in your heart, yet you have just placed Kills By The Water in the same position.'

Winter Man snorted his contempt. 'Kills By The Water is a different woman altogether. She makes free with every man she can lay her hands on! You would think she was gathering a conquest bundle to outmatch a Hidatsa's.'

'But it might happen. Butterfly is a jealous man.'

'And if it does, then I will know that I am the one who is the target for someone's spite.' His eyes searched out their distant companions. 'And I will have narrowed the possibilities considerably.'

The coldness of his tone made Hillside feel

uncomfortable. 'That does not say much for me,' he murmured.

Winter Man turned and slapped him on the shoulder. 'Not you, Hillside! You are as much my brother as if the same woman had suckled us.' He smiled broadly, but the smile did not reach his eyes, and when Hillside's expression failed to change, his smile slipped away completely.

'It is difficult,' he said. 'We are all strong-hearted Apsaroke, living our lives to the full, knowing that we will probably die young, hoping that we will die courageously. Our warriors are outnumbered many times, by Lakota, by Piegan, Shoshone . . . The list goes on. I would give my life for any one of our people, Hillside, and I have always believed that others felt as I do. To think that one might not sears the shadow of my soul.'

'Grave words. They would well suit the respected leader of a band. If anyone else had heard them coming from your lips they would have thought themselves touched by First Maker!'

Winter Man tossed back his long hair, and laughed. 'I should have known! I speak to you of my feelings and all you can do is make jokes.'

'I do not joke. In a few more years, when you have tried every woman there is to try, and finally got yourself a wife . . .'

Winter Man cut him short. 'A *wife!* You sound like a blackbird that can sing only one song! What do I want with a wife?'

Hillside lifted his head and gave him a look powerful enough to wither the grass. 'The question is,' he retorted, 'what woman would possibly want you as a husband!'

Moon Hawk repeatedly prodded the ground with her digging-stick, desperate to keep her mind on her chore. As a woman, collecting roots to supplement her family's meat-dependent diet was one of the many tasks she undertook, but because it was always dangerous to be so far from the village, women went on these forays as a group, for company as well as safety.

The day had been long, and hot for so late in the autumn. The women with Moon Hawk talked and sang as they worked, stopping every once in a while to pick herbs, play dice or simply to laze beneath the sun. Outriders had accompanied them to keep open a wary eye, but root-digging was women's work and the young men stayed at a distance, talking and laughing and singing among themselves. Such an expedition was not unusual and raised no speculations. Only Moon Hawk, Little Face and a few selected clan-grandmothers knew it had been organised with precision simply to intercept Winter Man on his return from a hunting trip.

Moon Hawk felt the tight clasp of her mother's hand upon her shoulder.

'The outriders have given the signal for approaching men,' she said briskly. 'Winter Man is on his way.'

'It might be Lakota warriors,' Moon Hawk offered, hard put, in her moment of nervousness, to decide which would be the worse.

'Nonsense! Even a child knows the difference between a hunting party and enemy raiders.' She pulled the red-painted yoke of her daughter's dress further on to her shoulders, making its bright shell ornamentation tinkle and dance against the elk-skin. A quick eye checked the blue and white beaded belt about her daughter's slim waist, and the subtly decorated leggings and moccasins peeping beneath her calf-length dress. She brushed a suggestion of dust from Moon Hawk's cheek.

'I should have painted your eyes a darker vermilion, I think, and added a little more to your cheeks.' She stood back and looked at her daughter's face. 'Perhaps not. After all, this is supposed to be a chance meeting, not a feast. Is it clear what you have to do?'

Moon Hawk nodded. Her teeth were chattering so much she dared not risk saying a word.

'And smile! Be confident! A faint heart does not win a man his coups and neither does it win a woman her man.'

A grandmother called a warning, drawing Little Face's attention, and Moon Hawk slipped away to her appointed place.

The grandmothers had instigated a little horse-play between the younger women and the outriders, who needed short encouragement to come down off their hill once they knew what was happening. No occasion for flirting was overlooked by men of their youth. The young people ranged themselves in two lines facing each other, the women with their roots piled at their feet for missiles. The ribald banter began, growing to almost a raucous harangue before the bravest young man attempted to cross the ground to take a kiss from the woman of his choice. He was met by a hail of small nobbly turnips, as were the rest, and then, amid thunderous shrieks and laughter, it was every man for himself. Into the midst of this rode the hunters.

Moon Hawk recognised Winter Man at once and her heart turned to jelly. What if he were angry? What if he called her a stupid little girl? What if he rode away without saying anything at all?

She let her eyes run over the others who rode with him. There was Hillside, Frost, Skins The Wolf and Walking Backwards. Between them they had had a good hunt, for a butchered elk and two big-horn sheep were lashed to a travois being dragged by a loose horse, and each rider had a small antelope slung over his mount's neck.

The hunters drew their horses to a standstill and looked on at the antics of their more youthful cousins with a mixture of amusement and disdain. Men who had counted coup did not begrime their prestige by entering into such games, but they all remembered when they had.

Moon Hawk had eyes only for Winter Man. He flanked the group, a mercy she gave thanks to First Maker for. She had no idea what she would have done if he had been surrounded by his friends. Despite being away from the village for more than four days, his raven-black hair was as immaculately dressed as ever she had seen it, its length almost touching his horse's rump, the quiff above his brow erect and as whitened as a swan's tail. His leggings were stained with mud and water to the knee, speaking much of his industry on the hunt. No shirt stopped the sun from shining on the bronzed skin of his back, and only a looped necklace of tiny bone discs adorned his well-developed chest. Moon Hawk's eyes traced the slight shadow of each rib beneath his muscled arm, and followed the expanse of firm flesh down past his breechclout belt to his powerful thigh. Just looking at him brought a thrill of expectation.

Moon Hawk put such thoughts from her mind and drew a determined breath. If she did not act now . . . She pulled back her arm and threw her chosen missile with accuracy. A small, shrivelled turnip caught Winter Man full on the base of the neck. Such a well-balanced rider needed more to unhorse him, but the blow made him lurch to such an extent that his horse shied. Regaining control, he swung round on his attacker, astonishment sharpening his high cheekbones and widening his eyes.

'Did you throw that?'

Moon Hawk swallowed her fear and lifted her chin haughtily. 'I did not mean to hit you,' she said. 'My throw was wild.'

'Wild? No woman's throw can be that wild!'

Moon Hawk flashed her eyes at him to give her words more vehemence. 'I slipped,' she said. She pointed behind her to some imaginary obstacle in the grass. 'Do you think I would waste a hit on *you*?'

She glanced across to the young people disporting themselves in the sunshine. As she knew he would, Winter Man followed her gaze. She looked back at him in time to see his face registering utter disbelief that any young woman would prefer someone of no account to him.

'I am Winter Man!' he bellowed indignantly. 'I am a Good Young Man.'

Moon Hawk gave a casual shrug of her shoulders. 'I know that.'

Her reply seemed to cut him to the quick. She took a step towards her friends.

'Ha!' Winter Man spat after her. 'Your lover seems to have deserted you. No *boy* waits for you that I can see.'

Moon Hawk's heart sang. He had drawn on the bait as

her mother had said he would. She quickly swallowed her smile of excitement and turned back to him with a look of disdain.

'Lover? *Lover?* I have no lover! I am chaste. There is not a man alive who can entice *me.*'

Before he could respond, she turned on her heel and strode off into the throng of kissing youngsters.

The temptation to turn and see if he was still watching her was great, but one she managed to ignore. She picked up her root-bag and pushed a few discarded turnips into it before sauntering over to where her mother was sitting with the older women.

Little Face, for all her easy stance, was as breathless as herself. 'You did it! You did it! Do not look back, now. I guarantee that he will be outside our lodge within a few days; then we shall put the second part of our plan into action.'

Her clan-grandmothers laughed and joked and pushed at one another, remembering with pleasure their own courting days and how they had led the young men a dance. Only Little Face had eyes for the departing hunters, but as she watched them laugh and taunt Winter Man, her smile faded and her lips turned to a thin line of concern.

'What is it?' Moon Hawk asked.

The smile again in place, her eyes darted back to her daughter. 'Nothing,' Little Face insisted. 'Everything went well. Did I not say it would? No man of his reputation could possibly resist such a challenge. His friends would laugh him to the peaks of the Shining Mountains and back!'

Moon Hawk smiled as her mother curled a protective arm about her shoulders and ushered her back into the welcoming throng of her relatives, but, deep within, her heart did not beat with the same fervour that it had. She wanted Winter Man for her husband, had always wanted him, but was this the best way of gaining what she sought? It was not altogether honourable.

CHAPTER TWO

MOON HAWK SPENT three anxious days watching for a sign of Winter Man, praying that he would show himself, fearing to turn round in case he stood there, looking at her.

'He will do nothing so obvious,' Little Face told her. 'He is a man, not a gawky youth. First he will make enquiries about you, and then he will watch you, but you will not see him until he wants you to.'

Moon Hawk tensed. 'You mean, he could be watching me at this very moment?' All along her back her flesh pricked and rose as if a hundred pair of eyes were burning into her. She did not know which way to look.

Little Face chuckled with amusement. 'Did you think he would sit outside our lodge and play a courting flute for you? That you would be able to walk over to him and take his hand in yours? Did you think gaining Winter Man for a husband would be so easy?'

Moon Hawk averted her eyes. She had not thought it would be easy at all, but, in truth, she had not contemplated the difficulties, either. When her mother had offered her a chance of gaining her heart's desire, she had jumped at it without noting how far that prize lay beyond her reach, or how far she might fall if she failed.

She set her jaw and raised her head. She would not fail. She was the woman for Winter Man—and she would make him see it if it was the last thing she did!

'I am hungry.' Bobtailed Cat knitted his brow and turned his face up to his elder sister towering so far above him. 'I am hungry,' he repeated.

The heat had slipped from the land and the sky was paling ready for the onset of twilight. Moon Hawk eased the tumpline which secured the bundle of firewood against her back, and offered him her free hand.

'Come. Mother will have a fine stew boiling on the fire and there will be roasted turnips if you are good.'

'I am always good!'

On their way back to the village, Moon Hawk spied a number of sticks dropped by another returning with firewood.

'Can you hand me those?'

'I am a man!' Bobtailed Cat retorted indignantly. 'I do not collect wood for fires. Do you want my friends to laugh at me?'

Moon Hawk altered the weight of the load upon her back and carefully bent low enough to pick up the sticks herself. 'You will have to fetch firewood when you go on your first raid, and water, too, or the Good Young Men who take you will chase you back to the village and sing derisory songs about you outside our father's lodge.'

Bobtailed Cat hung his little head, and muttered to himself, 'I am not a woman!'

Moon Hawk smiled indulgently at him. The years slipped by so quickly. Already he was acutely aware of what was expected of him. Soon he would be bringing a rabbit to the lodge, triumphant in his first kill. It would be a buffalo calf next, and then . . . She sighed. In no time at all he would be riding with the men. Would she be a wife then? Winter Man's wife? A chuckle of irony burned away any disturbing doubts. She would have young sons of her own by that time, and she would be telling them that collecting firewood was no work for a man!

Just outside the outer edge of the village another encampment had sprang up, and though the tipis were much smaller and far fewer in number, it was the same in most respects. Older girls were cooking over small fires, pretending to be wives and mothers. Some had little cradleboards upon their backs, and carried dolls made from deer-skin stuffed with buffalo hair. Others trailed younger siblings with them, claiming them to be their offspring. One girl even had her pony picketed by her half-size lodge and was proudly showing the rest that she was more than capable of handling a horse-travois, the large triangular drag-frame a woman used to transport her family's belongings. Not to be outshone, other girls had made themselves smaller versions to be harnessed to the wolf-like dogs which roamed the village.

Bobtailed Cat pulled back on Moon Hawk's arm. 'We are not going over to them, are we?'

'Your sister may well be hungry, too.'

Bobtailed Cat curled his lip. 'She will want me to be her son again.'

'I do not think so. It is too late in the day.'

Turtle saw them approach and ran to meet them. 'Look!' she called, waving a long stick on which were skewered several pieces of meat. 'Snow Rattle brought these for me to cook for him. I am his lover!'

Moon Hawk noticed her sister's beaming face and decided not to be too harsh in her reprimand. 'It is better that you be a chaste woman when you grow. You will gain much respect.'

Turtle shrugged her shoulders. 'It is more fun having a lover. I can ride on the back of Snow Rattle's pony when the boys have a victory parade.' Her expression became more serious, Snow Rattle and his pony forgotten. 'Do you think father will give me another pony to replace the one the Shoshone stole?'

'I do not see why not. If you help mother, and you do as our father wants the first time of asking, you will show that you are worth being given another pony.'

Turtle nodded, deep in her thoughts. Angrily, she kicked at a clump of withered grass. 'I *hate* those Bad Lodges! Stealing my pony . . .'

'Yours was not the only horse stolen,' Moon Hawk reminded her.

'I do not care! I would dance with their scalps if one was given to me!'

Moon Hawk raised a disparaging eyebrow. 'You are hardly likely to be offered a scalp just because your horse was stolen; besides, no one was killed in the raid, so I doubt the Good Young Men will be riding for scalps in any case.'

'I will not be offered one of the horses they bring back, either,' the girl muttered sullenly.

'I have told you, if you are good, father will give you

another. We are returning to the tipi to eat. Are you coming?'

Turtle shook her head and moodily stalked away, trailing the skewered meat behind her.

'No man will take her as a lover,' Bobtailed Cat said. 'She grumbles too much.'

Moon Hawk laughed out loud and took his hand in hers again. There were times when her youngest brother talked so much older than his years.

Winter Man! It was Winter Man. There was no mistake. He was sitting astride his dappled grey racer in the space between the two villages. He had come. He had *come*!

She drank in the sight of him as if he was the only sweet water in the vastness of a salt desert. How imposing he looked, dressed in his warrior society regalia. She had seen him in it before on many occasions, but this time, she knew, he was wearing it for her. There was a dignity in his bearing, in the way he carried the russet fox-skin cape over his broad shoulders. His leggings, too, were not of the usual elk-skin, but were made from scarlet cloth expensively bartered from the hairy-faced traders to the north. Across his back was slung the finest otter-skin bow-case any man possessed, and cradled in his arms was a cut-down musket, a single black-tipped eagle feather fluttering from the end of its shortened barrel. He was showing her his possessions, that he lacked for nothing, that he was a man who had the courage to take whatever he wanted; that he could—and would—take her if he so wished.

The racer lifted its forelegs in turn, tired of remaining so still. Winter Man calmed it with the lightest touch of his antler riding quirt, but it had altered its stance enough for Moon Hawk to see more of Winter Man's face. He had been painted vermilion and yellow; his arms, too, banded in the same favoured colours of the Fox society. Like an angry thunderhead, his dark hair spread out behind him, the sun glinting off each oiled lock as if feathers in a raven's wing. And there she was with twigs in her wind-blown hair and a great bundle of sticks upon her back! Oh, why come now? Why now!

Bobtailed Cat pulled on her arm. 'Are we going?'

Moon Hawk felt a trembling in her legs. She would have to walk by Winter Man. What should she say? How should she act? Her stomach tied itself in a hundred knots. If there had been another way to go she would have taken it, but, of course, there was no other way. That was the reason he was there. That was the reason he had chosen the moment, the only moment of the day when she was tired and dishevelled. Her indignation began to mount—and then she realised something else. He was not looking at her. He would not look at her, he would not even speak to her as she passed him. He was parading himself for the prized catch that he knew he was. The conceit of the man! Flaunting himself before her so that he could watch her drool over him. She would show him! She would walk straight by him and not even notice his *horse*!

She tightly clutched her brother's hand and headed towards the gap between the two nearest tipis where Winter Man and his grey racer stood as still as wooden carvings.

'And what have you been doing all day?' she asked of Bobtailed Cat in a loud voice.

He answered her, but she heard no more than a low murmur in the background of her noisy thoughts. Winter Man had painted his horse with his war honours so that she might be reminded that he was a man of valour. She could see hoofprints painted in red in an arc on its shoulder, telling of the many successful horse raids he had been a party to. There were black lines signifying the secondary coups he had gained, and red dots to indicate the number of times he had been wounded during engagements.

She was close to him now, not four paces away, and still his eyes had not so much as flickered in her direction. Curse the man!

'And have you enjoyed yourself?' she asked her brother.

What was that smell? Could it be . . . It was! Winter Man had rubbed himself with some mixture of herbs, the way lovers did, so sure of himself was he. She put a spring into her step and raised her chin a little higher as she drew level and passed him.

Bobtailed Cat slowed, pulling on her arm, and turned to look at the adorned warrior, his little face full of questions.

Do not say a word! Moon Hawk pleaded. Not now, please!

'Why is Winter Man sitting there like that?'

Moon Hawk felt her heart turn over. If she did not answer him he would make a fuss, but whatever she said would be heard by Winter Man. She pulled her wits about her and tried to make the tone of her voice sound as cutting as possible. 'Who?'

Bobtailed Cat pulled hard on her arm and pointed behind them. 'Winter Man!'

There was no other course now, Moon Hawk realised. She would have to acknowledge that she had seen him. Slowly, she turned round and looked behind her. As she had expected, his eyes were not on her, but she made a great display of looking him up and down, just in case he could see her out of the corner of his eye. She curled her arm about her brother's shoulders and began to lead him away. 'I really have no idea,' she told him loudly. 'Perhaps he is hoping to entice some man's wife. I hear it is a favourite pastime of his.'

The sound of the snort was unmistakable, and to Moon Hawk's practised ears it did not sound as if it came from Winter Man's horse. She did not look back, though, but kept walking, a smile of victory basking on her face. She might have instigated this odd courtship, but Winter Man was going to have to fight harder than that to take her!

She saw him again on each of the two following days. His approach was more measured, more subtle. The first time he was standing outside a neighbour's lodge discussing the relative merits of different saddle girths; the second he was washing down one of his notched-eared buffalo-horses in the creek when she went to refill the water-paunch. He did not look towards her on either occasion, and she did not look at him, but she knew he was only there because of her, and it filled the rest of her day with song.

'How long do you think this will go on?' she asked Little Face.

The older woman shrugged. 'It is hard to say. Until he tires of it, I suppose.'

'Tires of it!' Moon Hawk was beside herself. 'You mean, until he loses interest?'

'Oh, there is no chance of that. You threw him a challenge in front of his friends. Even if he wanted to ignore you they would not let him. You know what men are like. They make up the most derisive songs about each other for the most insignificant of causes. It is his reputation as a wooer of women which is being put to the test here. If it should be seen to fail him . . .' Little Face chuckled to herself. 'The longer you can keep him at arm's length, the more chance you have of keeping him for good. You must give him no encouragement—not any.'

Moon Hawk felt a twinge of despondency. Winter Man was being heedful of her only because of a dare. She had known it from the start, but it seemed harsh put so blatantly, so bound to failure. She carried on waiting, seeing him each day and ignoring his presence, until something happened which made her feel the sky had fallen in on her world.

She ducked into the lodge, almost tripping over the raised threshold in her hurry to be inside. Little Face looked up from the porcupine-quill embroidery she was working on.

'He is out there,' Moon Hawk stammered, 'sitting under a sunshade with Swallow in his arms. They are laughing and talking and . . . and he is kissing her and . . .'

'You should not have even seen them. If you have carried on like this in front of Winter Man's eyes, you will have lost everything. He is wily. This is a test to see how you will react.'

Moon Hawk let her gaze fall in her despair. Swallow. She was tall and lithe and beautiful. And she was lying in Winter Man's arms.

Moon Hawk watched her mother cross to the doorway

and lift the flap to peep outside. Little Face turned back to her, her eyes alight with excitement.

'Two can play at this game! Grind meat ready for making into pemmican for the winter. Work diligently outside the lodge under our sunshade and be most courteous to all who come to speak with you. Remember that.' Before her daughter could ask any questions, Little Face stepped out of the lodge.

Moon Hawk collected the items she would need from behind her mother's back-rest, and with a deep breath to steel herself, slipped out of the low opening of the tipi. Winter Man was still sitting under that same sunshade with Swallow. They had been joined by Hillside and his wife, and all four of them were laughing together and eating choke-cherry rounds. Moon Hawk studiously ignored them and set out the utensils of her labour beneath her own lodge's sunshade. She laid a piece of dried buffalo meat on the flat stone pounding-dish and started hammering at it with the maul until it crumbled. Tipping the pulverised meat into the centre of a clean skin, she began her work again. Laughter drifted to her across the heat-haze; the deep, gusty laughter of the men, of Winter Man. Moon Hawk did not look up, but try as she might, she could not ignore it.

A shadow crossed her hands and she raised her eyes to find one of her more elderly clan-grandmothers standing there, kneading her thigh with the heel of her palm. From the other hand dangled an empty water-paunch.

'Moon Hawk,' the old woman said in a loud voice, 'the young girls have gone swimming and left no water in the lodge. They have no mind for their duties. My leg pains me. Would you stop your work and fetch water for your grandmother?'

Moon Hawk stared first at the old woman's odd stance and then at her tired and care-worn face. She had seen her grandmother not half a day ago, cursing ferociously and running after a dog which had stolen a length of the sausages she had been making. What could she possibly have done to her leg in so short a time? She was about to ask when her perception suddenly cleared. There was

nothing wrong with the woman's leg, nothing wrong
with it at all.

Moon Hawk rose to her feet, her face full of concern.
'Of course, grandmother. You look tired. Rest here
awhile. I will bring you a fan to cool yourself.' She
helped the old woman to lower herself on to the robe she
had made her seat, and ducked into the lodge to retrieve
her own hawk-wing fan.

'Here, grandmother,' she said. 'I will be but a short
while.'

'You are a good grandchild, Moon Hawk. Many look
with favour upon you. You never desert your work.'

The old woman's voice boomed out far beyond the
reach of her own ears. Winter Man would have had to
have been deaf not to have heard every word. Moon
Hawk skipped down to the stream, unashamedly
laughing all the way.

She had no sooner settled herself back to grinding the
buffalo meat than Turtle arrived at her side. The young
girl thrust a boy-doll purposefully beneath her sister's
nose.

'Hail In His Eyes has been on a horse-raid and has
counted a grand coup on a Lakota warrior,' she
announced loudly. 'But I have nothing to blacken his
face with in honour of the deed.'

Moon Hawk suppressed a smile, and with an expressionless face told her sister that she would find
something. She brought out a piece of charred wood
from the lodge's fire-pit and offered it to Turtle.

'You do it,' she ordered, and offered the doll to Moon
Hawk's hands. Moon Hawk blackened all of his face as
any returning warrior would to announce that he had
taken the coup, and handed the doll back.

Turtle looked at her sister's handiwork and nodded
her approval. 'We should salute him for his bravery,' she
said in earnest.

'Of course we should,' Moon Hawk agreed, and the
pair threw back their heads and trilled loudly for the doll
in the way any woman would for a man who had risked
his life in the gaining of a coup.

As Turtle ran back to her friends, Moon Hawk risked

a glance in the direction of the other sunshade. Swallow was talking gaily, but, by the look on his face, Winter Man had no ears for what she was saying. Caught by a streak of sunshine flooding through a gap in the cut boughs above his head, his eyes were narrowed against the glare, his steady gaze only for Moon Hawk.

She turned quickly, picking up the maul to continue with her work. She hoped that he had not noticed her glance, but her heart sang just the same. She would win him. She knew, now, that she would win him in the end.

'He is not there again,' Moon Hawk stated emphatically as she entered the lodge. 'Three days have . . .'

She caught her mother's agitated movement and her eyes flicked over the low-burning fire to the semi-prostrate figure of Bear On The Flat. Her father's head was inclined to one side in a doze. A good ten years older than Little Face, his body was still firm of muscle, his eye quick and keen. Although a member of the esteemed Fox warrior society, he was more renowned as a fearless hunter than an adventurous warrior. He had gained five coups in his life, including taking a picketed horse from inside an enemy village, but these honours had not been enough to elevate him beyond being a Good Young Man and he had never led a raiding party in his own right. Exactly how much he knew of his women's plan to bring about her marriage to Winter Man, she was not sure. Little Face had soothed his affronted authority as head of the lodge over her refusal of the marriage enquiry from the family of Skins The Wolf, but she had not told him of their blatant manipulation of Winter Man. Such a course of action was not considered at all proper, and Bear On The Flat, had he been directly told of it, would have had no alternative other than to call a halt to it.

Moon Hawk eyed the reclining form of her father. He had not been in the lodge when she had left to refill the water-paunch, slipping out to a meeting of his clan-brothers after the family's large evening meal. She had not expected him back so soon. Turtle and Bobtailed Cat were playing together close to his feet and were making more noise than warriors in a victory parade without any disturbance to him. He could not possibly have heard her own words.

'He is asleep,' Moon Hawk hissed.

Her mother's grimace bade her be quiet. She was not so certain.

'I have told you about going out on your own,' Little Face whispered. 'You must be chaperoned at all times. It is imperative, now, that there must not be a hint of gossip about your character.'

Moon Hawk rolled her eyes, tired of her mother's constant remonstrations, but the words she heard came from another in a deep, baritone voice.

'It has always pleased me that my eldest daughter is strong in limb and pleasant of features. It pleases me even more to know that she is chaste like her mother. I would be the proudest man alive if she were to marry well, but I would warn the two of you to step warily. The land you tread has more quicksand than you think.'

With an affected snort and a trembling exhalation, Bear On The Flat resumed his doze, if ever he had truly been asleep. Moon Hawk and Little Face exchanged an astonished look and then suffocated a shared giggle. It was impossible for Bear On The Flat to give his blessing to their scheme, but at least they knew he was not going to reproach them from it.

Little Face began her monthly flow the next day and left the family tipi to take up residence in the small women's lodge used for such occasions. Late that night, in a bout of high spirits, Bobtailed Cat knocked the entire contents of the water-paunch over an embroidered robe. As quickly as she could, Moon Hawk caught up the edges and took the heavy skin outside.

It was a warm, starlit night without a breath of wind to stir her unbraided hair. Noises travelled in the clear air: horses whinnying far outside the circle of the lodges, the soft, slow beat of a drum and high-pitched voices raised in song, the giggle of lovers, the demanding cry of a baby wanting its mother's milk.

Moon Hawk spilled the water from the robe away from the door of the lodge and shook the skin several times to ensure that no drops still clung to the fine porcupine-quill embroidery, but it was damp in several places. She stretched it in her arms, ready to throw it over the roof of the sunshade, but drew it back into her body with a gasp. Deep in the shadow cast by the roofing-boughs a tall, slim figure was leaning casually against one of the supporting uprights. He uncrossed his ankles and stepped into the bright starlight. It was Winter Man. Moon Hawk's heart-beat doubled.

'I have stood outside many lodges waiting to speak to a woman within,' he said wearily, 'but this one . . .' He turned his lazy gaze on to the buffalo-skin tipi, the brightness of the fire within making it almost translucent. 'You are more closely chaperoned than a Sacred Woman. I thought I would grow old and lose my teeth standing here.'

A smile crept across Moon Hawk's lips, and she pulled the edge of the robe up to her nose to hide it from his sight.

'There is no need to cower behind that robe. I have not come to try to entice a kiss from you. I have a more willing partner waiting for my touch.' He inclined his head, indicating some other lodge lost in the darkness. Moon Hawk's joy evaporated instantly. She felt as though a bowl full of icy water had been poured over her head.

'You trilled well for your sister's doll. I have not heard you trill so well for the return of a Good Young Man.'

Moon Hawk affected an unconcerned shrug of her shoulders. 'Perhaps your ears were attuned to other voices.'

'Perhaps.'

Perhaps? Moon Hawk's eyes widened. Was Winter Man openly admitting his interest in her? Could she drop this pretence and at last speak of her love for him?

'We lost horses to the Shoshone during the last moon,' he said. 'Running Fisher is leading a raid against them in retaliation.' He raised his hand level with his waist and wavered it slightly. 'The horses of the Shoshone are not the best, but those Bad Lodges need to be shown that we will not tolerate their childish antics. I am among those going with Running Fisher.'

A chill ran down Moon Hawk's spine. He was going on a horse-raid. There was nothing untoward about that, she told herself fiercely. Wealth was measured in horses. Raiding horses from an enemy's herd was the principal way of acquiring wealth. Only frightened men caught wild horses and broke them to the saddle. There were no frightened men among the Apsaroke. Her father had been on many horse-raids and had never returned without a string of mounts to his credit. Winter Man, too, was well versed in the art. Why was she so fearful for him?

She watched him raise his hands and rest them on the cross-pole of the sunshade roof. The blue-grey starsheen glided over his tautening muscles; it reflected off the abalone shell gorget tied about his throat. His eyes bore into hers, cold and calculating and proud. Far away a wolf howled its mournful cry and the half-wild village dogs answered it in turns. The sound made Moon Hawk's flesh crawl. It was as if they had caught the scent of a fresh carcass.

'The others ride for wealth,' he said, 'but I have prayed to the Spirits. I have spoken with my Medicine. I will return with a single horse, and it will wear a short rope round its neck. I will hear you trill for me and see how well you do it.'

No! No! The words screamed inside her head. She had never intended this, never. To raid horses from an enemy's herd was bravery enough. Scattered in their hundreds on the hills about a village, men could take them and escape before the alarm was raised, but a picketed horse . . . A picketed horse was the pride of its owner. It was tethered to a tipi staking-pin outside the door of a lodge; an enemy lodge in an enemy village. One sound, one snort of the horse, one growl of the dogs, and that village would rise as one to rain death on to the intruder. On to Winter Man. He could not do this, not just to flaunt the deed before her, not just as part of this courting game they were playing—*she* was playing. First Maker, what had possessed her to start it?

She swallowed down the bile which fear had made rise into her throat. She would have given anything at that moment, made any sacrifice, to have been able to beg him to abandon his quest. Had he known her thoughts he would have hung his head in shame and gone high into the Shining Mountains to wail his grief like a wretched thing. Even though he might forfeit his life, she could not dishonour him that way. She took a breath to force courage such as his through her veins and lifted her head as any proud Apsaroke woman would on such an occasion. She only hoped that there was not enough light in the starsheen for him to see the tears standing in her eyes.

'Bring a picketed horse to this village and you shall hear me trill for you,' she said.

Winter Man did not smile. He did not give any sign that he had heard her words. As silent as a stalking cougar, he turned and walked away into the night.

CHAPTER THREE

When the sky had darkened and the stars were bright, the raiders left the comforts of their tipis and headed south into the night. One of the village guards, a Muddy Hand whose society had been elected to the duty for a season, counted eight figures past him, eight figures and two dogs, but no horses. Although the men were leaving on foot, it was a certainty that they would be riding back. He smiled as he watched them, memories of raids he had been on springing easily to his mind. His smile faded. Not every raid was as successful as it might be. Sometimes events overtook those who had so meticulously planned them. Sometimes the results were disastrous. It would not hurt to sing for these men. It would not hurt at all. He raised his arms to the sky and called upon First Maker to watch diligently over his brothers.

Running Fisher called a halt at daybreak, as was his custom. Winter Man had been chosen to accompany him on three other occasions and he knew the reason for the delay lay in a taboo connected with his Medicine. Being a pipe-carrier, a leader, was a heavy responsibility. Not only did Running Fisher have to acquire enough booty for everyone on the raid, but he had to ensure that none of his followers was lost to the enemy. No matter how large the booty, no matter how many coups were taken, if Running Fisher lost a man he would be disgraced. No one would follow him again until he could persuade the people that his Medicine had regained its former strength. Every ritual, every taboo of that Medicine, had to be strictly adhered to. Their lives depended on it.

Since seeking his first vision when he was only eleven years old, Winter Man had wanted to be a Good Man and lead his own raids like his father and three of his grandfathers. Mystics had prayed over him. Wise men had counselled him. He was a Good Young Man now, as were many of his age, but would he ever gain the honours he needed to rise to leadership? He needed three major coups to be considered. He had gained only one, the taking of a gun from an enemy.

The man had been a Lakota, a member of a scalp-raid the previous summer. In the ferocity of the hand-to-hand fighting, the Lakota had pointed the weapon directly into Winter Man's face. Perspiration beaded on his back as he recalled the moment. If that weapon had not misfired . . . If the powder had been dry . . . He threw aside the remembered hand of fear with a chuckle of irony. That day his Medicine had been stronger than that of the Lakota. The weapon had misfired. He had taken a gun from the hands of an enemy and gained himself a coup. When he wore his best clothing, he wore the shirt with the locks of hair on the sleeves. Everyone knew what the decoration meant, even visitors from other peoples who had come to trade. He was recognised. He was a warrior. Two more coups and he would be a Good Man. He would carry the pipe on his own raids—if he could prove that his Medicine was strong enough so that others would follow him.

A cake of pemmican landed by his moccasin. He raised his eyes and found Hillside grinning at him.

'Your thoughts are far away,' his friend said. 'Is it the horse you are wishing for, or the touch of that woman with the appealing dark eyes, the chaste one who cannot throw to save her life—or catch herself a husband?'

Winter Man smiled and broke off a piece of the foodstuff, but he did not reply to the taunt. He had been the butt of repeated jokes since the day they had returned from their hunting. Everyone in the village knew what had taken place when they had met the root-diggers. If Hillside had not spoken loudly of it, Frost had. There had been no escape for him. He had been so affronted by the woman's attitude that he had not realised the exchange for the challenge it had been.

It had left him in a delicate situation with Bear On The Flat, too. They were both members of the Fox society, Moon Hawk's father being an elder. He was not the sort of man to look upon lovers' games with a ribald eye, especially if the woman in question was his daughter, yet he had said nothing. He had remained almost aloof, as if such antics were below his dignity—which, Winter Man supposed, they were for a man of his standing.

Moon Hawk. He lay full length in the sun-withered grass, turning her name in his mind. She certainly had the haughty look of a hawk. The way she had ignored him—he still could not accept it without astonishment. If he had counted correctly, there would be a sliver of moon to guide their steps the next night. Perhaps it was an omen. He wished he had made enquiries into how she had come by the name. Bear On The Flat might have given it to her at birth to commemorate some deed he had done. She was, after all, his first daughter by that Piegan woman.

She, too, was chaste, he remembered. How many times had Bear On The Flat sat in the Fox lodge after the wife-stealing ritual and boasted of her chastity? No Lumpwood man had ever stood outside his tipi and called his Piegan woman out. He had been married to her for so many years that no one could remember the number. Winter Man shook his head in incredulity at his thoughts. His own father had divorced seven wives. What would it be like to share the same bedding-robes with a woman for so long? What would it be like to have a wife?

He caught his musings, drew them up sharply like a runaway horse. He did not want a wife. Making Moon Hawk his wife was not even the challenge. To entice her into being his lover, that was the challenge, though even as he dwelled on it he was no longer sure. He had had many lovers, had not regretted a single one, but none of them would ever be asked to notch the Sacred Tree at the height of the summer ceremonies. None of his lovers would ever know such an honour. Only the families of chaste women could carry that prestige, families with women like Moon Hawk.

'Have you spoken to her yet?'

The voice of Skins The Wolf was terse and, unlike Hillside's, devoid of all humour. Winter Man did not know what to make of him. He had been like this for days now, scowling or silent. At times it was difficult to know which was the worse. Despite belonging to opposing warrior societies, they had kept their childhood friendship. They were, after all, distantly related, not through blood as clan members, but through the marriage of one of their grandparents. Like a true brother, he had been the first to offer to guard Winter Man's back when he entered the Shoshone village.

'Of course I have spoken to her,' Winter Man replied, disdainfully waving his hand in the air. 'She trembled at my very nearness, hiding her blushes behind a robe she held.'

'Ha!' Skins The Wolf threw back his head and scoffed. 'That one would not tremble if she stood naked in the presence of First Man!'

Even as he heard the words, Winter Man felt his stomach lurch. All about him turned in horror to look upon Skins The Wolf. How could he be so unthinking as to tempt the goodwill of First Maker at a time like this? They were about to enter an enemy village.

Winter Man looked across to Running Fisher. He was the pipe-carrier. If he felt the breach of respect was too severe, he would order them to hang their heads and return to the village empty-handed rather than risk their lives in a venture no longer sanctified.

Running Fisher sat for long moments with his pipe-bag in his hands. No one spoke. No one wished to interrupt his meditation. Older than his followers, wiser for his experience, they waited nervously for his judgment.

'We go on,' he said.

Everyone sighed with relief. Skins The Wolf stood and raised his hand to the rising sun.

'However many horses I capture, I pledge half of them to the poor.'

Winter Man could hardly believe his ears. Half of them? If he had been so foolish as to say such a thing, he would have pledged them all!

They ran on. There were no paths to follow, no markers to point the way, but from the angle of the sun

and the individual peaks of the Shining Mountains rang-
ing along their right-hand course, they knew they were
leaving the hunting grounds of the Apsaroke and entering enemy lands. The dogs, brought by Otter Robe and
Spider to carry food and spare moccasins, trotted game-
ly along, their tongues hanging out in the late summer
heat.

The land undulated in increasing sweeps as the high
plains buckled into the foothills of the mountains. The
coarse grass, baked almost brown beneath the sun, gave
way to willow and gorse and lodge-pole pine. Jack-
rabbits fled in panic before the jogging raiders. Prairie-
dogs screeched their high-pitched warnings and darted
down their holes. A group of antelope stood and stared.
The heavy-limbed buffalo ignored them.

Running Fisher had picked two scouts to sprint ahead
and spy the land from distant hilltops. Hunts The Enemy
and Frost had donned their wolf-skins with pride and
raced on. Winter Man had been a wolf on four occasions
and knew the excitement the first sighting of their quarry
could bring. He had not been asked this time. He was
intending to gain a picketed horse, gain a recognised
coup. Running Fisher had felt that was enough for him
to concentrate on, and Winter Man had accepted the
leader's judgment and hidden his own disappointment.
A man gained prestige in the eyes of his peers by
discharging his duties well. The role of wolf carried
prestige. A man was nothing without prestige. Only the
men with the highest prestige, the highest war honours,
only those men were asked to take the burden of their
people upon their shoulders and become true orators.

The stars were growing bright in the eastern sky when
one of the wolves was seen running back towards them.
The jocular atmosphere of the little group changed at
once. Something was amiss. They were another night's
journey from the area of the Shoshone village sites.

Hunts The Enemy eased his pace and the others
crowded round him. His chest was heaving, but his
words were not strained.

'Bannock,' he announced. 'A party of five. They have
killed themselves a buffalo-cow and are roasting her

flesh over a small fire.' His eyes rested on each man in
turn. 'They are young.'

Young meant inexperienced. Five. It was a number
the eight Apsaroke would willingly take on. The thought
passed through every mind.

'They may not be alone,' Running Fisher said.

'Frost and I have watched them since noon. They
played in a creek like women, splashing each other and
singing songs. They smoked for a while, and chased
buffalo just for the fun of seeing them run before cutting
one out and killing it. It needed three arrows to bring it
down,' the wolf snorted contemptuously. 'None of their
number left to tell others of their kill. Frost circled round
them, but found no sign of anyone else. They are alone.'

'And asking to die,' Spider added.

Hunts The Enemy nodded. 'They have even let their
horses wander.'

Winter Man did not know whether this development
was a good thing or not. If they did attack the Bannock,
the raid would end. There would be no Shoshone horses,
no picketed horse to parade before Moon Hawk. There
would, of course, be the chance of a grand coup, the
touching of an armed enemy who was trying to kill the
coup-taker. The prestige gained through that act was
more than through the taking of a picketed horse, but he
would need both to be a Good Man. And what if he was
not quick enough? There were eight Apsaroke. Eight
men attempting to take the same coup. Even if all of
them succeeded, only the first to call the strike would be
allowed to drag a wolf's tail behind his moccasin. If
Winter Man was not the first, he would have nothing.

He thought of Moon Hawk, of her dark, beguiling
eyes gazing at him over the top of the buffalo robe that
night she had come out of the lodge. He thought of the
contemptuous look she had given him when they had
spoken at the root-digging. He, a Good Young Man,
and she had treated him shamefully in front of all those
old women. If he did not return with a picketed horse as
he had promised, he would forever hear her laughter
ringing in his ears.

'We are raiding horses,' Running Fisher said. 'Horses

from the Shoshone who dared to enter our lands to steal our own.' His arms were folded about his pipe-bag as if around a new-born child. He looked very grave, and went on, 'These Bannock have been given to us like wounded antelope caught in a thicket. They have been given to us as a test by First Maker. We shall not fail that test. We shall skirt the Bannock. We shall not show ourselves to them. We shall raid horses from the Shoshone. It is what I prayed for. It is what I was promised.' He turned away, indicating that there was to be no discussion.

They altered their route and took a wide circle round the Bannock, travelling until the sliver of the risen moon was high overhead. Running Fisher finally called a halt. For the first time since leaving the Apsaroke village, they wrapped themselves in their buffalo robes and stretched out on the ground to sleep.

Winter Man stared up at the silver arc almost lost in the winking stars. His thoughts were not of its beauty, nor of the stories his people told about its origin. His mind dwelled on the fine horse he would take, and on the moist lips of the woman who would trill to acclaim his victory. Perhaps, if he was very patient, those lips would kiss his own. It was a thought which stirred his blood.

It was still dark when Running Fisher bade them rise and begin their trek afresh. He called a stop at dawn so that he could meditate with his Medicine. Winter Man and Hillside gave prayers to the rising sun, asking that they might stand at the next dawn and give thanks for their deliverance. That night, they knew, would be the night they entered the Shoshone village.

Frost and Hunts The Enemy returned to the group just before noon. A village had been sighted. It was not particularly large, but had a good herd of horses distributed over the surrounding hills. Frost had witnessed a horse-race. A large roan had won it easily. The animal had been washed in the nearby creek and led into the midst of the village. A picketed horse. A roan. Winter Man decided that that was the horse for him.

They hid the rest of the day in a dry wash, joking and

sleeping and wagering on dice. Each one was nervous, but none would ever have admitted it to the others. As the shadows lengthened and the twilight grew, each took himself away from the group and spoke privately with his Medicine. There were rites to be fulfilled, taboos to be upheld, prayers to be sung. With the onset of night, they set off.

Winter Man, Hillside and Skins The Wolf went straight to the edge of the village. There would be little time, they knew, before the others began to cut horses from the herd. They would do it as quietly as they could, but horses were inquisitive creatures, easily unnerved. It took only one startled animal to set the rest in motion. Such a noise would bring every Shoshone alive down on them.

Winter Man crouched behind a woman's willow lodge, his friends at his shoulders. He was breathing hard, too hard, he knew, and perspiration was beginning to bead on his naked back. There was too much noise in the village, too much movement for the depth of the night. He could hear drumming from several lodges, and voices were lifting in song. The Shoshone were celebrating. He wished it were otherwise, but it was not. There was no point in waiting for them to sleep. The Shoshone could still be singing at dawn.

He hung his head, staring at the packed earth between his knees. His friends were waiting for his decision, for his instructions. Their lives depended on him now, the way all their lives depended on Running Fisher. Leadership was, indeed, a heavy responsibility. His head snapped up. His eyes took in the scene again. He turned with purpose to his friends and gave his instructions silently, in sign-language. They signalled their acknowledgments, and left him.

Winter Man moved outside the circle of the glowing lodges, watching every footfall for dry firewood and discarded possessions, his eyes staring into small impenetrable shadows in case he came across a dog. If he set a dog barking, he might as well stand and sing his death song.

He crouched low as he heard voices laughing in the

night. Two young men, decked in their finery. They passed on the other side of the tipi he hid behind and did not notice him. Winter Man strained his ears to hear what they were saying, as he knew a little of the Shoshone tongue. Their peoples did not always think of each other as enemies, but the young men's words were spoken too quickly for him to grasp.

He moved across the gap into the shadow of another tipi. There was a horse picketed outside its door, a chestnut, a fine horse, but not the one he was seeking. He had told his friends that he would take the roan. To change his mind might place them in jeopardy. A man brazenly courted ill-luck by changing his mind once a raid had been mounted. Winter Man padded on. He caught sight of Hillside moving between the tipis some little way off, and sent a silent prayer to First Maker that his friend should keep his head down. Of Skins The Wolf he could see no sign. Then he saw the horse. The roan.

There was no wondering at how it had won its race so easily. The length of its leg was truly amazing. He had seen long-legged horses at the fur-traders' fort to the north. He had even bartered all his skins for one after seeing it run, but it had been no good as a buffalo-horse, and had not been strong enough to survive the harshness of the winter; but this horse, this roan . . . Its parentage was mixed. It had the sturdy body of horses he knew well. This one would live to graze the spring grass. It would live to produce young of its own. How Moon Hawk would look when he paraded *this* horse in front of her!

The lodge was quite dark. No sound came from it that he could hear. Perhaps the occupants were singing in another tipi. Winter Man stole round its outer rim, to the edge of the shadow cast by an adjacent lodge. He spied Hillside. Hillside could also see him, because he gave the signal that meant all was well. Winter Man looked for Skins The Wolf, but his friend must have been too well hidden for him to be noticed.

Winter Man eased himself into the starlight, made brighter by the silver moon. The roan saw him and pulled slightly on the restraining rope tied about its neck. Winter Man stood a moment, letting the animal see him, showing himself for what he was. Slowly, he advanced upon it. The roan eyed him with distrust. Winter Man began shushing to it, holding out his free hand so that the horse might take his scent. His other hand loosened the plaited riding-thong from his belt, ready to slip the loop over the animal's lower jaw. He advanced further, attempting to stroke the horse's nose. It bared its teeth at him, bared its teeth like a dog. Winter Man's blood ran cold. If the horse began to shy . . .

'Quiet, horse,' he whispered. 'I am Winter Man. You are my horse now. Accept me as your rider and I shall tie red streamers in your mane. I shall paint my honours on your coat and ride you in parades so that all might gaze upon you and say, "Winter Man's horse is the most prized among all the Apsaroke horses."'

The roan pricked its ears at his words and eyed him afresh. It seemed a little quieter. Winter Man smoothed his hand down its neck and across its shoulders. It stamped a hoof and flicked its tail, but it did not try to pull away from him. He looped the riding-thong and slipped it about the horse's neck, deciding that a choke harness might be a prudent idea. The animal snorted, annoyed that it should be meddled with.

Winter Man licked his own lips as he prised the horse's apart and eased its jaw open. It had good teeth, the sort that could bite off a man's fingers. Carefully, he moved the jaw-thong into position and tightened it.

He was ready.

He expelled his held breath and raised his head to signal to Hillside, but Hillside was frantically signalling to him. Away to the left, two figures were walking slowly between the tipis. They seemed to be bent, large shouldered. Lovers—sharing a robe. And they were walking towards Winter Man.

He ducked beneath the roan's neck to stand in its shadow. Yes, lovers. They were engrossed in each other. If the horse did not whinny and he did not move, they would come and walk straight by him and not notice his existence. He watched them come towards him. His heart beat so hard that it hurt his ribs. Keep still, he told himself. All he had to do was keep perfectly still. He glanced across to where Hillside had been standing, but there was no sign of him. He had retreated into the shadows. Winter Man looked back towards the lovers. His stomach lurched. There were three figures now, one behind the other two. Skins The Wolf! What was he doing?

In a moment of horrified perception, Winter Man realised exactly what Skins The Wolf was doing. He was getting ready to count a grand coup—in the middle of a Shoshone village.

Everything moved slowly then, so very slowly, yet so terrifyingly fast. The cry that leapt from the mouth of Skins The Wolf could have been heard clear beyond the edge of the village. The Shoshone unravelled himself from the robe and his lover's arms with admirable speed, but he was not quick enough to dodge the blow Skins The Wolf delivered with his fist. The man fell to the ground as the Apsaroke's cry of victory rent the air. His call was still jangling in Winter Man's ears as the Shoshone woman began to scream. Skins The Wolf silenced her with a single blow from his stone-headed club. She fell heavily, knocking into her rising lover. Skins The Wolf dealt another blow, and, without a single look around him, darted away between two lodges.

Winter Man grasped the roan's mane and heaved himself on to its bare back. All around him people were spilling from tipis, wondering what had happened. Winter Man drew his knife and cut the restraining rope which picketed the horse, leaving the loop and a short lead dangling from its neck. Free at last, the roan skitted backwards on its powerful hind legs. Winter Man crouched low upon its back, trying to control it with his knees, trying not to look conspicuous. He glanced about him, his nerve ready to fail him. Where was Hillside?

The roan shied. It rose on its hind legs, a deep bellow forcing its way up its throat. Every Shoshone in the village looked at Winter Man. Their cries were unintelligible to him, but he knew what they meant. He had to get out of there. He had to get out of there quickly.

He fought with the roan, finally bringing it under his control. A searing pain streaked across his naked back. Men seemed to be all around him. He pushed one down with his foot, lashed another in the face with the end of the riding-thong. Then the horse was moving, kicking out with its hooves, lengthening its stride. A tipi loomed in front of it. The horse veered to the left to be confronted by a propped-up travois. The roan leapt it as fluidly as a springing cat. Winter Man felt the blood surge in his veins. He would escape. He would live. Freedom was his!

Where was Hillside? He looked behind him. No one had caught a horse to follow him. No one, not even the enraged Shoshone. He reined in the roan and turned it back towards the village. Hillside was in there somewhere, without a horse, without a friend to die beside. Winter Man kicked the roan, kicked at its belly until it galloped like a true spirit-dog, streaking its mane and tail out behind it in the wind it created. They were upon the lodges before Winter Man realised. The Shoshone threw themselves aside as they galloped through, curving this way and that to create more confusion. The frantic pace fired the roan. It hardly needed a touch of command. It was, indeed, a spirit-dog sent by First Maker. Winter Man filled his lungs and cried out the fighting call of the Fox warrior society. Almost at once he was answered. Hillside was still alive.

Winter Man dragged the roan to a standstill and looked in all directions. A crouching figure darted from the shadow of a nearby tipi. Winter Man's fingers sought his sheathed knife before he realised it was Hillside. A hand was raised. A hand was lowered. They clasped each other about the forearm and Winter Man pulled Hillside up behind him. He felt the fletching of an arrow pass his face and he kicked the roan into motion. The Shoshone were organising. Their initial surprise had been swept aside. They would be running for their horses, ready to give chase.

'Go! Go! Go!' Hillside shrieked in his ear.

The two Apsaroke went like the wind itself. Winter

Man gave the roan every encouragement and the roan gave them all its speed, so sure-footed that it did not falter at the creek. It did not hesitate as the land broke up into a series of narrow gulleys. It leapt them with ease, one and two and three. All Winter Man had to do was to keep heading it where he hoped the other Apsaroke were waiting.

They came upon Running Fisher long before Winter Man expected to. He was alone, sitting astride his captured mount, the riding-thongs of two others held in his hand. Hillside slipped from the back of the roan on to the back of one of the spare horses.

'Change your horse!' Running Fisher commanded. 'The roan is tired.'

Winter Man shook his head. The roan was tired, but if he changed mounts now, he might lose it. 'Skins The Wolf?'

Running Fisher pointed ahead and kicked his own horse forward. Hillside and Winter Man followed him. Winter Man repeatedly thrashed the end of the riding-thong across the horse's rump, forcing from it reserves of speed and endurance it had not known it owned. At any other time Winter Man would have continually praised it for such a feat, glorified its triumph, but his mind was full of confusion and doubts.

Skins The Wolf was alive and well. Running Fisher had already given him a horse, but . . . but Skins The Wolf had been on *foot*. To have arrived before himself and Hillside, he must have run from the village as soon as he had taken the coup. Winter Man would not accept that it was possible. He and Skins The Wolf had been on horse-raids since early manhood. It was inconceivable that one so experienced could not have been aware of what would happen as soon as the coup was called. He had known Hillside and himself were there. He must have done.

The other members of the party had cut a large number of horses from the unguarded herd on the hills surrounding the Shoshone village. Running Fisher had sent them on ahead while he had waited alone for his three remaining men. They waited now, the horses rested, the men crowding around Skins The Wolf, eagerly listening to details of his coup.

Winter Man felt his heart grow heavy as he rode towards them. There were many questions still in his mind, questions to which he had found no ready answers.

Hillside slipped from his mount's back before it had fully drawn to a halt, almost running in his haste to reach Skins The Wolf. He hit him in the shoulder with such force that he nearly knocked him off his feet.

'You could have killed us!' he roared.

Skins The Wolf stared at him. Spider and Otter Robe stared, too. Hillside was boiling with such fury that he could hardly speak.

'Your foolery nearly cost us our lives!'

Skins The Wolf squared his broad shoulders and took a menacing step towards his accuser. '*Foolery?* I gained a grand coup. You saw me gain it. Are you going to stand before these men and say that you were blind?'

Running Fisher cut between them, separating them with his arms. He looked quickly from one to the other, finally resting his gaze on Skins The Wolf.

'What is this?'

Skins The Wolf beat his chest with his closed fist. 'I gained a grand coup,' he said, his pride glowing in his face.

Ignoring Hillside, Running Fisher turned to Winter Man and called him into the circle. 'Did you see this coup being taken?'

Winter Man's stomach knotted. He had known he would be asked to verify the deed. What was he supposed to say? A man never lied, it was an outrage against one's Medicine, against First Maker, but could he stand before others and accuse the friend with whom he had shared so much over the years of leaving himself and Hillside to die at the hands of the Shoshone?

He twisted the riding-thong about his fingers as he stood before Running Fisher. The tired roan nuzzled at his neck.

'It was a good coup,' he said in a clear voice. 'A man and woman were walking between the tipis. Skins The

Wolf gave warning of his presence. The man turned to attack him and he took the coup, knocking the man to the ground. The woman began to scream and he hit her with his club.'

'Smashed in her skull,' Skins The Wolf qualified with enthusiasm. 'I felt it shatter beneath the blow.'

'She fell on the man as he was trying to rise. It gave Skins The Wolf time to strike him, too.'

Winter Man looked straight into Running Fisher's eyes. Running Fisher stared unflinchingly back into his.

'And then?'

Winter Man could not say it. There had to be a reason for Skins The Wolf doing what he had, some fact of which he was not aware.

'And then?' Running Fisher repeated.

'I cannot say with certainty what happened next. There was much confusion. I had taken the picketed horse and . . .'

'You were not upon its back! I gained my coup first.'

Winter Man felt his jaw sag open, and quickly gritted his teeth to cover his astonishment. From his own lips Skins The Wolf was telling him that he had known their positions. He had simply ignored their safety. Winter Man did not want to believe what he was hearing.

'Winter Man *had* gained the picketed horse,' Hillside countered vehemently.

'I had not cut its restraining line,' Winter Man said. 'I was waiting in the shadow of the horse for the two Shoshone to pass me.'

'They would have seen you,' Skins The Wolf snorted.

For the first time since he had been called as a witness, Winter Man turned to look at him, and he did not like what he saw. Skins The Wolf was brimming with self-admiration. He could hardly keep himself from strutting before them all.

'I do not think so,' Winter Man answered thickly. 'I do not think so.'

'Then the coup was good?' Running Fisher asked. Winter Man had to acknowledge that it was. 'It seems to me that you gained your coups at the same time within the sight of one another. Both will stand. Neither will be devalued. It is rare that honours are gained simultaneously, but it does happen.' He looked from one to the other of them for sign of objections. There was none. 'Then that is how it will be told.'

Skins The Wolf threw his arms up in jubilation. Whatever Running Fisher said, a grand coup always took precedence over a picketed horse. He curled his arms round the shoulders of Otter Robe and Spider and led them away to tell them, yet again, of the details.

Winter Man turned away, thankful to be able to tend to his new horse as an excuse to be away from the others. He had begun to rub the roan with grass when Running Fisher drew close.

'Is there anything you wish to tell me?'

'Tell you?' he echoed.

'That you would, perhaps, not wish the others to hear?'

Winter Man forced himself to look at the pipe-carrier. It was obvious the older man knew something was amiss.

'Skins The Wolf took a horse from me a good while before you and Hillside came into view,' Running Fisher prompted.

Winter Man ran his hand under the roan's belly, giving him the opportunity of averting his eyes. 'I have said. There was much confusion.'

An ominous silence was held between the two. It spoke much of Running Fisher's true belief. He dropped his gaze and began to turn away, pulling himself up and looking back at his subordinate.

'A man always holds the truth in his heart. Sometimes his words are the same, sometimes they are slightly different. Keep the truth in your heart in your heart, Winter Man.'

Winter Man watched Running Fisher walk away into the darkness, his chest and stomach heaving until he felt bile rise into his throat. He turned to the roan and pushed his face into its flank in an attempt to hide his anguish.

Keep the truth in your heart in your heart. He had been called a liar. As near as possible without the word being spoken, he had been called a liar by a pipe-carrier, by a

Good Man. Never change your story, that was what he had been warned. Never speak of what is truly in your heart now that you have denied its existence.

The shame. The humiliation.

He felt a hand drop heavily on to his shoulder and shuddered under the impact, believing his thoughts had been discovered. It was Hillside.

'I am sorry. I did not mean to be so harsh. I am angry with myself. That back of yours will need a salve on it.'

Winter Man worked his shoulders. 'It does feel stiff.'

'A lance skimmed you, I think. Your Medicine was strong today.' Hillside showed him his arm. It was covered in dried blood from shoulder to elbow. 'I was nicked by an arrow.' He chuckled. 'Both our Medicines were strong today.' His amusement faded. 'What did Running Fisher want with you?'

Winter Man wondered, fleetingly, if he had the courage to speak of his dishonour, then realised he needed someone to confide in. 'He wished to know what was truly in my heart. I could not tell him. He called me a liar.' He hung his head. Would he ever be able to hold it high again? He heard Hillside's gasp of astonishment, and the pain in his chest increased until he had to grasp the roan for support.

'To your face? He accused you to your face?'

Winter Man shook his head. 'His words were couched very well, but he will never trust me again.'

'Will he . . . Will he say this to others?'

'He will have no need to. He will pick men to ride with him and he will not pick me. How many times will that happen before others wonder why? I am disgraced.'

'No,' Hillside told him. 'You are not disgraced. Running Fisher came to me, too, but I added nothing to what you had witnessed before us all. I am not disgraced. You are not disgraced. It is Skins The Wolf who has disgraced himself.

'Why did he do it? He was there to guard your back, not to take himself a coup. He could have killed us. Why did he do it?'

'Perhaps he could not resist the opportunity when it presented itself.'

Hillside scoffed. 'A man says that in defence of a boy on his first raid, not in defence of an experienced man like Skins The Wolf.' He shook his head, himself not wanting to believe what had happened. 'To gain such a coup and then turn and run, leaving us to the Shoshone . . .' He raised his head, waving a finger at Winter Man. 'You came back for me,' he said. 'You had escaped and you rode that horse back into the Shoshone village to rescue me. I told Running Fisher that, and I shall recount it to the village when we return. I shall recount it to the members of the Fox society. I shall not forget that you saved my life.' He patted Winter Man on the arm, and walked away.

The roan turned in a tight circle and came to nuzzle at its new owner. Winter Man slipped a hand under its jaw and patted it. He should have felt exhilarated gaining such a coup, taking such a fine horse. Songs would be sung about the deed. Songs would be sung about his rescue of Hillside. He would be paraded around the village, his valour brought to the notice of everyone. His family, his clan, they would all be proud of him. The women would trill for him. Moon Hawk would trill for him. None of it would wipe away his shame. That would be with him for ever.

CHAPTER FOUR

'Is it true? Are they back?'

Moon Hawk's eldest brother gazed at her in open-mouthed astonishment. Adult siblings maintained a strict sense of dignity in their exchanges. His sister's lack of propriety embarrassed him. He turned to their mother and spoke directly to her.

'Bear On The Flat sends me to tell you that Running Fisher has returned with horses and coups. He said that you would be eager to know.'

Little Face took a step towards him, smiling. 'Thank you, my son. Were there any injuries?'

He shook his head. 'Not that I have heard. There will be much singing tonight. Here, I have brought you something.' He opened his hand and showed her the slender dentalium shells he had hidden there. 'They will look well hanging from your ears.'

Little Face uttered her delight as he tipped them into her offered palm. 'You are a good son, Antelope Dancer. You make a mother proud.'

He smiled, nodding his acceptance of her thanks. Without a glance towards Moon Hawk, he bowed his head and went out through the door opening.

Little Face glanced at her daughter, and frowned. 'If you talk to him like that again, he will refuse to visit us while you are here.'

'I am sorry, Mother. I did not think. I am . . .'

'I know. I know. You have been like it for days. I do not know which is worse, falling over Winter Man every time I leave the lodge, or coping with your anxieties when he is away from the village. I shall be pleased when it is all over.'

Moon Hawk relaxed a little, and smiled. 'Mother . . . You know you are enjoying every moment!'

'Perhaps,' she mused. 'But I shall still be pleased when his family offer you an elk-tooth dress.'

An elk-tooth dress. A wedding gift. It was all Moon Hawk could dream of, that and lying in Winter Man's arms.

'Do not stand there like something carved,' Little Face admonished. 'Bathe. Dress. I must paint your face and oil your hair. He will be here soon!'

The face of Skins The Wolf seemed to be set in a permanent scowl. While Otter Robe had dressed his hair and attached bright beaded temple ornaments to the thin braids he wore in front of his ears, Spider had painstakingly painted his eyes vermilion and his face black, the honour colours of a coup-taker. Running Fisher had divided the captured Shoshone horses, generously keeping no more for himself than he had given to his men, but Skins The Wolf could speak of nothing but the group of boys they had met some little while before.

'They will have run straight to the village and told everyone that we are here. What surprise will there be when we ride among the lodges now?'

It was the third time he had said those same words. Hillside bent his head nearer Winter Man's ear as he applied vermilion to the torn skin of his back.

'He likes to hear his own voice. He sounds like a prairie chicken trying to encourage a mate.'

Winter Man turned his blackened face so that he could see Hillside out of the corner of his eye. 'You sound like something, too, ridiculing his every move.'

Hillside narrowed his eyes. 'I carry a fire in my chest for him, the way he has treated us. I do not know how you can remain so calm.'

Calm? Winter Man nearly laughed. Was that how he looked to Hillside? Was that how he looked to them all?

'I feel unworthy. I have gained a coup, taken a picketed horse . . .'

'. . . and rescued me.'

Winter Man sighed. 'I do not feel that it should be my shoulders these honours should be heaped on.'

'Then whose shoulders should they be heaped on? Those of Skins The Wolf for deserting us? Your only mistake was to protect him by not disclosing all you saw to Running Fisher. It is too late to alter that now. It is gone. It is past. Your honours are good. You will stand tall and raise your head high. What will people think if you skulk into the village hiding your face? What will Moon Hawk think? She will be waiting for you to pass her lodge.' He slapped Winter Man playfully on the shoulder. 'Say that she will not be there, all coy and affecting a tired disinterest, while she wears her most prized clothing for you. Ah, you will feel differently when the celebrations begin.'

Winter Man hoped so.

When Running Fisher felt the time was right, he told his men to mount their horses. They began at a sedate pace, singing songs of valour and cunning, but as they neared the tipis they eased their mounts into a trot, finally entering the village at a gallop, driving the stolen horses before them.

The village erupted in its excitement. There were calls and shouts. People waved painted robes and ran alongside the horses of the returning men. The air was filled with dust and noise; the women's continuous high-pitched trilling punctuated by the deafening booms of powder guns. Round the village, the stolen horses were driven by every tipi so that all might see and admire them.

Once the horses had been shown, Running Fisher paraded his men: Skins The Wolf to the fore in recognition of the precedence his grand coup took, Winter Man behind him, leading the roan, the wolves came next, in honour of their duties, and finally Hillside, Otter Robe and Spider in a line bringing up the rear. They stopped outside the lodge of Running Fisher so that his family and clan members could hear the deeds of the raid and applaud his leadership. They stopped outside the lodge of Skins The Wolf so that he could re-enact the taking of his coup for his family. They stopped outside Winter Man's lodge so that all there might hear at first hand how he had come to take the roan and save the life of Hillside. Slowly the raiders made their way through the rejoicing village, stopping before a group of Lumpwood society members who sang songs for Skins The Wolf, and again before a group of Fox society members who sang songs for Winter Man.

It was as Hillside had predicted. The jubilation forced all melancholy thoughts from Winter Man's mind. He was treated as a hero – and he felt like one. He told his tale time and time again, showing off the red-painted wound upon his back, emphasising his bravery as custom bade he should. One of his clan-grandfathers, a mentor since before the time of his vision quest, recalled the other deeds he had accomplished: the taking of a gun, the striking of a second and a third coup, so that the people might know and remember that he was a Good Young Man with a strong heart, destined for mighty things.

Swallow came to hug him and bathe in his glory. Several of his cast-off lovers did the same, but not Moon Hawk. He wondered if she had been standing outside her father's lodge as the men had paraded by it. He had made a point of not looking, half hoping that she would seek him out herself.

As the sun slipped towards the mountains and the clamour of the village began to subside, Winter Man felt a new excitement kindle within him. He was pleased Moon Hawk had not come to fawn over him the way his lovers had. Very likely, it would have meant an end to their game. But she had not come. The game was still on – and it was his turn to play.

Moon Hawk stepped into the lodge, dropping the flap over the door behind her. She stood a moment, looking over her mother's shoulder as Little Face ladled food into wooden bowls for the two children. Her gaze flitted to the willow back-rests at the rear of the lodge, and beyond to the tipi-lining where the brightly painted war exploits of her father were displayed for all to see.

Where was Winter Man?

She raised her eyes to the apex of the lodge, to the hole where the faint smoke curled through. The sky was no longer the piercing blue of the afternoon. It was

darkening before her eyes, darkening into twilight.
Where was he?

'Do you want some of this?' Little Face asked, lifting
the ladle.

Moon Hawk shook her head. 'I cannot eat.' She began
to pace back and forth beside the door.

'He will not appreciate a bag of bones,' her mother
murmured. 'And I shall not appreciate your wearing a
delve inside the doorway for the rain to soak into.'

Moon Hawk lowered herself on to a buffalo robe and
tucked her legs beneath her. She had put on her best
dress for Winter Man, the one with the tiny mirrors
fastened to the shoulders, the one with the heavy beadwork running in lines across her breasts and along each
sleeve. Free from the restraining braids she wore when
working, her hair cascaded in undulating waves over
her shoulders and down her back. Had it all been for
nothing? Was he lying, now, in Swallow's arms? Was he
gazing, now, into her dark eyes?

The buffalo-skin covering of the tipi shook beneath a
single sharp blow above the doorway. Even the children
stopped eating and looked up in surprise.

'Ho! Women of the lodge! Come out! Come out and
admire a Good Young Man worthy of the title!'

Moon Hawk opened her mouth to cry out in her joy,
but remembered herself and stifled it. Little Face, her
eyes twinkling, ushered her daughter out before her.
Even Turtle slammed down her bowl and rose to her
feet. As far as she was concerned, 'women of the lodge'
included her, too.

Winter Man's appearance had changed drastically
from when he had ridden by the lodge in the parade. He
wore new leggings, each strip of the skin fringing bound
with dyed porcupine quill-work at the base. His moccasins were striped in blue and white beadwork from heel
to toe, and from his wrist hung a carved elk-horn riding
quirt, its tanned leather strap covered in bright red trade
cloth and edged in coloured beadwork. His face was still
blackened in honour of the coup he had taken, but his
raven hair had been plaited in numerous thin braids
which snaked down his back. To the temple braids that

brushed each cheek, slender pipe-bones had been attached. From their tips the white down of an eagle spurted upwards, balancing one either side of the raised, whitened quiff of his hair. Painted rings on his upper right arm proclaimed how many coups he had taken in his life. Vermilion circled the scar of an old wound on his chest. He sat proudly astride the roan, his back rigid, his head held high. The whites of his eyes sparkled like stars in the black night of his face as he watched Moon Hawk's appreciative gaze run over him.

'Winter Man is here,' he announced loudly, so that all near by might hear and listen, too. 'A picketed horse I told you I would gain, and a picketed horse I have gained.' He reached along the roan's neck with his quirt to touch the loop and line which dangled from its neck, just in case she had not seen that it was there.

Moon Hawk noticed, too, the decorations painted on the captured roan: hoofmarks denoting other successful horse-raids, bars across its nose for its rider's coups, red circles about its eyes. Tied into its flowing mane were thin red cloth streamers.

'See the length of its legs.' He pointed again with his quirt. 'When Winter Man steals a picketed horse, he steals the best in all the land!'

With a flick of his wrist he brought the thonging of the quirt down on the horse's rump and urged it into motion with his knees. Despite its having no saddle, his body swayed with the movement of the horse as though he were a part of the animal. He galloped it away from the tipi a distance, turned it, and galloped it back again, drawing it to a shuddering halt a pace from Moon Hawk. He turned his dark eyes to her, daring her not to agree with him.

'Is this not the best horse in all the land?'

'Yes,' she answered. 'It is the best horse in all the land.'

He tossed back his head in his acknowledgment and walked the roan in a tight circle to show it off to her again.

Moon Hawk had eyes only for his back. She had not been mistaken. Vermilion accentuated a fresh wound.

She felt her stomach knot, but forced herself to smile at him as he turned back to her, a studious frown crossing his face.

'I have passed this lodge once today, but I did not hear any women trilling for my bravery.'

Moon Hawk took a deep breath and threw back her head, her heart filling with all the love and pride she felt for him until she thought it would burst in her chest. She opened up her lips and sent forth a roulade of sound in the highest pitch she could manage, hearing her mother and Turtle joining her in the honouring. Other women, standing nearby and watching the spectacle, added their strident tones, but Moon Hawk knew, at that moment, that Winter Man had no ears for anyone but herself.

Moon Hawk's note faded through lack of breath. Others faded with her. She eased her straining neck and looked up at him astride his painted horse. What would he say now? What would he say to her?

'It is true,' he began, quietly this time, his words meant only for her. 'You trill well. When the stars shine above us, come to the lodge of Running Fisher. I would have you sit behind me and trill for me again.'

Without waiting for a reply, he smacked the horse's rump and urged it into an immediate gallop. Moon Hawk stepped out to watch him leave, then turned to Little Face, her arms outstretched in unashamed exultation.

'He has asked me to the celebration! He has asked me to sit behind him!'

Six lodges distant, standing alone in the deepening shadow of a sunshade, a broad-shouldered man raised the edge of his buffalo robe to hide his blackened face from the fast approaching rider. As Winter Man passed him, he lowered it again, returning his cold gaze to Moon Hawk. He was too distant to hear her words, but the fine dress she wore was clear to his eyes, as was the joy brimming in her face as she alternately hugged her mother and waved her arms in the air in her excitement. Skins The Wolf watched her a moment longer before reeling away, his resentment deepening into a snarl about his thinly drawn lips.

*   *   *

The family of Running Fisher had been cooking since the end of the victory parade. An active man could easily eat several pounds of meat at one sitting, and there would be eight to feed, not to speak of their wives and lovers who would sit behind them, as well as drummers, singers and other invited guests. There was roasted meat from the buffalo, antelope and elk, delicacies such as tongues and hearts, maize bartered from the earth lodge people in the east, gathered nuts and berries, and a variety of roots.

A man gained prestige in being fearless in all his deeds, his family and clan by aiding him in his material needs. They had willingly given food for the feast, as Running Fisher had willingly distributed his newly-acquired horses among them, making up the numbers from his own small herd when he had found there were not enough to go round. A Good Man was an overall provider, a distributor of wealth, and Running Fisher would not be the first, or the last, to make himself destitute in ensuring that his people were well cared for. His standing, his honour, depended upon it. If ever he were so unthinking as to commit an act which would discredit him, his family and clan would bear the shame as well. No one would be allowed to forget, and the disgrace would follow one generation into the next.

Such troubling thoughts were kept well to the back of a Good Man's mind, yet they stood stark and alive in Running Fisher's head as his gaze swept the inner circle of his laughing followers. To his left sat Skins The Wolf. Opposite sat Winter Man and Hillside. Before the raid, when he had asked the village Crier to announce their names, and they had sat in his lodge to smoke his proffered pipe and vow their allegiance to him, the three had sat together. Now they were apart, and although Skins The Wolf had glanced at them, both Hillside and Winter Man had steadfastly refused to look the other's way.

What had happened in that Shoshone village? Hillside's anger had been like that of a rabid dog before Winter Man had stood witness to the taking of the grand coup, and afterwards he had acted as if it had never been. What did Winter Man hide in his heart? And why did he hide it? Of all his chosen men, he was the one with the makings of a Good Man, but his character had to be beyond reproach. Why did he court dishonour and disgrace?

Running Fisher's heart grew even more leaden as he thought of the future. He would lead other raids, but could he have their names announced again for all to hear? Could he trust them again as he had trusted them before? If not, whom was he to ignore? All of them, or just Winter Man? His name had been announced on three previous raids which Running Fisher had led. People expected Winter Man's name to be called. To pass him by for another would be the same as cursing him. The responsibilities held by a Good Man were heavy. Why did Winter Man have to make them worse?

A rattle of deer-hooves on the outside of the lodge covering quietened the hubbub within. Running Fisher straightened his back, his mind shedding his troubled thoughts as a duck sheds water from its plummage.

'Who wishes to enter?' he called.

'Moon Hawk,' came the reply.

Running Fisher smiled to himself. So, Winter Man still played the lovers' game. 'Enter, Moon Hawk.'

A bent head, a bright, vermilion-painted hair-parting, a flash of mirrors on the shoulders of the dress she wore, and Moon Hawk had entered.

She stood upright, her fingers unconsciously clutching at the edges of the buffalo robe slipping down her upper arm. It was warm inside the lodge. She would have no need of it, felt embarrassed for bringing it. The others would mock her, she knew. She had thought she had arrived early, but so many were already seated. She let her gaze run around the circles, the women outside, the men in, their feet towards the low-burning fire. They looked at her, Otter Robe, Spider, Skins The Wolf . . . She felt her eyes widen as his gaze bore into her, his blackened face unsmiling, unyielding of the thoughts behind it. She looked away, desperate to be rid of his stare, desperate to see the welcoming smile of Winter Man. All she saw was his back, the painted flesh-wound arching across his body in the dancing firelight. He was deep in animated conversation with Hillside and was paying no attention to the doorway, or to her.

She stood there, growing more uncomfortable by the moment. Never had she attended a celebration for returning warriors before. She knew of the expected etiquette, had been reminded of it by her mother before leaving their tipi.

'Be very careful how you act,' Little Face had told her. 'All eyes will be upon you there, both the men and the women. If bawdy jokes are told towards the end, do not laugh with the others. You are chaste. Act as you should. Blush and hide your face. They may mock you in turn, but they will also respect you for it. When your name is spoken later, these things will be remembered.'

Moon Hawk tried not to blush now. When was Winter Man going to turn and acknowledge her presence? A gentle smile, that was all she wanted, something to boost her wavering confidence.

She risked another glance in his direction and caught, not his eyes, but Hillside's. The speed with which he averted his gaze stunned her, and forgetting herself, she kept her eyes on him, watching him raise his fingers to rub the side of his nose. He was whispering to Winter Man.

A clammy hand wrapped itself about her heart and squeezed. The two of them were plotting – plotting against *her*.

She raised her eyes to stare at the decorated dew cloth, at the rattles and bags suspended from pegs above it. She would not be intimidated, she told herself. She would not let them intimidate her. But she was. She knew she was. The tipi had grown so silent. Every eye was on her, making her cheeks burn with embarrassment. Her vision began to blur as unshed tears forced themselves behind her eyes. She wished herself anywhere but there.

Do not cry! Do not cry here! As if in response to her own commands, she tensed the muscles in her back and raised her chin defiantly. Spiteful man! She would not give him the victory he sought. Playing with her like this.

Why had she believed he had asked her here out of . . . Oh! Curse his heart! It was she who was the fool!

Her eyes rested on Running Fisher, sitting solemnly in his place at the back of the lodge, his wife beside him. No matter how much Moon Hawk wanted to, she could not turn and leave now that she had called her name and had been asked to enter. To do so would dishonour those who lived within the lodge. It would dishonour her, too. People would speak of it for months, pointing and turning aside their eyes. Winter Man had well and truly trapped her.

'Who is it you are to sit behind?' Running Fisher asked. He opened his arms widely, indicating all who sat with him. 'I have many fine men.'

Many fine men. Moon Hawk's anger subsided. Running Fisher, despite his expressionless face, knew well what was happening and was offering her a way of fighting back. She would take it with both hands, she decided, and then she would see how Winter Man liked being held to the ridicule of others!

'I come to honour the man who bore his duties well and his wound bravely. I come to sit behind . . . Hillside.'

Even Running Fisher could not keep a straight face. He motioned Moon Hawk around the back of the circle, and she made her way to her place amid much subdued laughter and the waving of feather fans to hide it. While others turned their heads to look at her, Winter Man kept his eyes on the fire at his feet. Grinning from ear to ear while trying hard to maintain the sense of propriety the occasion demanded, Hillside welcomed her with an outstretched hand. She touched it in response and made herself comfortable behind him.

'You know my wife, Jay?'

Moon Hawk looked anxiously at the young woman beside her. She had spoken Hillside's name without a thought to how his wife would react, but from the glint in her eye, Moon Hawk knew she had an ally.

'We are of the same clan,' Jay stated loudly. 'You honour me by honouring my husband. May our lodge be ever open to you, for sunshine will follow in your footsteps.' There were more giggles and titters as Moon Hawk thanked her.

'You see my husband's wound,' Jay continued, drawing Hillside's arm towards them. 'It heals well, but if one such as you would touch it and say a quiet word, I am sure it would heal the quicker.'

No one hid their laughter this time. Even Moon Hawk thought it was going a little too far. Men painted their wounds and scars so that all might know how brave they had been, but it was tantamount to an insult to lavish such sympathetic attention on a mere flesh-wound. Hillside, though, took it all in good part, even retelling, in stirring tones, how he had come by it.

Despite wanting to ignore him, Moon Hawk found her gaze straying towards Winter Man. When the others laughed at something Hillside said, he remained steadfastly still. She could see nothing of his face for the thickness of his curtaining hair, but she doubted that he even smiled. He had struck her a blow, no doubt he had believed a winning blow, but she had deflected it and struck him back. No man liked to be bettered by a woman, especially in front of his friends.

She had not wanted this. It had been his doing; yet every instinct told her that she should be the one to offer the hand of reconciliation, if only she knew how, if only she dared risk the pain of his rebuff.

Her gaze followed the line of his hair, the curve of his shoulder muscles, the ugly gash across his back. The wound was inflamed and had no need of the vermilion used to enhance it. Perhaps she could offer him a salve for it. She had trilled for his courage as he had wanted. Surely he would accept a salve?

The rattle of deer-hooves announced another visitor.

'Who wishes to enter?' Running Fisher called.

'Swallow,' came the reply.

Moon Hawk's heart thudded. *Swallow?* Had Winter Man asked her, too?

She sat back, as far from him as she could manage, humiliated by her own sense of appeasement, by the extent of his duplicity. What had been his scheme? Had he hoped that she and Swallow would fight over him?

Swallow was called inside, and the lodge fell into a deathly hush on her entry. She stood in the doorway, her dark, almond-shaped eyes enhanced by the vermilion she had painted in a fish's tail around them. Moon Hawk glanced at her and looked away. No matter how she had her mother paint her face, she never seemed to look as beautiful as that.

Swallow's bright smile was fading, a look of perplexity crossing her high cheekbones. No lodge filled with so many could stand so silent without a reason.

'Who is it you are to sit behind?' Running Fisher asked her.

She flashed him a smile. 'Winter Man.'

The assembly erupted into life with knowing looks and stifled giggles. Swallow made her way around the circle. 'Have I missed a joke?' she asked.

'Ignore them,' Winter Man told her. 'They are women. Sit behind me. Let me feel your soothing touch.'

Moon Hawk watched him raise a hand to greet her and felt a flame of jealousy ignite within. When Swallow slipped her fingers through his to caress the back of his hand, Moon Hawk gritted her teeth and looked away.

Swallow seated herself and spoke warmly to the woman on her right. She turned to her left to greet the woman there, too late realising who it was.

Moon Hawk steeled herself and met her eye to eye as she watched Swallow's features darken. She had no wish to make an enemy of the woman. Winter Man was using them both, one against the other. Moon Hawk wanted to say something friendly to her, but the words refused to form on her lips.

Winter Man's bronzed arms were reaching back for Swallow. She paid him no attention, unable to take her eyes off Moon Hawk.

'A kiss,' he murmured, his voice no more than a mewing coax. 'A kiss from those moist lips of yours.'

Swallow struck him across the face with the long fringes of her sleeve. 'You try to make a clown of me, Winter Man, and I will send my brothers to visit you!'

Her threat, spoken savagely through clenched teeth,

brought gales of laughter from the onlookers, startling her. Moon Hawk did not know where to look or what to say. It was Jay who reached across to lay a comforting hand on Swallow's arm.

'Believe me, Swallow, this laughter is not for you. Moon Hawk sits behind my husband to honour him.'

Swallow shot Moon Hawk a withering look. She did not believe a word.

There was a sharp thudding of a drum, and order was gradually restored. Running Fisher began the speeches, calling upon all to retell the part they had played on the raid. The women trilled after each man had spoken. Skins The Wolf and Winter Man stood and re-enacted the taking of their coups. Again the women trilled and the drummers beat their drums. Food was distributed and eaten heartily, and then the singing began, to go on long into the night.

Each time Swallow touched Winter Man, Moon Hawk ached inside. Her indignation had worn thin again, and without it to sustain her she was a captive of her own heart. She loved Winter Man, had loved him for many years, had wanted to be his wife since the blossoming of her womanhood. How could he look at so many others and not at her?

When the time came for the women to dance with their men's weapons, Swallow was first on her feet, Winter Man's stone-headed club in her hand. Immediately Moon Hawk felt her arm being nudged, and turned to find Jay offering her Hillside's brass hatchet. She tried to refuse it. She had no stomach for this type of wagering. Her battered emotions were too open, too sensitive, but Jay was adamant and pressed the weapon into her hands. Moon Hawk dragged herself to her feet and followed another woman to the doorway where a space had been cleared for the dancing. At least, she reflected, she was not having to dance alone against Swallow. She tossed back her head and tried to lose herself in the sounds of the rattles and the drums and the singing.

Hillside altered his position and leaned close to Winter Man's shoulder. 'She dances well.'

Winter Man's head snapped round and a pair of narrowed eyes glared at him. 'Who?'

Hillside did not miss his friend's harsh tone, and he grinned widely. 'Why, the woman who dances with my weapon to honour me, the small one with the slim, enticing frame.'

Winter Man turned his head away, but Hillside was not finished with his goading.

'I leaned against her when the food was being passed. Her body is soft. Her thighs are firm.'

Winter Man inclined his head, his teeth almost bared in a tight-lipped grimace. 'Perhaps you should tell that to Jay – or perhaps I should. I am sure she would be interested to hear your thoughts.'

Hillside shrugged his shoulders. 'My wife likes her. They are as sisters, and sisters . . .'

Winter Man turned away. He knew what Hillside was intimating. When a man married the first daughter of a household, he took the right to marry the succeeding daughters if he was able to support them. Jay and Moon Hawk might not have shared the same parents, but they were clan-sisters.

He found his eyes upon her, dancing in the doorway, without realising he had consciously made the decision to seek her out. He had kept his eyes from Moon Hawk throughout the celebration, but whom was he hurting, her or himself?

She was slim, he noted, and small compared to the other women who swayed beside her. She had a bewildering quality, too, one he was not certain she was aware of herself. One part of him wanted to ridicule her, to taunt her; another wanted to encircle her with his arms, not as a lover—yes, as a lover—but also as a protector, to do nothing but hold her, make her feel secure. He could not readily understand it. He was not sure that he wanted to.

The beat of the drumming altered as one song changed into another. The dancers revolved, their unbraided hair and the long fringes of their dresses fanning out like swirling branches of a pine sapling. Moon Hawk slipped closer to the door, Swallow closer to the fire-pit.

Winter Man pursed his lips as he regarded the woman who honoured him by dancing with his club. Nothing had turned out how he had planned. Nothing.

'If I were to be asked . . .' he heard Hillside murmuring in his ear.

'You are not asked!' he snapped. He flung up his arm and signalled for the nearest drummer to pass the drum to him. Once it was in his hands, he beat the stretched skin harder than ever, forcing the accompaniment from his lungs until he felt his throat constrict with the strain.

The singers were hoarse, the drummers tired, the dancers could dance no more. Running Fisher's wife apportioned the remained food as gifts and the couples began to drift away.

Hillside stood outside the lodge, his arm round his wife. There was a chill wind reaching down from the Shining Mountains, heralding the coming snows. Moon Hawk clutched the edges of her buffalo robe about her shoulders, pleased she had brought it after all.

'You sang well for me tonight,' Hillside told her. 'I am truly honoured.'

Moon Hawk smiled. He meant it, she knew, no matter what had been intended in the beginning.

'Shall we walk with you to your father's lodge?'

She shook her head. Jay was shivering.

'I do not wish you to walk alone with a heavy heart,' he added.

Moon Hawk's pretence of good humour peeled away from her like the skin of an over-ripe fruit. Hillside was speaking of Winter Man, and he was right. No matter how she had acted during the celebration, she had been deeply hurt by Winter Man's rebuff. The game they played had ceased to be a game for her. She had realised that while watching Swallow dance with his club, dance until she nearly dropped, staking her claim on Winter Man for everyone to see. The two of them had been the first to give their thanks to Running Fisher and leave the lodge, leave arm in arm, no doubt to find a more secluded spot to share the rest of the night.

It was over. She would not look at Winter Man again.

She could not take this kind of pain a second time.

She forced a smile for Hillside. 'I am well,' she said. 'Do not concern yourself with me. Every child has to burn itself before it knows not to touch the fire.' She lifted her hand in farewell and turned to walk away.

Hillside pulled his wife closer to him as he watched her leave, sighing heavily as Moon Hawk disappeared into the deep shadows between the lodges. 'Though I would give my life for that man, I would say to his face he is a fool!'

'Then take no time to tell him so,' Jay retorted. 'There is one who will not be long taking meat to that lodge, I am sure.'

Hillside held her at arm's length, the starlight catching the questioning glint of his eyes. 'Who?'

'Skins The Wolf.'

Hillside felt the coldness of the wind about his shoulders. His easy smile died on his lips.

'Did you not see the way he kept looking at her?'

'No,' he said. 'I did not notice.'

Jay gave a disparaging rattle deep in her throat. 'Men never do.'

Hillside barely heard her. His eyes were seeking the darkness for a sign of Moon Hawk, but the silver starlight and the impenetrable shadows offered no clue to which route she had taken. He should have walked with her, he realised. He should have insisted on escorting her back to her father's lodge.

CHAPTER FIVE

MOON HAWK DALLIED awhile. There were few noises in the village, few tipis showing the subdued light of an inner fire. Most people were asleep. She wanted to be sure that her family, too, was asleep, before entering the lodge.

The evening had been a battle as far as Moon Hawk was concerned. She felt emotionally drained. She could not face her mother's prying questions nor the silent condemnations she knew would stand naked in her father's eyes. Tread warily, he had told her, and she had ignored him. She had gone to the celebration, her heart full and open, believing the game she had begun with Winter Man to have served its purpose and be over. He had not seen it that way, and she accepted, now, that he never would.

When she paused to look up at the stars, they blurred one into another as her eyes filled with tears. She wiped them away, angry with herself for allowing them to rise. She would not cry because of him! She would not! Had she not turned his intended humiliation on to himself? Had she not remained aloof while everyone around her had laughed? She had gained the victory in that encounter, not he!

Her fierce tirade died in her breast. It was a poor victory that made her feel so wretched; no victory at all.

She pulled her painted buffalo robe tighter about her shoulders. The wind was keen and she was cold, but she would wait a little longer before venturing near the family lodge. If one of her parents asked if she had enjoyed the celebration, she could not, with certainty, trust herself to answer without shedding tears. In the morning, after sleeping, if she slept at all, she might be able to look back on this time of misery with more composure, but it was a hope she had little faith in.

A dog growled close by, startling her. She swung

round to face it, afraid that it might try to snap at her ankles, but she could see nothing in the darkness. It growled again, low and throaty, unsure of what it was defying. Moon Hawk felt her muscles tighten. It was not growling at her. The familiar shadows of the nearby lodges took on a sudden malevolence. As she peered into them, their density seemed to alter. Perhaps silent spirits were playing there; but a dog never took fear of kindly spirits, only of more human intruders. Her salival glands brimmed unnaturally. Perspiration oozed cold and clammy down her spine. Enemy raiders waited until night to venture into a village. They slunk in the shadows of tipis wanting to cut free a picketed horse, wanting a coup, or a scalp, or a prisoner.

She stepped back a pace, uncertain which way to turn. She was standing in the open moonlight for any eye to see, she knew she was. Where were the Muddy Hand guards? Had they been evaded? Were they lying dead? Which way was the safe way to run?

'Do not cry out.'

The voice was Winter Man's. She knew it was as soon as she heard the first syllable of his words, but her fear had built so fast inside her she could not stop herself. A figure leapt at her from the darkness, powerful fingers grasping at her shoulders through the thickness of her buffalo robe.

'Quiet! Do you want an arrow to sprout its fletching from my back before I can shout "Hold"?'

She raised her eyes to the angry face above her head. 'Winter Man!' She spoke his name like a prayer of deliverance and sagged against him, the tension leaving her body in shuddering fits as his grip on her shoulders eased.

'Who is that?' called a voice from a nearby tipi.

'Stay your hand! It is Winter Man.'

There was a guttural grumble from within the lodge. 'Do you never sleep, Winter Man? Take your sweating loins elsewhere.'

Moon Hawk felt his arm snake around her shoulders, felt him guiding her away. Her shaking legs seemed incapable of supporting her.

'You are trembling. I frightened you.' Slim fingers gently smoothed her hair. She heard him chuckle. 'You truly thought I was Lakota.' The laughter left his voice. He pulled her closer. 'You would have made easy prey, standing there in the moonlight. You should have thrown yourself into the shadows, screamed until your lungs burst . . .'

Moon Hawk opened her eyes, her lashes flicking against the cool skin of his chest. There was such concern in his voice. He cared. He *cared* about her. She raised her eyes, wanting to see his thoughts held starkly in his face, unable to believe what she had heard. His head was closer to hers than she had expected it to be. His blackened face, hidden in the full shadow of his head, offered nothing, but she could feel his breath warm upon her cheek. Upon her mouth.

There was a tightening in her chest and abdomen. She let slip the buffalo robe and put out a hand to push him away. It stopped against the solid muscle of his chest. His skin felt so warm to her chilled fingers. His heart was thudding against his ribs. Or was it hers? She did not know. She was not sure what she . . .

The burning heat of his lips seared into her own, flinging the confusion of her thoughts into a bottomless whirlpool, never to be retrieved. So delicate was his touch, yet so charged with power. As his lips rose, hers rose, too, clinging skin to skin until his pulled free. A new sensation overwhelmed her as his moist tongue skimmed the dryness of her parted lips. And then he bore down on her once more, stronger this time, the tenderness gone, his tongue lunging hard again and again into her mouth, into every hollow, every crevice, reaching for her throat.

Alarms screamed inside her head as she shuddered under his onslaught. She tried to pull away from him, but her neck was caught in the crook of one arm. His other was tight about her waist. The thrill she had felt at his touch turned to fear as she realised she was locked against him. There was no escape from his demanding mouth.

And then his lips were gone and she was breathing

cool, crisp air again, sucking it inside her in great lungfuls, trying to stifle her rising panic, trying to clear her spinning head.

'Do not struggle.' His lips brushed her cheek, her eye, her brow, delicate again, like the touch of a butterfly. 'I am too ardent, I know. I forget myself.' The iron grip of his arms relaxed a little. 'Have no fear of me, Moon Hawk. My only wish is for a kiss from those moist lips of yours.'

Her breath froze in her lungs . . . *moist lips of yours*. She had heard those words before. That very night. He had spoken them to Swallow. He had left Swallow's bedding robes to come hunting her!

Her fear of him was gone. Anger exploded inside her with the ferocity of an overloaded powder gun—anger for him, for herself, for the way she cared when he did not. The knuckles of her clenched fist hit his ribs before she realised she wanted to strike him. Pain raced through her hand and up her arm and she jumped back, more startled by that than by his grunt and the relaxation of his grip. She crouched down suddenly, touching the cold, hard ground with her fingers to steady herself, and she ducked underneath the circle of his arms, leaving him nothing but the buffalo robe to grasp for. Free of him, her only thought was to run.

'Leave me this robe, and I shall wear it as a gift!'

His threat stopped her retreat as certainly as any physical restraint. She turned to look at him, astonishment opening her mouth, but robbing her of words. It was a woman's robe he held. Her robe. Everyone knew it to be hers from the design she had painted on its surface. Surely he would not parade it about the village as his?

'You would not wear my robe and say it was a . . .'

'I would say nothing; but you are right, Moon Hawk. There are many who would see it in my hands and think you gave it as a lover's gift. No one would visit your lodge to ask you to notch the Sacred Tree in the summer ceremonies.'

He altered his stance, draping the robe casually over one shoulder. The moonlight caught his face, the brightness of his eyes. He was laughing at her.

'You are beneath contempt!' she spat.

'Perhaps, but it is better than having to chase you round the village. I only want to talk to you, Moon Hawk.'

'Talk to me! You hide in the shadows, frightening the dogs, because you want to talk to me! You pounce on me out of the darkness because you want to *talk to me*! What talking was it when you had me pinned in your arms?'

'It was only a kiss.'

'And no doubt you will make a song about it to sing to your friends!'

'A man does not boast about a single kiss. A kiss is nothing.'

She tried to speak again, but her indignation overwhelmed her. She did not know which was worse, the way he had taken the kiss, or the fact that he considered it nothing.

He extended a hand towards her, the blue-grey star-sheen glinting off the rings on his slender fingers. 'This meeting is not as I intended, Moon Hawk. You thought I was Lakota and you were fearful. I did not mean to frighten you.' He took a step towards her and she took a step backwards. He stayed where he was and lowered his arm.

'I had been waiting outside your lodge for such a time. You did not come. I—I thought you had left with another.'

'Another?'

His answer did not come easily. 'With Hillside.'

Moon Hawk stared at the tall silhouette before her, at the thin braids fluttering from the nape of his neck like ribbon streamers in the rising wind. Left with Hillside? What was he saying?

Winter Man jerked a hand. 'He is well regarded among the Good Young Men, honourable and courageous. I know he wants Jay to carry a son for him soon. He—he has discussed with me the merits of acquiring a second wife to ease the burden of her work.'

Moon Hawk's indignation rose like a geyser at the hot

springs. 'A second wife! You think I would be a second wife to . . . I will be no man's second wife!'

She saw him shrug. 'You called his name and sat behind him.'

'I did that to . . .' She caught herself. He knew very well why she had called Hillside's name. 'You tried to humiliate me in that lodge. You asked me to go and sit behind you and then you ignored me.'

'I only wanted to hear you speak my name. If you had spoken my name, I would have accepted you with pride for all to see.'

Moon Hawk scoffed. 'You say that now, but what of Swallow? What were you intending to do when she announced herself at the lodge? Were you hoping we would fight over you? She nearly tore my eyes out for sitting within arm's reach of you!'

'I did not know Swallow would come. I did not . . .'

'How can you stand there and say you did not know she would come? She is your lover!'

'Mine and two other men's.'

Moon Hawk raised her eyebrows. 'Do I detect a certain resentment?' she taunted. 'Perhaps if you were to curb your own lust a little you might attract a more chaste . . .' She clamped her teeth down on the words, but the damage had been done.

'A chaste woman? But I thought I had, Moon Hawk. I thought I had.'

He was moving towards her again, swaggering now, sure of his advantage. Why had she said it? Why? What had possessed her to be so foolish?

'Stay away from me!'

'Stay away? But that is not what you want, is it, Moon Hawk? *You* who threw the turnip at *me*.' He paused a stride from her, a wolf eyeing its helpless prey. 'What is it that you do want, Moon Hawk? Tell me now.'

She drew her hands in front of her, clasping them together in an attempt to stave off her misgivings. How could she tell him what she wanted. He would laugh.

'Do you want me to follow you about the village like a puppy dog, playing you tunes on a courting flute, desperate for one of your smiles? I will not do it, Moon Hawk. I would rather cast my spirit into the limbo of eternity by cutting my own throat!'

He was becoming excited, very demonstrative. Moon Hawk was not certain if it was truly a display of how he felt, or an act to frighten her. He was talking so quickly that she had no time to think.

'No! That is not what you want of me. You want me to dress as for war and ride you down as you collect water from the creek. You want me to haul you over my saddle and carry you away, throw you to the ground and rip your dress from neck to calf with the cold blade of my knife. You want me to . . .'

'No!' She almost screamed the word.

'Then what do you want, Moon Hawk? Tell me now, for I tire of this game of yours.'

Game? Who was playing games now? His tone was as quiet and flat as if he had been speaking to his own grandmother. Moon Hawk realised she had been out-manoeuvred. She was angry and embarrassed, and she let both emotions do her talking.

'Meat,' she said stiffly. 'I want you to bring meat to my lodge.'

Winter Man's laughter was loud and harsh. She would not be goaded, she told herself fiercely. She would remain outwardly calm, even if she did not feel it.

'Then give horses to your father and brothers?'

'Yes,' she said. 'I will be your wife.'

'*Will* be?' He laughed again. 'Your mind is muddled. It is Winter Man you are speaking to. I take lovers, not wives.' His voice took on a harder edge. 'And when I feel the time is right for me to take a wife, I shall decide who she will be.'

'I will not be your lover, Winter Man.'

'Then go and sleep alone, Moon Hawk. I have no desire for a little girl who is too afraid to give herself to a man.'

He threw the heavy robe at her. In the darkness she misjudged its speed, and part of it landed on her head. When she had pulled it aside and drawn her hair from her eyes, Winter Man was striding away between the tipis.

Tears forced themselves into her eyes, blurring her vision. She had been wrong. The game had not been over. Had she played it a little more deftly, she might have won, but she had lost, lost Winter Man for ever. She clasped the robe tightly to her and buried her face in its softness.

The sun was high, but the cool wind robbed the land of its heat. Thick grey clouds rose above the white peaks of the Shining Mountains and scudded eastwards over the Apsaroke village. Hillside and Winter Man were sitting outside Hillside's lodge, fletching arrows ready for the last big buffalo hunt of the season.

'I tell you, I did not know Swallow would be there.'

Hillside openly guffawed.

'I did not! Two nights before we left for the Shoshone village she told me that she had given her heart to Strikes The Drum and would look at me no longer.'

Hillside rolled back his lips in a derisory gesture. 'She could not keep her hands off you when you paraded the roan.'

'She and others. The others did not come to Running Fisher's lodge for the celebration.'

'But Moon Hawk did, and she danced with *my* weapons.'

Winter Man did not rise to the taunt. He kept his eyes on the berry-wood shaft in his fingers, taking great care with the positioning of the long split feathers at the notched end.

'I heard my mother-in-law talking about you this morning,' Hillside continued.

Winter Man felt his chest tighten. He had noticed the looks and the pointed fingers. Everyone in the village seemed to know what had taken place after the celebration.

'You and Moon Hawk must have made enough noise to wake half the tipis.' He chuckled. 'Am I to know, too? Is the game you play with her still in progress?'

Winter Man raised his eyes and glared at Hillside. 'The game is over.'

He saw his friend's grin fade, watched his laughing

eyes take on a defensive sheen. Winter Man looked away, shamed at the severity of his own reply. What was this anger which rose inside him every time Moon Hawk's name was mentioned? And to show it to Hillside, of all people . . . They had grown into men together, shared their triumphs and their defeats, their lovers, their fears, the dangers of the fight. They had entered the Fox warrior society together and Winter Man had always thought of them leaving it together, in death, in one final, glorious act of valour. Why could he not speak to him of Moon Hawk? Why could he not understand, himself, what he was feeling?

'She has the body of a woman, but the mentality of a child. I have no time for it,' he said.

'Then you will not feel slighted if another takes meat to her father's lodge?'

The tinge of jealousy Winter Man had felt the night before flamed anew. He made himself look into Hillside's eyes, made himself smile with an amusement he did not feel. 'So, you have decided to take a second wife.'

Hillside shook his head, his brows knitting. 'No. Jay went to the women's willow lodge this morning.' He looked pointedly at Winter Man, his dark eyes heavy with concern. 'It is a full turning of the seasons since I took her as my wife. Either my seed is not strong enough, or she is barren. I am not the first man she has known. She had lovers before she came to me, but never a sign of any child.' His gaze fell. His shoulders sagged. 'She cried so much when she saw her flow. I could not comfort her.'

Winter Man lowered his gaze, too, feeling guilty for the thoughts he had harboured.

Hillside slammed his fist into the ground between his crossed ankles. 'Curse me for my foolishness! Why did I have to talk to her of a second wife? I did it in innocence, I swear I did. I was telling her how I would look after her when she carried my child, how I would get another woman to tan the skins and gather wood and do all the heavy work for her.' His anger faded. 'Now she waits for me to take another wife so that I can hold a son in my arms. Winter Man, I could not hurt her that way. I would rather die shrivelled with age without ever having held a child of my own, but I cannot make her believe that.'

Winter Man reached out and grasped him firmly by the arm. There were no words to help his friend, but he had to show he grieved with him. Hillside raised his head, and the two exchanged the single bond they had shared for many years.

Hillside smiled, faintly at first, and then with a stronger grin. 'Come,' he said. 'Brighten my heart. Make me laugh. Tell me what passed between you and Moon Hawk in the depths of the night. What challenge did she cast before you this time?'

Winter Man made his words heavy with irony. 'No challenge. An order.'

Hillside raised his eyebrows in astonishment. 'She would give an order to a Good Young Man?'

Winter Man flicked his hand in the air. 'She is chaste, remember. She believes it carries her above the etiquette the rest of us are bound by. She wants meat to be taken to her father's lodge as a preliminary to our marriage.'

'She ordered you to take meat to her father's lodge?' Hillside's eyes were growing wider by the moment.

Even Winter Man was finding amusement where none had existed the night before. 'Demanded it!' He feigned horror, and his friend roared with laughter.

Winter Man pursed his lips and smiled a little. He had intended to ignore Moon Hawk totally, to smooth the ruffled feelings of Swallow and carry on with her as before, but as he spoke to Hillside and watched the light burn in his eyes, an idea was born in his mind.

Hillside inclined his head like an attentive bird. 'You have thought of something. Tell me.'

Winter Man straightened his legs and eased himself back on one elbow. It was a good idea. A great idea. One with as keen an edge as a freshly-honed blade. One that would cut so deeply that Moon Hawk would never dare to raise her eyes to his again.

'If she wants meat taken to her lodge, I should take

meat to her lodge. We all should. I think, Hillside, it is time we went courting.'

It had been five days since the celebration at Running Fisher's lodge; five days since the disturbance afterwards, which had brought knowing looks, pointed fingers and undisguised giggling from nearly every woman Moon Hawk had met. She hardly dared to drag her eyes from the ground as she went to collect water from the creek. She would not have left the lodge at all except for the condemning silences she received from her father. Everyone in the village knew, or thought they knew, what had passed between Winter Man and herself that night, and as she saw it, the truth was no better than the rumours. She had disgraced herself, and it would take many days of hard and constant work to atone for her behaviour. If she ever saw Winter Man again it would be too soon—yet her lonely nights were filled with thoughts of him, of how their relationship might have blossomed if the spirits which watched over such things had helped a little more.

Moon Hawk was standing up to her knees in water. The long skirt of her dress was drawn between her legs and caught tightly in her belt to stop the edges from being soaked. She was looking for a stone, a certain type of stone, to replace those lining the fire-pit in the tipi. In ordinary circumstances new stones would never have been sought at that time of the year, so close to the village moving to its winter site, but Little Face felt as responsible as her daughter for all the gossiping being carried on about their lodge, and she knew only too well how easily gossip leapt from one subject to another. No one would point a finger and say that the lodge of the Piegan captive was ill kept and dirty. No one would whisper in her husband's ear and say that she was unworthy and should be divorced.

Moon Hawk lifted a flat red stone from the bed of the creek and showed it to her mother. Little Face squinted at it a moment and then nodded. Her daughter tossed it on the bank, where it clinked against others they had thrown.

'Have we enough now?'

'Two more.'

Moon Hawk grimaced. Her legs were cold, her fingers tingling. She could no longer feel her feet.

'Hi-ee! Hi-ee!'

The excited calling turned their attention to the bank. It was Turtle, running towards them as fast as her little legs could carry her. Her face aglow, her chest heaving, she could hardly speak for lack of breath.

'Meat! At the tipi! Father says . . . you have to return.'

Moon Hawk stared at her, not daring to believe it was true. Meat had arrived at the lodge. She extended her arms to Little Face, wanting to share her delight with a woman who understood.

'He has brought meat! After all he said, Winter Man has brought meat!'

'Not just Winter Man,' Turtle countered. 'Lots of men! Frost, and Hillside, and Spider, and . . .' She extended her arms and shrugged. 'Lots.'

The smile slipped from Moon Hawk's lips. She felt herself shudder. She looked to her mother, desperate to hear someone pour scorn on Turtle's words, but Little Face was already climbing out of the water. Moon Hawk watched her snatch up her leggings and moccasins and begin to hurry back to the village, her precious fire-pit stones forgotten.

Only when her mother was lost to her sight did Moon Hawk pull her wits about her and drag herself on to the bank. It was not possible, she kept telling herself. Winter Man would never hold her to such ridicule. The dropping of a joint of meat at the lodge of an unmarried woman was a recognised courtesy, a sign of goodwill to all those who lived within. It was a sign of a suitor's intentions. He made no speech as he left the meat and the head of the lodge gave no acknowledgment of acceptance, but all knew that the young man would be standing outside the tipi at dusk in the hope of talking to the one he desired. A woman might have more than one suitor, but not in the way Turtle had described it, not Frost and Hillside and Spider—all friends of Winter Man.

Moon Hawk stared at the joints of meat piled high on a robe outside the entrance of her father's lodge. There were many, too many to count, too many for an honourable show of intent. People were gathering, pointing, sniggering. She had never sought to discredit Winter Man. Why was he doing this to her?

If there had been somewhere for her to run and hide, she would have run and hidden herself, but in a village of skin tipis where everyone could hear a raised word, there was no place to find the solace she craved. She entered the lodge like a shadow. Little Face was sitting there, her head bowed, the children one on either side of her, silent and pensive. At the rear, leaning against his back-rest, Bear On The Flat stared into the dull grey ash of the fire-pit. The atmosphere could not have been more desolate if they had just learned that a close relative was dying.

'Why is this lodge suffering this humiliation?' Bear On The Flat asked in a low tone. 'Why has my daughter —and my wife—brought such disgrace upon my name? Have I not kept you both well over the years? Have I not loved you and protected you, honoured you in my speech and thought and actions so that others would honour you, too? The men who brought that meat to this lodge had laughter in their eyes. They mock the solemnity of the occasion. They mock you for your impudence. They mock me for not guiding you with a firmer hand. Those men are my brothers. They are of the Fox society. *My* warrior society. I shall never be able to hold my head high again!'

Moon Hawk closed her eyes in an attempt to stem her rising tears. There was no apology she could offer to her father, no words to show the remorse she felt. She had never intended him to suffer such ridicule, had never expected such herself. It had been a game, just a game to make Winter Man notice her.

They sat there, a family in silence, until the daylight melted into dusk. There was movement outside, talking, subdued laughter. Her mock suitors would be coming to stand by the lodge, waiting for her to step out and speak with them. She wished she could curl up and die like a leaf dried in the autumn wind, such was her pain. And then the calling started, the calling from the watching crowd.

'Moon Hawk! They are waiting, Moon Hawk!'

'Come out, Moon Hawk! Come out and meet your suitors!'

'Everyone is here, Moon Hawk! The whole village waits to see you do your courting! What a choice there is for you!'

'He stands here, Moon Hawk. Winter Man stands here. Do you not want him now?'

Their laughter rang in her ears. She bowed her head until her brow reached down and touched her bent knees. She prayed for the people to stop but their taunting was endless, and when she could pray no more, she cried.

CHAPTER SIX

'SOMEONE HAS SMOKED against you,' Hillside maintained. 'You are cursed.'

It was an explanation that had sprung readily to Winter Man's mind, but one he had dismissed as too grave to contemplate. The Apsaroke had many mystics. They worked for the good of the people, but any one of them could, if he desired, resort to sorcery to gain whatever end he wanted—or he could be paid to do so on behalf of someone else. Charms and potions to entice the ardour of the opposite sex were well used, but smoking against someone—cursing them—was not.

There were stories, of course, of jealous mystics who had fought each other with sorcery. Winter Man had never witnessed such battles, but his oldest grandmother had, far back in her childhood. She had told him the tale during the long winters of his boyhood, and he had heard her tell it again to his nephews and nieces. It still made his flesh crawl across his bones. It did now, as he thought of it again.

'I cannot believe that,' he said forcefully. 'I have never done anything harmful to any of our people.'

'You have wrapped your robe about the wives of other men,' Hillside reminded him.

'I never sought them. They came to me, you know that. Besides, I was always very careful not to enrage their husbands.'

'And Squirrel's husband?'

Winter Man had been thinking about her. The sight of her, bruised and bloodied, hiding herself in her shame at the rear of her tipi was still etched deeply in his mind. Knowing that he had been the cause of it was something no mere transfer of wealth could adequately redress. Had the spiteful person who had whispered lies in Butterfly's ear also had a hand in the shaming of a fellow Fox society member?

He forced his ringed fingers through the thick locks of his hair. He could blame that on no one but himself. It had been he who had asked his friends to take meat to the lodge, he who had spread the word to the younger members of the society in the hope that some of them might do the same. He had only meant to bait Moon Hawk as she had baited him, but there had been so much meat, so many men standing outside the lodge in their finery. And the people who came to watch . . . shouting and laughing and calling out their obscene comments as if Moon Hawk were some disgraced enemy. In his wildest dreams he had never envisaged the appalling cruelty of the scene. He had never meant it to have such far-reaching effects. He had tried to calm them, tried to disperse the men who had stood with him, but those he had touched had laughed and treated his actions as a goad. He had found his only course was to stand aside and let the encounter run its natural path as quickly as it was able. But he had shamed Moon Hawk, and in shaming her he had shamed not only her father, but all the members of her family.

'What happened to the meat?' he asked Hillside.

'Moon Hawk and her mother were seen distributing it among the lodges of the poor before dawn. None of it has been given to their relatives.'

Winter Man had feared that. Moon Hawk's father was treating the meat as if it were tainted with ill-luck. He would not offer it to his relatives in case that ill-luck passed to them. In all honesty, Winter Man could not say that his precautions were unfounded. He arched his neck, staring up into the grey, rain-laden clouds. 'Has Bear On The Flat been seen today?'

Hillside shook his head.

'I have shamed him.'

'It is not you.'

'It *is* me!' Winter Man sat upright, his back rigid. 'I have shamed him. I have shamed the man who spoke for me when I first entered the society lodge. How can I enter it now? I have to make amends—and quickly. I shall take horses to him.'

'You cannot take him horses, not after leaving meat at

his lodge. He will consider it a marriage gift.'

'Then I shall marry Moon Hawk.'

Hillside flung up his arms in despair. 'You are not thinking straight! He feels he has been shamed. By you, he thinks. He would not have you for a son-in-law if you took him horses that could leap the stars!'

'A pipe then, so we may smoke together and seal the breach I have created.'

'He would have to be approached by a third person on your behalf; someone who commands a great respect. A Fox member, preferably. Running Fisher would be ideal if you could . . .'

'How can I ask Running Fisher? I lied to him, remember? He made it quite plain that he no longer trusts me. Do you think he would even look at me after what he witnessed last night?'

Hillside shook his head. 'Each path we think to take is blocked to us. You have been smoked against, Winter Man. There is no other explanation.'

'Then what am I to do? I dare not entreat a mystic to work on my behalf. If he has not the power to overthrow this sorcery, who knows what ill-spirits might be let loose upon the people.'

'Perhaps you need another spirit guardian.'

'My Medicine has always been strong.'

'Until now.'

Winter Man raised his eyes to the Shining Mountains, their peaks enshrouded in thick grey cloud. He knew snow already lay on the upper reaches; it could be seen glistening on clear, moonlit nights. Only a desperate man undertook a vision quest so late in the year. There would be the sweat-bath, the songs and prayers, the travelling to the place, four days of fasting . . . He opened his left hand and traced the scarred remnants of his smallest finger. He had taken his first vision quest on the threshold of manhood. He had sung and cried and sacrificed his flesh, wailing for the spirits to take pity on him—and one had, finally, and he had honoured it ever since. His Medicine was strong, Winter Man knew it was, and he did not wish to court its indifference to him by attempting to gain a second when there was no need.

'I shall wait until after the hunt before I decide.'

Hillside pointed a finger towards his face. 'That is another thing,' he said. 'Why are the buffalo so late? This time last year we were fat from eating heart and liver. The women had dried the meat and tanned the skins, and the village had moved to its winter site. It is connected. I know it is.'

'The buffalo have been late before.'

'I tell you, it is not natural.'

Winter Man rose to his feet. Hillside made to follow him, but Winter Man waved him aside. 'I wish to walk alone. There is much I have to consider.' Hillside nodded and the two friends parted.

Winter Man left the tipis and made his way out to the surrounding pasture. The grass was short and thin, more brown than green. Even the coming rain would not be enough to replenish it. The village would have to move soon, buffalo or no buffalo. If the horses did not get fresh grazing they would begin to grow ill and die.

His new roan recognised him as he approached and swung its heavy head from side to side in greeting. Winter Man scratched it between the ears and it whinnied its appreciation, making him smile.

'How Moon Hawk looked when I paraded you before her!'

His smile faded. He had tried to keep Moon Hawk out of his thoughts since the twilight of the day before. How was she feeling? He did not dare to guess. Would she ever look at him again? Would he see her eyes light with pride the way they had when he had taken the roan to show her? Hillside had been right. Her father would not accept him as a son-in-law, not now. The finality of that knowledge made Winter Man's heart heavier still. He had never intended to take Moon Hawk as his wife, no matter what she had wanted. A passing lover, perhaps, but never a wife. So why did it pain him so much to know that she would never be his? There was no sense to it.

The rain came lashing down just after midday, turning the spaces between the lodges into wide puddles and muddy patches. The smoked buffalo-skin tipi coverings shed the water well. Their poles were smooth and knot-free, and only an occasional drip fell into the fire-pit below the smoke-hole.

Moon Hawk could hear voices raised in song. A group of women had gathered in one lodge to sing and talk while they embroidered brightly dyed porcupine-quills on items of clothing, or on robes which the hairy-faced traders would be willing to exchange for their red cloth, coloured beads and metal goods. Moon Hawk had spent many a happy afternoon at such gatherings, but she had not been invited to this one. Neither had her mother.

The singing stopped. The dull hammering of the rain and the occasional whinny of a horse were the only noises to be heard. Then there was laughter, uproarious laughter, that split the air like a peel of thunder. Moon Hawk felt her chest constrict. They were laughing at her, those women in that lodge; telling old jokes of the antics of foolish young maidens, and inserting the name of Moon Hawk among them.

She raised her eyes and risked a glance at Bear On The Flat. Her father sat motionless, as he had all that morning, the steady rise and fall of his bare chest the only sign that he lived. A bowl of sliced buffalo tongue, his favourite delicacy, lay untouched by his moccasin. Little Face had put it there in an attempt to communicate with him, but it had been to no avail. Moon Hawk wished he would openly castigate them, anything to break this interminable, soul-destroying silence.

A movement of the door-flap startled her. At a time like this, who would attempt to enter without announcing their presence? Winter Man? Her heart began to lift. Had he come with gifts of apology? She willed it to be him, coming to set right all that was wrong. Her hopes sank. It was her older brothers. From the look in their dark eyes she knew they had not come on a mere social visit. Antelope Dancer held his pipe-bag in his hands. They had come to smoke with their father.

Runs His Horse reached over and unhooked the water-paunch from its peg above the wood-pile. He tossed it into his sister's lap without a flicker of expression. Moon Hawk gathered its neck in her hands as quickly as she could, but she was not able to stop its contents from spilling down her dress. Tears welled in her eyes, blurring the paunch and her hands into one congealed, shapeless image. Her brothers had every right to be angry, she told herself, every right. Even her clan siblings would be hiding their faces in shame.

'Mother.' It was Antelope Dancer who spoke, his words measured and without inflection. 'Take the children to my lodge and wait there until I return.'

Little Face rose at once. She lifted Bobtailed Cat into her arms and silently ushered Turtle out of the lodge before her.

Moon Hawk rose, too, the paunch still clutched in her hands. She was not to go to her brother's tipi, that had been made perfectly clear. Antelope Dancer did not want her there. His wife did not want her there, either. It was hardly surprising. She left the lodge in the wake of her mother, unable to lift her head and look either of her brothers in the eye. She walked between the tipis as quickly as she was able. The rain had lessened to a drizzle, but few people were to be seen outside their lodges, a consolation she felt particularly grateful for.

The creek was in flood, its clear waters now turbid and unpalatable. Moon Hawk stood before it, watching twigs and hunks of grass root riding its undulating back. There was little point in filling the paunch at once, since the men would be smoking for quite a while, perhaps until the twilight. She shuddered as she thought of the return of the twilight. It would mirror her shame, drag cutting remarks back into her mind. It would make her think of Winter Man. She heaved a trembling breath into her lungs and began to walk upstream.

Why had Winter Man been so harsh in his rebuff of her? If his attack had been confined to herself she could have understood, but to include her family? Her father? She would never have believed him possible of such cruelty. How could she have spent so many sleepless nights dreaming of his touch? The very thought of it made her cringe and shake herself. He had intended to frighten her, that night of the celebration, hiding in the shadows like an enemy ready to strike. And what had he said? That he thought she had left with Hillside. Hillside! The sheer gall of the man! She stamped her foot hard as she walked on, not caring about the mud she splattered up her leggings and the bottom of her dress, oblivious to her surroundings and the rushing of the creek.

To think that at one time she would willingly have become his lover! Thanks be to First Maker—and to Little Face—for turning her from that course. He would have taken her chastity and made a song about it to sing to his friends. And what would she have had left? Nothing!

Water oozed cold between her toes, bringing her to an abrupt halt. She stared down at the absorbent moss creeping up the sides of her soaked moccasins, and then ahead and around her. Could she have walked so far without realising? Had she reached the marshy hollow already? She raised an eyebrow, surprised by what her eyes were showing her.

The village, and the flat land upon which it was sited, were well behind her. Here the ground rose quickly to twice her height, creating a deep cut through which the creek ran in a wide arc. It had changed its route several times over the seasons, silting up one track in a drought, creating another in a flood. The thick earth it had deposited drank heavily from the incessant water passing at its edge, and had become a refuge for a rich variety of marsh plants, both short and tall. Even during the hottest summer, when the creek no longer ran, a hole dug here at dusk would be full of reviving water by the dawn. It was a place well-noted by her people, a place that had saved a party of thirsty travellers on more than one occasion.

Moon Hawk retreated a few steps, veering to the rise of the bank where the ground was marginally firmer. Trees grew there, with thick, dark roots criss-crossing the surface in great profusion. She used the roots as stepping-stones, climbing up to find a place to sit. Water dripped on to her from the yellowing leaves, but she paid no attention. Though the drizzle had stopped, there was no sign of the sun peeking through the heavy cloud. If she had to stay away from the lodge until darkness fell, this was as good a place as any. She pushed errant strands of wet hair from her eyes and wrung out the sodden skirt of her dress. She had a strike-a-light bag hanging from her broad belt, and thought of finding fuel for a small fire, but the leaf-litter was damp, and she was not very cold, so she decided against it. If only she had had the forethought to bring something to do—sewing, quill-work, anything—it would have given her something to concentrate on, something to blot out the images of Winter Man that kept rising, unbidden, into her mind. Curse the man! Why did she have to keep thinking of him?

At first, she believed the sound was inside her head, some self-induced torment to add to those spinning endlessly there, but it became louder, more insistent. It was a flute. Someone close by was playing a courting flute. And he was playing it for her. *Winter Man*. Was he going to ridicule her for ever? Was he going to persecute her until she went mad?

She heaved herself to her feet, glaring wildly in all directions. Where was he? She would tell him what she thought of him and disregard the consequences. She would not be treated like this!

'Winter Man! You say you are a Good Young Man worthy of the title. Why are you hiding in the bushes? Show yourself!'

The high, wavering notes of the flute died in the middle of a phrase. Away to her right there was movement among the birch fronds, then they were drawn back, and a broad-shouldered man stepped into the open. Moon Hawk snatched at her breath, almost toppling backwards over a curled root as every instinct told her to run. It was not Winter Man at all. It was Skins The Wolf.

His face, still blackened in honour of the coup he had taken, creased into a frown. 'Winter Man? He derides you before all the people and the next day you expect him to be playing a courting flute for you?' He slapped the flute across his thigh, an action Moon Hawk found unnerving.

She shook her head. 'No. You do not understand. I thought the flute was being played by him to mock me.'

Skins The Wolf eased his stance significantly. The heavy winter robe he wore slipped from one shoulder, uncovering his arm and the loops of different necklaces draped across his painted chest. A yellow hand-print spoke of a prisoner he had once taken. Behind his right moccasin he dragged a decorated wolf's tail, his latest acquisition, for winning a grand coup in the Shoshone village.

Moon Hawk's eyes widened in alarm as she surveyed him from his brightly beaded moccasins to the eagle and hawk plumes tied neatly into the back of his hair. Surely he had not come to court her? His family had already made an advance on his behalf, and it had been refused. What was he doing here?

Skins The Wolf inclined his head a little. His mouth opened as if he were about to speak, but it was some time before he selected his words.

'I think Winter Man has played his game,' he said. 'He has laughed. Others have laughed with him, but I was not one of them.' He shrugged a little, and took a step towards her. 'I do not have his heart, so cannot say for certain how it beats. Many would say that he has been overly favoured by First Maker. Since manhood he has never needed to hunt for lovers. I can understand how you were drawn to him.'

Moon Hawk felt his steady gaze envelop her, and she tensed herself against it.

'He would have made a good provider for you, I admit. He is well skilled in all the hunting arts and, of course, he is brave and courageous in his quest for honours—as I am. We have often ridden together on the war trail. If the Lumpwoods had not specifically asked me to join their ranks in place of my grandfather when he died, I might well have joined the Fox society with Winter Man.' He paused, and his voice seemed to drift on the air. 'There was a time when I had hoped that he might affiliate himself with the Lumpwoods, but . . .'

His attention snapped back to Moon Hawk. She thought she saw a hunted look flicker in his eyes, but it was so brief that she could not be sure.

'You are wet and cold. Here.' He shrugged the buffalo robe off his shoulder and took the heavy garment in one hand to offer it to her.

She shook her head, uncertain how to refuse it without offending him. She wanted to take nothing from his hands in case it was misconstrued as the giving and accepting of a gift.

'I am damp.' She laughed a little. 'But I am not cold, truly.'

His hand remained extended. She felt the flesh rise on her arms like that of a plucked goose. He was still a few steps from her. She hoped that his eyesight was not sharp enough to notice.

At last he nodded his acknowledgement of her decision, and draped the robe over his shoulder once again. Moon Hawk breathed a quiet sigh of relief. She wondered how she might excuse herself from his company, and then it was too late, for he was speaking again, slowly, picking his words, being careful of his manner.

'It is early yet, I know. Your heart still bleeds with the pain Winter Man has brought it, but I want you to know that I look upon you the same way as I . . . Did you know that my family had initiated an honourable offer of marriage on my behalf?'

Moon Hawk felt her mouth turn dry. 'Yes,' she murmured.

Skins The Wolf tossed back his head, making the length of his unbound hair rise and fall like a horse's tail. 'That offer still holds good, though I shall have none of these quiet consultations that my family insisted upon before. I shall take meat to your lodge, openly, so that all the village will know you have a true suitor. Then I shall give horses to your father and to your brothers, and my family will provide you with an elk-tooth dress. We shall have a fine lodge to call our own, and . . .'

'No!' The word forced itself through Moon Hawk's clenched teeth before she realised. It silenced Skins The Wolf at once. She saw the flash of his dark eyes, and desperately cast around for some way of deflecting his intentions.

'I am unworthy,' she said. 'You are a Good Young Man with creditable coups to your name. Your family would not want you to take such as I as an honoured wife. The people have long memories. There would always be someone who would point at you and say, "He took a shamed woman as his wife." It might mean the difference between being a man who leads and a man who is led.'

'I have no care for what the people think of me,' he retorted sharply. 'I am strong. I am determined. I shall gain the coups I need to become a pipe-carrier. No matter what the people say of me, I will not be turned from what I want.'

And he wanted her, Moon Hawk could see it plainly. She stared at him, wondering what to say. A shudder raced down her spine. There was such conviction in his stance. She was not going to be able to dissuade him. But she *had* to.

She spread her arms, almost in supplication. 'My father is very angry with me. I am to live with my shame until the village moves to its winter site, and then . . .'

'Your father knew nothing of the original offer of marriage! He was never told of it. That Piegan captive of his took it upon herself to refuse the offer without even the pretence of negotiation!'

Moon Hawk shrank back. Skins The Wolf was angry, very angry. He flung his arms in the air as he spoke, whipping the courting flute back and forth like a thong-less riding quirt. This was what it would be like being married to him, Moon Hawk realised, cowering from his wrath and the blows which would follow it. She would not marry him. She would never marry him, no matter who insisted upon it.

Skins The Wolf took a step towards her, and Moon Hawk backed a pace. She was alone there, far from the village, far from any ear who might hear her pleas for help. She had to keep away from him.

The flute jabbed towards her chest. 'Your words are mere excuses! Your heart still beats for Winter Man!'

Moon Hawk lifted her chin defiantly. 'Yes! And it always will! I will never be your wife. Hear my words and know them to be true, Wolf. I would rather be taken prisoner by the Lakota than lie in your bedding robes!'

His blackened face contorted in a rage Moon Hawk thought no man could possess. She saw the courting flute lift in his hand and she ducked instinctively, but he did not throw it. He brought it down with a howl of indignation, shattering it on a gnarled root at his feet. She did not wait to see more, but turned and ran.

Skins The Wolf launched himself forward to grab at the back of her dress, but the heavy robe he clutched snagged on the broken branches of a bushy sapling, impeding his momentum and altering his weight. The smooth sole of his moccasin slipped on a wet root and he lost his balance, so that it was all he could do to stop himself from toppling sideways. By the time he had regained his footing, Moon Hawk was out of his reach.

He hesitated a moment, weighing his options, and then forced his tensed muscles to relax. Let her run! He would not chase her. Not this time.

He raised his hand, uncurling his fingers to look at the shattered remnants of the delicately carved courting flute that he had lavished so much time and energy on. An utter waste. He snapped his fingers back over it and flung it towards the rushing creek, but it fell short of its intended mark. The mire weed welcomed it with tiny open fronds. They curled about its decorated shaft, wiping clean its red paint, which drifted on the still water like blood oozing from a wound. And then the flute was gone, dragged beneath the surface, suffocated by the weight of weed that clung to it.

CHAPTER SEVEN

MOON HAWK did not dare to tell her mother of her encounter with Skins The Wolf, and because her clan-relatives were steadfastly shunning the family, there was no one in whom she could confide. She had never felt so alone in her life.

For days she lived in fear of meat being left at the lodge, for she knew that if Skins The Wolf did make a second offer of marriage, her father would insist upon her acceptance. The vain hope that Little Face might oppose such a decision was short lived. Her mother sat with her head bowed and her shoulders slumped, hardly offering a word to anyone.

Moon Hawk had seen women act like this before, women newly-captured from enemies of her people, the quality of their lives entirely dependent on the whim of their captors. She had given them no thought, hardly noticed their existence, and had never associated her mother with such women. Little Face had been taken so many years ago. She had borne Bear On The Flat children now grown to adulthood. It seemed inconceivable to Moon Hawk that her mother should still feel her position so threatened, but, of course, except for her children, Little Face had no blood relatives, and certainly no clan-relatives, to whom she could turn. She was as alone and as vulnerable as she had been the day Bear On The Flat had carried her into the village as his personal possession.

Moon Hawk watched her father with a new and searching eye. He presented a cold edge of his nature, not just to herself as she had believed, but to everyone in the lodge. It was as if he were resolutely distancing himself from his entire family. There was no sign of affection for anyone, least of all for his wife of so many years. To know that she was the sole cause of this made Moon Hawk feel utterly wretched.

The sighting of the migratory buffalo was a time for both relief and joy among the Apsaroke. With the threat of winter starvation removed, the old ones openly told stories of their youth, when food had been so scarce they had been reduced to eating the village dogs and boiling hide-scrapings for soup. It was a time when life was breathed afresh into the lodge of Bear On The Flat, and Moon Hawk lost no time in giving thanks to First Maker in her prayers.

Although her father still rode out on raids against the enemies of their people, it had been some seasons since he had gained himself a coup. His hunting skills, however, were renowned. No one, it was said, showed greater courage in the swirling dust of the surround, when the heavy-shouldered buffalo were stampeded and made to run in a circle. There, the hunters rode abreast of their chosen prey and let loose an arrow directly into the heart or the lungs. A misplaced arrow would only enrage the animal, making it twist its head in an attempt to disembowel the horse which galloped beside it. Like every other Apsaroke, Moon Hawk knew that more men died of injuries sustained in the hunt than ever they did from those inflicted in combat.

Waiting for the signal for the start of the hunt was always an occasion for agitation and excitement. Scouts had been sent to watch the herd and report its movements. It was imperative that the buffalo be engaged as close to the village as possible, so as to simplify the transportation of the heavy carcasses and the butchered meat. There was always the threat of some over-eager hunter ignoring the needs of the many and slipping away from the village to try his luck on his own. Such behaviour often frightened the herd away a great distance, and it was one of the last roles of the year for the appointed Muddy Hand guards to watch for such miscreants. Anyone caught attempting to leave the village was severely dealt with, his tipi ransacked, his weapons broken.

Bear On The Flat had four well-trained buffalo-horses. Moon Hawk watched him put them through their paces on the outskirts of the village. On several occasions she had been allowed to ride with him, to stand sentinel some way from the milling herd and hold his spare mounts until he needed them. She was not to be asked this time, she knew. She had seen him speak to one of his brothers. A younger cousin of hers would be riding out with him before the dawn. She would follow with the women on the slower horses, dragging unladen travois out towards the site of the kill.

She hung her head. How long would it take her to regain her former position in her father's affections? Would he ever forgive her? It seemed so long since she had thrown the turnip at Winter Man that it felt like a different lifetime. If she had known then . . . But would she have averted her eyes? Would she have cast him from her thoughts? From her thoughts, perhaps—but never from her dreams. She had spoken in anger to Skins The Wolf, anger and defiance, but her words had been true enough. Her heart beat for Winter Man. It always had. It always would. Oh, that his heart might have beat for her!

The buffalo hunters left in the cold darkness of pre-dawn. By sunrise, all from the village were up and moving, bringing in horses from the surrounding hills to saddle and fit them with travois harness. Women, young and old, rode in family groups, some with babies in cradleboards strapped to their backs. Older children rode mounts of their own, or sat on the travois platforms to be bounced along behind the horses. Dogs loped back and forth between the throngs, eager for the freshly killed meat they knew would be theirs. There was chatter and songs and games of I-spy. Older boys, carrying their own bows and quivers full of arrows, darted after prairie chicken and hare which the column startled from clumps of vegetation. Such exuberance only emphasised Moon Hawk's feeling of isolation as she rode beside her mother. To be ridiculed was to be set apart, to be shunned, to be forgotten. It was the harshest judgement the people could impose, the harshest judgement for anyone to bear.

It was well into the morning before someone spotted the rising cloud of dust that marked the killing-ground.

The area was far dryer than that chosen for the village site; the soil was thin and vegetation sparse. Outcrops of grey, blue-veined rock jutted towards the sky. Boulders and loose stones littered the deeply undulating land, making negotiation slow and difficult for the horses pulling travois.

Buffalo carcasses lay on every side, arrow-fletching sprouting from their dark woolly coats. Most were already dead. An occasional animal was to be found bellowing in agony, but it was soon despatched by a woman wielding an axe or long-bladed knife.

Moon Hawk slipped from the saddle of her horse and toured the stiff-legged animals, inspecting the distinctive markings on the arrow-stubs, looking for her father's. One was protruding from the carcass of a two-year-old cow, thought to be the best in quality of both meat and hide. She called her mother over and left her to begin the butchering, while she went in search of another. She found the next some distance away, and set to work herself.

Every part of the buffalo was to be used, for it would be an offence against the animal's spirit to discard any item as unworthy. Besides, Moon Hawk knew that the best way of appeasing her relatives was by the courteous offering of gifts. She would give Antelope Dancer a tail to use as a fly-switch, Runs His Horse a pouch to carry the lead balls for his new gun. She would make ladles and cups and a black-powder carrier from the horns; bags for her clan-sisters from the tanned skins, and cushions stuffed with woolly buffalo hair for her grand-mothers. There would be a toy for every child, and moccasins for those too old to play with them. Every-thing would be as elaborately decorated as Moon Hawk could possibly make it. She knew that she would be working on the items until the spring thaw set in, but the knowledge only made her more determined to complete the task. Having her time so fully occupied might help keep her thoughts from wandering too often to Winter Man. It might also make her father more tolerant of her.

She paused a moment, searching the skyline for a sign

of the hunters. If her father had killed a reasonable number of buffalo he would be in a good humour; he always was. She would risk speaking to him directly, and would ask for his forgiveness. It might heal the breach between them, or some of it, at least.

The buffalo-cow was close enough for Winter Man to reach out and touch. Gritting his teeth against the ache of his straining muscles, he drew back his elk-antler bow, took aim and released the arrow. It disappeared, fletching and all, into the shaggy animal. There was a gasp from the beast, as though an over-stretched bladder had been punctured, and the beady black eye swivelled in its socket to glance at the departing rider before its legs collapsed beneath it.

A lung. Another direct hit. His aim was good today, Winter Man reflected. He reached for the fletching of another arrow; already the quiver was half empty. He grinned to himself. His sisters would be working for days to tan the skins and dry the meat.

Through the swirling dust his eye glimpsed an undulating wave in the surging mass of brown woolly coats in front of him. In an instant Winter Man had grasped the bow and arrow firmly in one hand, gripped the black buffalo-horse tightly with his knees and thrust his free hand into its long waving mane. The sudden drop into the gulley made both man and mount shudder with an impact so violent as to have unhorsed an unsuspecting rider, however proficient. For one heart-stopping moment Winter Man did not think the black stallion was going to recover quickly enough to escape the stampeding buffalo behind them, but it sprang forward, almost like an antelope, and matched the running buffalo stride for stride up the steep bank and back on to the level ground.

Winter Man let his held breath whistle between his teeth, and gave his horse an enthusiastic pat on the neck. It was the second sheer-walled depression they had come across without warning: the area seemed to be riddled with them. It was not a good place for a surround.

He calmed the blood-flow through his veins by taking a deep, dust-laden breath, and cast about for another suitable kill. There was an angry bellow to his left, and instinctively he drew the bow and twisted his body in its direction ready to despatch the charging bull before it gored his horse. He found the bull to be a cow, which tripped and fell before he had a chance to let loose the arrow. Beyond its humped back another hunter rode —Bear On The Flat.

Their eyes met. The older man's unnerving gaze penetrated Winter Man to the bone. Without blinking against the clinging dust, Bear On The Flat brought forth a fresh arrow and notched it in his bowstring. Winter Man's eyes widened as he felt a hollow bubble burst in his chest. Bear On The Flat was going to fire at him!

His muscles tensed to pull back on his own bow even as the thought flashed through his mind, but he found he could not raise the weapon, not even in the defence of his own life, not against Bear On The Flat. The memory of the shaming reverberated along every sinew of his body. In his stupid arrogance he had humiliated a fellow Fox, humiliated him beyond any honourable man's endurance. He saw the glint of the metal arrowhead and knew it for what it was, a judgement from First Maker. The thundering of stampeding buffalo roared in his ears to show him the manner of his death, and his courage failed him. He let slip his bow and drove both his hands into the black's thick mane, praying for oblivion before he slid from its saddle and fell beneath the crushing hooves.

The horse shied. In his surprise, Winter Man clung tighter. And then there was no ground under the black, it was pawing uselessly at air as man and mount and bellowing buffalo fell down and down and . . .

Winter Man was coughing so hard that his chest hurt. Each breath he took seemed more dust than air. It was choking him. He felt dizzy and sick, and then he realised it was not the coarse hair of his horse's mane that was slipping through his fingers, but dry, gravelly earth. He flicked open his eyes to a glaring, swirling brightness which seared into his eyeballs and forced his lids to close. He fought with his reeling senses, forcing his mind to clear. Something was dragging him. To its lair? For food? The fear of such a grisly end focused his will and his strength, and he lashed out wildly with his arms. One moved. The other felt as if it had been sliced open and was being filled with red-hot coals. He cried out, but the voice he heard was not his own.

'Winter Man! Help me, Winter Man! Push with your feet. Push with your feet!'

His Medicine-helper? He did as it bade, and found strength in his legs.

He did not seem to be turning over, yet sometimes he felt the ground hit his knees, and sometimes it lay behind his calves. With each exertion the pain grew worse and his grip on his senses lessened, until he was not certain if the jerking movement was real or an imagined sensation. And then his head was tipping back, pulling the length of his body behind it; down, down, into a bottomless abyss that was warm . . . and cushioning . . . and black.

Winter Man focused his sight first on the depth of the shadow and then beyond it to the blue-grey particles of gravel that made up the wall before his eyes. As he stared at it, a thin layer peeled away and fell in a small, dusty cloud on to his face. Where was he? Wherever he was, he was going to have to move before more fell and he suffocated.

There was a grunt from behind him, and Winter Man tensed. A licking flame of pain raced along his neck and across his shoulders, but he gave no sign of feeling it, his attention centred on whatever threat lay beyond his line of vision.

A tearing noise. A gasp. A man in pain? *Bear On The Flat.*

Winter Man eased himself on to his back and finally became aware of what was wrong with him. His left arm was useless, his shoulder twice the size it should be. He gasped, and then relaxed to allow the jangling of raw nerves to subside. When he looked at Bear On The

Flat, the older man was sitting upright in the sun, gazing down at him with a mixture of concern and expectancy.

'Can you see me?'

Winter Man tried to speak, but found his throat full of dust. He coughed to clear it, bringing himself more distress.

'Clearly?'

'Yes.'

'Good. I thought that wound on your brow might have blinded you.'

Winter Man could feel no wound. He lifted his good hand to investigate his head with his finger-tips, and found a lump of gravel and dust, hardened, he reasoned, with his blood. Despite its unlikely composition, it acted like a dressing, stemming the flow of his blood, and it would be foolish to remove it. He concentrated instead on his surroundings.

Bear On The Flat had pushed him under the overhanging bank of a dry wash—the dry wash that had yawned abruptly before the running buffalo and which had swallowed him and his horse. He turned his head to the left and to the right. Where was his horse? Where were the buffalo? He could see only one. The shaggy animal was on its side, its limbs stretched stiffly in death. Many buffalo had stampeded over the lip of the wash. They would have fallen one on top of another to be gored or crushed. He had seen it happen before, had heard stories of the old ways where such traps had been planned in advance of the herd. For a man to be caught in one was regarded as certain death, but Bear On The Flat must have dragged him free. Bear On The Flat had saved his life.

Taking his limp arm in his strong hand, Winter Man struggled out from beneath the overhang and carefully eased himself to a sitting position. He had believed his fellow Fox member had wanted to take his life. First the shaming, then to think so badly of him . . . He dared not look him in the eyes, yet he felt the need to say something, to offer aid, or encouragement, some simple act of contrition to alleviate his sense of guilt.

He pointed to the older man's bloody legging. 'Were you gored?'

Bear On The Flat nodded. 'By my own bone. It will mend, I think, though I cannot be certain about the ankle. Perhaps that is shattered.'

Winter Man watched him for a moment. Beads of sweat stood out on his skin, and his breathing was more laboured than usual, with an occasional narrowing of his eyes. Apart from that, there was no sign of the pain he bore. Winter Man chastised himself for not carrying his own pain with the same resolve, and he straightened his back.

'Is your shoulder broken, or dislocated?'

'I do not know.'

Bear On The Flat grunted. 'I could not tell, either. The swelling is too great. Star Ghost will know. He has healing in his fingers and will make both of us stand tall again.'

Winter Man glanced at the bloody legging and the awkwardly placed foot. He might stand tall again, but he doubted if Bear On The Flat would. 'How long have we been here?'

'We shall be found. Have patience.'

Winter Man felt an initial rise of resentment. He did not lack patience, but was merely trying to prolong the conversation. His eyes caught Bear On The Flat's. The older man could not mask the pain held in them, and his pain, Winter Man realised, was great. He smothered his sense of irritation.

'You saved my life,' he said. 'I shall not forget. When my shoulder is healed, I shall hunt for you.'

'It is you who saved my life, I think. You dropped your bow and clung to your horse. I was astonished by your action, and in my astonishment I looked where you looked, and I saw the edge of the wash in time.' He lowered his gaze, then raised it again. 'Why did you drop your bow?'

Winter Man cast about in desperation for an excuse he might offer, but none came to mind. It might, he decided, be better if he opened his heart and did not try to conceal his embarrassment. He had wanted to speak to

Bear On The Flat for some time, to apologise for the shaming, but no opportunity had presented itself. Perhaps this was the moment.

He looked the older man full in the eye. 'I dropped my bow because I thought you were going to kill me.'

There was no roar of indignation, no exclamation of rage. Bear On The Flat sat stolidly before him, a gentle pursing of his lips the only guide to his thoughts. Winter Man's stomach took a sickening lurch. His instincts had been right. Bear On The Flat *had* been going to kill him.

'Why did you drag me clear? You could have left me. I would have been crushed.'

Bear On The Flat shrugged. 'I have said: your action saved my life. Besides, stroking the hand of death opened my eyes. It showed me my pride for the foolishness it was. To have left you would have been dishonourable. I would have walked in unworthiness for the rest of my life.'

'I know such a state,' Winter Man admitted. 'I have walked in it since the day I asked the young men to take meat to your lodge. I never meant to shame you, or Moon Hawk. My apology is useless, but I give it.'

'Every man acts according to his heart. Sometimes there are regrets, sometimes not. It is the way of a man's life. If he did not act in this way, he would be as a dead thing and have no heart at all. If you were to bring meat to my lodge a second time, it would be accepted with dignity.'

Winter Man gazed at him in stunned silence. Meat? Again? He had not thought to take meat a second time. Was Bear On The Flat saying he would like him for a son-in-law—or was he commanding him to become one?

He covered his growing disquiet as best as he could. 'I am surprised that you would want to accept me after what I did.'

'Your heart is strong. You would be a good provider. I have always known it. That is why I never stopped the game my daughter began with you. I should have done, I know, but I wanted her to marry well.' He looked at Winter Man in earnest. 'I wanted her to marry you.'

He eased his leg a little and looked again at Winter Man. 'I have watched you from your youth, from the time you first joined the Fox society . . .'

'You spoke for me. I have not forgotten.'

Bear On The Flat nodded at the distant memory. Winter Man watched him smile to himself, and his forebodings grew. Bear On The Flat was taking too much for granted. If he did not speak plainly, the moment would be lost.

'I must tell you that, even during the game with Moon Hawk, I thought of it only as a game. I was not looking for a wife.'

'I know.' Bear On The Flat was nodding again, lost in his own reverie. Winter Man wondered if he had understood what he had said.

'I see much of myself in you. I, too, had many lovers when I was young with never a thought of taking a wife. We were raiding horses from the Piegan and a friend dared me to take a prisoner. I dared him back.' He chuckled, remembering the moment, and then his expression became troubled.

'I had never known a woman so frightened—not of me. She trembled when I touched her, when I held her in my arms. She was so young—timid, like a rabbit-child. I could not have hurt her. If I had been stronger in my heart, not afraid of the songs which would have been sung about me, I think I would have taken her back to her people. But I kept her, because I was afraid.'

He chuckled again, this time to hide his frankness. 'To this day I do not know her true name. She thought that if she revealed it, I would bind it with charms and turn her into a fish, or some such thing, so I called her Little Face. She accepted that. She accepted me.'

Winter Man had to concentrate hard not to let his amusement reach his lips. What was all this talk of 'accepted'? *Loved* was the word he would have used. Bear On The Flat was brimming with it, even now, after . . . how many years? Twenty? Winter Man could just imagine him in his youth, following her every nervous movement, tongue-tied beyond belief—another Hillside; perhaps even worse. Bear On The Flat had to be touched by First Maker to believe that the two of them were alike in anything.

However, it did not alter the fact that the older man expected him to become his son-in-law. Perhaps he should have felt honoured—Bear On The Flat was an elder of the Fox society and held in high esteem by his fellow members—but Winter Man did not feel honoured, he felt cornered, cunningly manoeuvred into a trap from which there was no escape, first by a daughter, and then by her father. He had told Moon Hawk that when he chose to take a wife, he himself would do the choosing. It seemed that such a natural course was not to be allowed him, after all.

The two men sat in silence. There seemed nothing else for them to say to each other. Winter Man nursed his shoulder. Bear On The Flat eased his broken leg.

They were spotted as the shadows lengthened towards dusk. The hunters swarmed down the steep-sided wash to crowd round them, voicing their concern, marvelling at their escape.

Star Ghost was brought to see to their injuries. He staggered towards them on crooked legs which he was never destined to cure, and tended to Bear On The Flat first. Winter Man watched as the healer cut open the blood-soaked legging and deftly fingered the leg and ankle. The only time Bear On The Flat cried out with his pain was when the broken bone was aligned for the makeshift splint. Winter Man felt the man's agony for him and gritted his own teeth against it. His time, he knew, would come soon enough.

Men carried Bear On The Flat up to the waiting horses, and Winter Man watched Star Ghost lurch towards him. Instinctively he tensed against the healer's onslaught, and he had to force himself to relax. He had suffered wounds before, and knew that he had to accept the pain willingly. To fight against it only made it more intense.

'Can you lift your arm?'

'No.'

'Have you any feeling in it?'

'A tingling in my fingers and the outer edge of my

forearm. The rest is numb, or pain.'

Star Ghost took Winter Man's hand and gently manipulated each finger, slowly following up through the wrist and lower arm to his elbow and inflamed biceps.

'You are perspiring more now than you do during a sweat,' a deeper voice offered.

There was something in the tone of the words which cut through Winter Man's pain and caused him to raise his eyes. Skins The Wolf stood with his back to the sinking sun, the detail of his features lost in the red-gold radiance surrounding him. Winter Man was aware only that he was standing; standing, whereas all the other men were crouched. He had not even taken his bow-case from his back. The silhouette of its fluttering fringes had all the appearance of the wings of a diving hawk.

Star Ghost's probing fingers jarred a raw nerve, and Winter Man winced against the heightened wave of pain.

'Just dislocated—as far as I can see. Lie on your back.'

He felt a supportive arm against his spine and leaned against it until his weight was cradled in the soft earth.

'Do you want a moccasin to bite on?'

Again that tone which elusively defied definition. This time Winter Man's eyes did not have to seek Skins The Wolf; Skins The Wolf stepped abruptly into his line of vision. Out of the direct glare of the sun's rays, he had no difficulty in reading the man's expression. It was haughty, condescending even, devoid of all compassion or concern.

A fragment of memory flashed through Winter Man's mind—his report to Running Fisher of the taking of Skins The Wolf's grand coup after the raid on the Shoshone village. There was the same overbearing stance, the same strident conceit. Skins The Wolf was standing there, taking a kind of twisted pleasure in watching his pain. Winter Man felt his blood run cold, and then it began to run very hot.

'I need nothing to bite on,' he rasped. 'I am not going to cry out.'

Someone wrapped strong arms about his waist. Another took his good arm. A third held his legs. It felt as if they were trying to crush his bruised body. He turned his gaze from Skins The Wolf and forced all thoughts of him from his mind.

The sky was very blue, he noticed. A buzzard was circling idly overhead. He would not cry out, he told himself. His breathing would remain steady.

Star Ghost took his useless arm, gently at first, and then he pushed his foot into Winter Man's ribs below his armpit. His shoulder and spine, and half of his body, it seemed, were consumed in a conflagration of agony that showed him what it would be like to be torn limb from limb. There was a grinding of bone and a snap like a bow-string, and he was freed from all restraining hands to lie quivering like a freshly-caught fish.

His eyes stung with the salt of his own sweat, and his resentment built afresh as his thoughts returned to Skins The Wolf. He looked for the man, but there was no longer any sign of him in his line of vision. Winter Man felt cheated.

'Move your fingers,' Star Ghost told him. He found he could—just. 'Make a fist.' That was beyond him. Star Ghost grunted. 'I shall visit you in your tipi to apply a poultice. Help him up, someone.'

'I need no help. I am not an invalid.' He waved away the proffered hands and dragged himself to his feet. His legs felt weaker than he had expected, and for a moment he wished he had not been so hasty.

The climb up the side of the wash was arduous, and he did not protest when a powerful arm gave him the lift he needed. Hillside was waiting at the top for him.

'Winter Man! I have been searching half the day for you! I thought to find no more than a greasy mark on the grass! How good it is to see you!'

There seemed no suitable reply to Hillside's exuberance, so Winter Man did not offer one. He glanced impatiently beyond his friend's shoulder, and his eyes caught on a knot of people. Bear On The Flat was being laid on a travois ready for travelling. Little Face was kneeling beside him, her hands locked about his. Crouched at her shoulder was Moon Hawk.

As he watched, she raised her head and their gazes

locked. She looked pale, Winter Man thought, and
tired. He saw her walk forwards a few paces—forward,
towards him—and then she stopped. She slid her palms
down the sides of her dress and clasped her hands
nervously in front of her. She was waiting for him to walk
towards her, waiting for him to acknowledge her.

'Go on,' Hillside growled at him. 'Now is your chance
to make your peace with her.'

Winter Man swivelled on his heel and rested hard eyes
on him. 'To what end? I was chosen for a husband long
ago. What I think or do alters nothing. I am to be
married. Are you not overjoyed?'

Hillside gaped at his overt show of sarcasm, but he was
left with no chance to reply as Winter Man strode
purposefully away to an unsaddled buffalo-horse.

Caught unawares by his own confusion, Hillside
turned to Moon Hawk for an explanation, but she was
already drifting back to her family. With her shoulders
slumped and her head bowed down, she looked the soul
of dejection. He felt sorry for her. He felt angry for her.
This hurt-and-hurt-again game had gone on long
enough. When was Winter Man going to see that?

CHAPTER EIGHT

FOUR DAYS HAD passed since her father had been brought back to the village. To Moon Hawk it felt more like four months, her sense of guilt was so crippling.

She had been skinning a buffalo some distance from her mother when she had heard that her father was missing. She had felt sick. There had been no doubt in her mind that his disappearance was directly linked to the dishonour she had brought upon the family, and, driven to distraction with worry, she had taken her knife and cut her arm, offering her own blood in sacrifice to First Maker so that her father might be found alive.

And then news had come that Winter Man could not be found.

She had been overwhelmed by desolation. The hunt had been abandoned; all the men were searching for them. No more could be done, yet she had wanted to cut the travois from her horse and search for him herself, search for ever if necessary.

Fresh word had arrived. They had been found— together and alive. How she had ridden to the spot! How she had whipped at her horse to make it move faster over the uneven ground! The men had been bringing her father up from the wash when she and Little Face had arrived. She saw his agony as they carried him. She saw the splint and the bloody legging, but he had been alive and not in mortal danger, and her fears had rested on him only temporarily. Winter Man had been nowhere to be seen. Where was he? How badly was he hurt? Was he *dying*? They were the thoughts which had filled her mind, crowding out all others. It had been almost more than she could bear to stay at her mother's side as Little Face had knelt by her husband to take his hand in hers.

Like a Sacred Being, Winter Man had appeared before her even as she was looking for him. One moment there was no one on the edge of the wash, the next he stood there with Hillside. To see him safe, standing there unharmed . . She had wanted to run to him, to hug him, to cry, to laugh—and he had stood there, as cold and unyielding as stone. He had looked through her as if she had not existed. She had died inside, shrivelled in on herself like a dried autumn leaf.

Moon Hawk dragged the heavy buffalo-skin she was working on back on to the bank and pounded at the hair with a stone to rid it of water and congealed blood. Why did she keep allowing him to hurt her? Why did she keep hurting herself? It was over between them. Why could she not accept that?

She stood outside of herself a moment, and almost laughed as she contemplated her agitated thoughts. *Over?* There had been nothing between them to be over. She had read love into his every look, into his every gesture, making herself believe what she felt was true for them both. And at the very end, when she had learned that both Winter Man and her father were missing, who was it who she had feared for the most?

She hit the skin again and again in her self-loathing. She was stupid, she told herself. Stupid!

She wiped her face with the back of her wet hand, oblivious of the other women working and talking around her. Again she pushed the skin into the creek to rinse it, and dragged it to the bank once more, to squeeze it and roll it ready to take it, and those she had already washed, back to the lodge for the next stage in the tanning process.

The sky was heavy with cloud, and between each tipi small fires burned to give smoke and heat to assist the drying of the meat, which hung in long thin strips over high racks built above them. Aged grandmothers and young pregnant women shunned the back-breaking work of tanning in favour of the messier duties of slicing meat and cleaning the usable innards. Little Face was sitting outside the family lodge patiently showing Turtle how to empty and prepare the long lengths of intestines to be used later for sausage-casings. The girl was so engrossed in her task that she did not notice Moon Hawk approach, but Little Face raised her eyes and her gentle smile turned into a bright grin.

'Go into the lodge. Food is waiting for you.'

Moon Hawk dropped the wet hides by the tipi and shook her head. 'I am not hungry. I shall wash the other hides.'

'Moon Hawk . . .'

She caught the sharper edge of her mother's voice and turned her eyes to her, expecting to see a frown. Little Face had chastised her gently, but often, during the past few days, for not eating enough, or for looking sad, or for working too hard without rest. Bear On The Flat's incapacity, or perhaps his close brush with death, had loosened the cold atmosphere that had hung between the pair since the shaming. Even in his pain, Bear On The Flat was hardly to be seen without a ready smile for his wife or his children, and Little Face seemed to have shed half her years with the weight of her relief at having him returned to her alive.

'Moon Hawk . . .' Little Face lowered her voice, but the warmth still radiated from her smile. 'Your father wishes to speak to you.'

Moon Hawk gazed at her mother a moment, and then at the grey skin of the tipi covering as if, with an effort, she might be able to see through it and discover the reason for her father's request. She had no need to fear his words. More often than not now, Bobtailed Cat was to be found sitting contentedly with his father's arm round him, listening to hero stories. On two occasions she had seen Turtle walk up to him and set a kiss upon his head for no more reason than his being there, and she had been rewarded in return by a hug and loving words.

No, it was not his response Moon Hawk feared, but her own to him. Again and again she had failed her father, if not in actions, then in thoughts. She should have thrown herself down wretchedly before him and begged his forgiveness for the misery she had brought, but somehow she had not been able to bring herself to do so, blinding her reasons with the excuse that there had been no opportunity.

She ducked into the lodge and stood just inside the

doorway. Her father was sitting against his willow-stick back-rest, his chin curled in on to his chest. He looked as if he were lost in a doze. Moon Hawk did not wish to disturb him; she knew that his nights were not filled with restful slumber. A quiet moan escaped his lips, almost like a sigh, and she saw the tightening of his sun-bronzed skin over his cheekbones as he winced. The small wooden bowl by his side had held a pain-killing infusion of crushed bark. Now she saw it was empty.

'Shall I boil another potion for you to drink?'

He raised his head quickly, startled, she thought, by her presence. He smiled a warm smile, like that which had sprang so readily to her mother's face.

'No, not yet.'

He lifted a hand and pointed beside her, near the door. The package, bound in hide, was unmistakable in its shape and its position inside the lodge. Meat had arrived from a suitor.

She stared at it, and the question seemed to take a long time to form on her lips. 'Who—who is it from?'

'Winter Man.'

Her gaze jumped back to her father. 'Winter Man?'

He nodded. His smile rose up his face to brighten his eyes. 'He brought it soon after you had left for the creek. It is a pity you were not here to witness it, but perhaps he planned it that way. This courtship of yours has not always run smoothly. Perhaps he feared you would throw it after him!'

She looked down at the parcel again to make sure it was still there. 'I do not understand,' she murmured. 'He does not want me. He made it plain.'

'When a man narrowly escapes death, it often makes him see things differently.'

Moon Hawk frowned. Winter Man had narrowly escaped death before, on several occasions. By every account she had listened to, he had escaped it during the horse-raid on the Shoshone village. He had not seen things differently after that. Yet, even as she was doubting the sense of it, a warmth, an excitement, was building inside her. Every hope she had ever held was blossoming afresh. The constancy of her love had finally seeded itself within his heart. She could still be his wife. She *would* be his wife!

She felt the pressure of a hand against her back and stepped away from the door. When she turned to share the news, her brothers were standing there, intent on the package at their feet. Antelope Dancer hung his head and groaned. Runs His Horse was more forceful.

'It is true! It is *true!*' He raised his hands in his disbelief and swung hardening eyes on Moon Hawk. She backed a pace as she saw a snarl contort his lips. 'It is all round the village! No one can talk of anything else! Was there no one here to push his rancid meat down his throat!'

There was an awkward silence as the three siblings glanced at their father leaning against his back-rest, incapable of moving. Runs His Horse shrugged off his unthinking comment with a grunt, and made to pick up the parcel. 'I shall do it.'

'You will not touch it!' his father snapped. 'It was not given to your lodge. You no longer live in this one.'

Runs His Horse stared at him. 'You are not thinking to keep it? Not after the shame he brought to you—to all of us?'

'He brings it with a good heart.'

'Good heart! We are being laughed at by every family in this village! Are you going to let him bring horses for her, too?'

'I am hoping he will.'

In his rising anger, Runs His Horse flung an arm across his body. 'Nothing will make me accept horses from him!'

'Then I shall not offer you any; for—hear me, my son—I am the head of this lodge and of this family, and as such the gifts will be offered to me. Whether I accept them, if they come, will depend on Moon Hawk.'

Her heart thudded as she heard her name being spoken, and as she knew they would, all eyes turned to her. She fought to keep her head high beneath their scrutiny. Her father was right: it was her choice. She was not going to allow herself to be brow-beaten by her brothers.

Antelope Dancer took hold of his brother's arm, but

Runs His Horse thrust him off and pointed a threatening hand towards her breast.

'Do not think to look to my lodge for gifts to reciprocate his. As far as I am concerned, he can buy you like a captured woman!'

Antelope Dancer clasped his arm again, this time tighter. 'You have said enough!' He turned anxious eyes to their father. 'We shall leave. We thought Winter Man was trying to shame the lodge a second time. Obviously we were wrong.'

Runs His Horse tried to speak again, but his brother hustled him out of the tipi. Moon Hawk was left gazing at the open doorway, fearful that her marriage was going to split the family.

'Take no heed of him,' her father told her. 'When he sees how happy you are with Winter Man, he will change his mind.'

The day dragged. Towards the end of the afternoon, Little Face began to fuss round her daughter, insisting that she leave her work and bathe and dress ready for when Winter Man stood outside the lodge that evening. She painted her face and brushed her hair, rubbing dried flower-petals into the thick locks to make it smell sweet after the day's labours. Moon Hawk sat wordlessly throughout, remembering with mixed emotions the last occasion she had been dressed like this. The evening had not gone well for her. She wanted to hope for better this time, but dared not. She could not stand to be hurt again.

The shadows lengthened. Twilight lingered, but the day's cloud had not dispersed and the darkness of night came quickly. Of Winter Man there was no sign. Turtle kept watch from the doorway, lifting and dropping the edge of the flap as her enthusiasm rose and waned alternately. Little Face talked. She talked about anything and everything to keep the lodge from slipping into total silence. Moon Hawk busied herself embroidering porcupine-quills on a strip of elk-skin. She tried hard not to feel hurt by this latest rebuff. She told herself again and again that she had been expecting it, that it did not matter. But it did matter, especially after what her brother had said. It mattered to her, and it mattered to her father.

'He is here! He is here!' Turtle jumped up and down in her exuberance. Little Face visibly relaxed, but Moon Hawk attended to her stitching as if nothing had been said.

Her mother touched her arm. 'He is waiting for you, Moon Hawk.'

'Let him wait.'

'No!' Her father was adamant. 'There has been enough of these games! Go out to him now.'

Moon Hawk laid down her sewing and stepped out of the tipi. Despite the chill edge to the autumn air, her hands were sticky with perspiration. She wiped them down the sides of her dress and looked across at Winter Man. He stood a few paces from the lodge, from anyone's lodge, so that what words passed between them would remain secret to them both. She took a deep breath to steady her wildly beating heart, and walked towards him.

There was something about him that seemed odd to her; she was not sure what. He did not seem to be so tall, so awe-inspiring. He was not standing straight, that was it. He was slouching. Was he in pain? Had there been more damage to his shoulder than a dislocation? Was that the reason for his late arrival? And she had believed he had kept her waiting on purpose!

Feelings of guilt stirred within her. She stifled them. The robe he wore, the warm robe that he would wrap about them both, was not painted with his war honours; it was plain. No ornaments kept the breeze from pulling at loose tendrils of his unbraided hair. There were no rings on his fingers, no paint on his face. His moccasins were undecorated, and so, too, were his leggings. She peered closer. One legging had a tear in it along the shin. Winter Man had come to court her in rags!

As she stood before him, he opened up the robe ready for her to step close to him. His left arm was supported in a sling, the shoulder wrapped bulkily with soft skins holding a poultice. His chest, too, was bare of either painted marks of valour or decorative necklaces. If too well fed, he looked the poorest man alive.

'The snow-winds draw closer. Have you such a feel for the cold that you do not wish to share my robe?'

Even as he spoke, Moon Hawk felt the downy hairs rise on her skin, but she was not certain whether it was due to the cold or to some instinct of foreboding. She stepped within the open robe, and he closed it behind her. Only then did she realise the extent of her mistake. He was so much taller than she, that where the upper edge of the buffalo-skin reached his ears, it completely enshrouded her head. She was trapped inside it, her face level with his upper chest. Heat radiated from his body, but she found no pleasure in it. The smell of him appalled her. Stale sweat and horse dung assailed her nostrils. He had not even washed!

An image of him sitting astride his grey racer flitted through her mind. He had been dressed to perfection then, adorned as a warrior should be adorned, his body scented to arouse her senses. Bitter tears sprang to her eyes. She forced them back.

'The women of my family are decorating a dress with elk-teeth for you. A fine tipi is being prepared for our use. I have picked out the best horses from my string to be given as a gift to your father and brothers . . .'

It was all Moon Hawk had ever hoped to hear from him, but not like this; never like this.

'Why are you doing this to me?' There was a quiver in her voice that she had hoped to mask.

'Doing what?'

Her resentment leapt like flames from dry kindling. 'This!' Without thinking, she gestured with her hand and inadvertently brushed the backs of her fingers along his ribs. She balled her fist immediately and let it slip down by her side again. 'Everything,' she said.

'You have not stood within a man's robe before. Perhaps you do not know what is said.'

'I know a man does not come courting in rags! You should list your coups, tell me how good a provider you will make.'

'Do clothing and adornments make a man?'

His quietly-spoken question caught her off balance,

and she shook her head. 'No, I suppose not, but it is a measure of his worth, his self-esteem.'

'And my coups . . . You know what coups I hold, how good a hunter I am, how many horses I have captured from our enemies. What point is there for me to list them?'

She felt her exasperation rise once again. 'Because— because that is the way it is done!'

'Which is it you want, Moon Hawk, the man or the marriage ritual?'

She drew breath to reply, but the words never came. For the first time in her life, she was not sure. She looked up towards the sky, hoping to find answers in the clouds, but all she saw was Winter Man's shadowy face looking down at her.

His eyes seemed unnaturally bright in the darkness. She watched him blink, once, twice; watched his gaze rove over her face, felt it, like a dragonfly's wing, brushing her skin and her hair. Why could he not encircle her with his arms and draw her into him, hold her as if he never wanted to let her go?

'Well, Moon Hawk . . . Which is it you want?'

A trembling anxiety rippled through her. Dared she say it? Dared she leave her heart open for his knife again?'

'I—I want to be loved!'

The robe grew taut across her back, pushing her towards him. She felt his arm slip about her waist as he drew her into the contours of his muscular body with a firmness which made her pulse race.

'I can love you, Moon Hawk. I can take you in my arms and carry your spirit to places you have not dreamed of.'

Slowly, so very slowly, his face descended to hers. With an aching moan of an expelled breath, his moist lips opened and took possession of her mouth, her heart, her very soul. She cut loose her soaring senses, letting them fly wild and free. His hand rose up her spine to lock into the thick hair at the base of her skull and she felt her head being pulled backwards. His lips left hers to run rampant over the soft flesh of her throat, and she clung

to him, her unleashed passion racing beyond her rein.
With an almost inaudible growl, he bared his teeth to
ravage at her neck. A muffled cry of ecstasy escaped her
parted lips, and a desire she had never known before
burgeoned in her slim body, tightening her breasts,
gnawing at her abdomen. She wanted him! She wanted
him as she had never wanted anything before.

His caresses stopped. She felt him tremble against
her; or was it her against him? She could not be sure.
Every sinew of her body was vibrating with the rapture
he had released. He held her tightly, crushed her in his
powerful arms so that her hands could not reach for him,
so that she could not even move. He placed a soft,
fleeting kiss on her cheek and then one on her neck. His
finger-tips gently brushed her skin, not arousing her
now, but soothing her, calling her passions down from
their dizzy heights, down back to the place of their
slumber; a place, Moon Hawk realised, they would
never return to now that they had tasted the freedom his
touch could inspire.

Winter Man cupped her face in his slender hands and
luxuriated in the searing heat of her cheeks—a woman
on fire. He ached to kiss her, to feel the craving erupt in
her again, raw, untamed, unaware of its potential or its
delights. It took an immense surge of will to deny
himself. He eased his hands down her neck on to her
shoulders, calming her, calming himself.

'I think . . .' he murmured into her hair. 'I think I shall
bring horses to your father as soon as our tipi is ready.'

If not before! he added to himself.

CHAPTER NINE

WINTER MAN SAT on the damp earth watching his string of horses quietly grazing the remnants of the autumn pasture. He had gathered his mounts together away from the tipis to decide which and how many he would give as gifts to Bear On The Flat, but his mind was reluctant to dwell on the etiquette surrounding the exchange of bridal gifts. He had laid awake most of the night thinking of Moon Hawk, arousing himself with memories of the way she had responded to his kisses, dreaming of future nights when they would be together.

The tingling anticipation of lying with a willing woman was nothing new to him, but he could not remember when it had been so fierce, or had lasted so long. Making love was an enjoyable pastime, but so were racing horses and wagering on dice. Each excited his spirit in its own way, but only for a short time. What Moon Hawk had fired within him was possessing his senses to the exclusion of all else. He had not given thought to it before, but every one of his numerous lovers had known a man before they had lain with him. He had accepted it without concern; after all, it meant he could enjoy without having to teach. Yet, holding Moon Hawk in his arms had shown him how wrong he had been. Innocent of the pleasures she could offer or thrill to, her sexuality stretched before him as pure and unsullied as a fresh fall of snow. What power lay in his hands! To watch her grow from a dormant seed into a woman alive with the knowledge of her own sensuality . . . What a source of fascination! And he could have lost her, acting like a fool because of his wounded pride!

He resented the way Bear On The Flat had manipulated him, it was true. On occasions he resented Moon Hawk, too, so sure was she of gaining him, but he regretted, now, his decision to stand before Bear On The Flat's lodge in the poorest clothes he could find. He felt ashamed of the aggressive sense of elation he had experienced when he had seen the disappointment on Moon Hawk's face. The rest of the marriage ritual—the offering of horses and gifts to her father and brothers —he would do with such flair that the people would talk of it for years. He would make Moon Hawk's face light again.

'You are deep in thought. Have you decided how many horses you are going to offer for her?'

Winter Man raised his eyes and smiled at Hillside. 'Not yet. How many do you suggest?'

Hillside shrugged his shoulders and crouched opposite him, pulling idly at a tuft of grass. He looked wary, Winter Man thought, and then he remembered how abrupt he had been after the hunt, when Hillside had welcomed him as one returned from the dead. He regretted that, too. It seemed that there were a great many things he was regretting. Since the beginning of the summer the normal stability of his life had been turned upside-down. It was almost as if First Maker had tied his spirit to an unbroken stallion and whipped the animal into flight.

'You seem very certain that Bear On The Flat will accept horses from you.'

'We have settled our differences.'

'What about his sons? Will you be offering horses to them, too?'

'It will be expected that I should.'

Hillside raised his eyebrows and chuckled. 'Are you ready to receive them back with their legs slashed?'

Winter Man frowned. The thought had crossed his mind. Antelope Dancer was a Fox, like himself. At the last society meeting he had simply stood and walked away when Winter Man had approached. His younger brother, the hot-headed Runs His Horse, belonged to the Lumpwoods, and Winter Man had heard from his own relatives that the young man was losing no opportunity to denounce him. Slashing the legs of offered bridal horses was something he might not wish to pass by.

'I think I shall give them all to Bear On The Flat,

saying that they are for him and his family, and let him sort it out.'

'You will have to judge the number you offer him. If his sons refuse to help him collect reciprocal gifts for your family, you may unwittingly insult him by giving more wealth than he can return. Remember, his wife is a captured woman. She has no relatives of her own to turn to.'

Winter Man rubbed a hand down his face and shook his head. 'It would have been so much easier if Moon Hawk had just eloped with me!'

Hillside laughed. 'Perhaps, but you will not regret it when you see the joy held in her face.' His head rose a little and his tone changed. 'Riders,' he announced.

Winter Man narrowed his eyes and peered into the hazy distance. A group of men on horseback were trotting towards the village. He fought to bring the image into focus, to distinguish one man from another. Hillside, trying to do the same, raised himself to observe them from the advantage of his full height. Too late, Winter Man recognised the leader. He called Hillside back down, but the movement had been spotted and the riders veered from their original course to seek out the two men. Hillside groaned when he saw who rode to the fore.

Skins The Wolf kicked his horse into a gallop as he neared them, reaching Winter Man and Hillside before his companions. He drew his sweating mare to a shuddering halt, creating a cloud of dust which engulfed the three of them.

'Ha!' With bright, unblinking eyes and a full grin, he flourished a fresh scalp. 'Is there to be no salute for me?' he demanded.

'We are not women to trill for you!' Hillside retorted. 'Whose was that?'

'A lone Lakota.'

'A *lone* Lakota?'

Skins The Wolf nodded, showing a little begrudging admiration. 'He was on foot, too. He jammed his lance into the ground as if it were a society staff and stood and fought us with a knife and axe. He fought like an angered bear. None of us could get close enough to count a major coup on him. He died bravely.'

'What about the main party?' Winter Man asked.

Skins The Wolf looked at him with distaste. He exuded the same belittling manner Winter Man had noticed at the wash. 'You have the deafness of the old,' he sneered. 'The Lakota was alone.'

'He was not a wolf scouting for a raiding group?'

'I have said, he was alone.'

The two exchanged their unblinking gaze, the hostility crackling between them. Skins The Wolf averted his eyes first, turning to look over the horses grazing near by.

'Are these the mangy beasts you are hoping to buy Moon Hawk with?'

'I am not buying her. I am taking her as an honoured wife.'

Skins The Wolf openly guffawed. 'That is not what I am hearing. You will be lucky to be offered a handful of beads and a moth-eaten robe in exchange! Runs His Horse spat on the meat you took to the lodge.'

Winter Man stifled his irritation and kept his voice steady. 'I did not take it for him. I took it for Little Face.'

Skins The Wolf curled his lip. 'She is a captured Piegan.'

'Bear On The Flat seems to hold her in esteem.'

'He is an old man with a shattered leg.'

'He was not when he took her.'

Skins The Wolf had no ready reply to that, and Winter Man took the opportunity of addressing another member of the gathered horsemen. 'Spider! You gained the Lakota's bow! It is a good coup. The women will trill for you tonight.'

Spider lifted the captured weapon above his head to whoop his triumph, but the cry died in his throat as the lance of Skins The Wolf swung down towards Winter Man's face.

'And I took his scalp! I killed him with this lance. See, the blood still marks the blade.'

Winter Man saw. The point of the blade was so close to his nose that it was no more than a blur, but he saw the dark stain along the length of the slender metal, and he saw the wildness in the angered man's eyes. A quiet menace crept into Winter Man's voice.

'A soiled edge is apt to dull. You should take care with your weapon, Skins The Wolf. You may need it to defend your life.'

A grin creased the man's face, baring his straight, white teeth. If he had drooled saliva, Winter Man would not have been surprised.

The blade rose abruptly as Skins The Wolf returned it to its upright position. Winter Man saw the flash of the metal before his eyes and felt the rush of the vicious point as it swept by his cheek, but he did not flinch. Skins The Wolf laughed uproariously, turning to his riding companions to share the joke, but the most they could give was a forced chuckle and an awkward smile. Without offering another word, Skins The Wolf pulled on his mount's jaw-thong to turn its head round, and struck its loins with his riding quirt to spur it into motion. The other men turned their horses and followed, leaving a cloud of dust to descend on the two men left behind them.

Hillside blew the soft yellow powder from his face. 'You may regret goading him by saying that.'

Winter Man supported his injured shoulder with his good hand, and raised himself to his feet. 'I do not cower before the Lakota. I am not cowering before him.'

Hillside rubbed thoughtfully at his ear. 'Do my eyes look like his when I have taken a coup?'

Turning on his heel, Winter Man began to walk towards his horses. To his knowledge, no man's eyes looked like that, except, perhaps, during the raging heat of battle, and the fight with the horseless Lakota could never have been considered a battle, even in its widest sense. The whole episode left Winter Man with a bitter taste in his mouth.

That evening the celebrations were particularly vociferous. Star Ghost had visited Winter Man during the afternoon to manipulate his shoulder and apply a new poultice. As he watched the re-enactments of

valour, his shoulder burned with a pain he had not
known since the day of the hunt. Perhaps it coloured his
view of the proceedings, he was not sure, but it seemed
to him that a great deal was being made of the killing of a
single Lakota, no matter how bravely the man had
fought. Skins The Wolf had had himself painted to
signify all the coups he had previously taken, and was
parading before his clan-relatives and fellow society
members as though he had taken another grand coup,
when all he had done was skewer a man on foot with his
lance while he had been on horseback. Spider had been
the one to take the Lakota's bow—a true coup—yet he
was not gaining half as much recognition.

Memories of the horse-raid against the Shoshone
filled Winter Man's head, reminding him of the way
Skins The Wolf had acted there and afterwards at that
celebration. Images of Squirrel came to him, too, mer-
cilessly beaten by her husband because of someone's
vicious lies. Hillside had said the spite could not have
been directed at him, but Winter Man was not so sure
any more.

He waited two days for the excitement to die down
before instructing the village Crier to strike the drum
and call news of his impending marriage. He scrubbed
himself in the creek and dressed in his finest clothing,
including his red trade-cloth leggings and the coup shirt
with the hair pendants ranged along the sleeves. His
father painted his face with his honour colours, and his
mother, tearful, this being the last occasion, brushed the
length of his hair until it shone, plaiting the locks which
fell down his back and whitening the quiff above his
forehead. She attached long blue-bead drops to the
short locks in front of his ears so that they brushed
against his cheeks, and into the back of his hair she tied a
circular quilled ornament from which fluttered clipped
hawk and his black-tipped eagle feathers. Lastly, his
mother slipped about his throat a necklace of beads and
short red-painted bird bones; an item not over-large or
gaudy, simply something she had made for him. He
thanked her and hugged her to him, and she sent him to
his bride.

Outside his family tipi an older uncle, Rain Catcher, was waiting to lead the procession through the village. Winter Man smiled at him and cast an approving eye over the intended gifts for Bear On The Flat. Six of his best horses were picketed there, each bearing some minor present on its back: a freshly-tanned robe, a parfleche of dried meat, or a saddle-bag full of items donated by his relatives. He strode over to his roan and swung himself up on to its back. His uncle took up the lead rein of the bridal horses and urged his own mount into a walk. The others followed, Winter Man a discreet distance to the rear.

The route the procession took to Bear On The Flat's lodge was the most roundabout possible. Every tipi was passed, so that the occupants could see the gifts being offered. Again and again, so that none might miss it, Rain Catcher sang the praises of his nephew in a high, piercing voice.

> Look all who have eyes,
> Here comes a worthy man.
> He is a Fox.
> His name is Winter Man.
> He is a Good Young Man with coups to his name.
> See the shirt he wears.
> See the colours he is painted.
> He defends your lodges.
> He kills your enemies.
> His name is Winter Man.

Bear On The Flat's tipi loomed before them, and Winter Man felt dread claw at his heart. No one stood outside it. Even the door-flap was closed.

Had he chosen his moment wrongly? Had the man's sons influenced him to change his mind? What would he do if no one came out, if he and his bridal gifts were ignored? He would leave the village. He would have to! Everyone would laugh at him. Skins The Wolf would laugh at him. He would be disgraced.

Rain Catcher walked his horse up to the tipi covering and struck it a heavy blow with his riding quirt.

'Ho! People of the lodge! A worthy man brings gifts!'

He backed his horse away from the tipi and sat patiently to wait.

The waiting seemed endless, and then the flap was raised and Antelope Dancer stepped out. Winter Man felt his stomach twist—Antelope Dancer was going to speak for the family—but no, he turned back to the opening. Taking his father's offered arm, he helped him out into the sunshine. Little Face followed with the children; last came Moon Hawk.

Winter Man drew breath at the sight of her. She was wearing a dress of whitened elk-skin, tanned so finely that it clung to the curves of her body as if it was a part of her. Across the shoulders and down the elbow-length sleeves, a short fringe of sky-blue beads cascaded and tinkled in answer to her every movement. Circles of red quill-work emphasised the fullness of each breast, and a belt the thickness of three fingers the narrowness of her waist. At thigh-height, long, slender thongs of skin had been fastened with patches of red trade cloth all round the skirt, forming a fringe which stopped just short of the bottom of her dress. If she had twirled about, they would have lifted horizontally away from her in a wide fan. Her leggings were decorated with vertical stripes of red and yellow quill-work; the moccasins on her tiny feet embroidered to match.

Winter Man let his held breath escape and slowly raised his eyes to her face to see if she was looking at him. Her head was down, her thick, dark hair falling freely from the vermilion-painted parting on her crown. He spoke to her in his mind, willed her to look up at him, and slowly, finally, she did.

Their gazes met. Winter Man's heart swelled within him until he thought it would burst through his ribs. Her eyes were painted vermilion; a spot, too, highlighted the bone of each cheek, but he was sure he saw the blush of her own colour spread across her face. There was certainly a shy curving of her lips. And then she cast her eyes down again, acting as a chaste maiden should when confronted by her proposed bed-fellow.

Bear On The Flat shrugged off the attempts of his son to help him, preferring to stand alone, but painfully, on his broken leg with only a slender crutch to support him. He, too, wore his best clothing and his honour colours, something which was conspicuously missing from Antelope Dancer. Of Runs His Horse there was no sign. Perhaps harsh words had already been spoken within the family and the younger son had refused to be present at the meeting. Winter Man worried, afresh, that the young man might ride up to hurl abuse and shame him, but Little Face was smiling confidently, obviously expecting no such interruption.

Rain Catcher saw his moment and began his speech. 'My nephew has asked me to speak for him on this occasion, and because he is a man of honour, a Good Young Man with creditable coups to his name, I have accepted this role with pride. He seeks your daughter, Moon Hawk, in marriage, and offers these gifts in good faith.'

Rain Catcher spread his arm in the direction of the horses, and Bear On The Flat pursed his lips non-committally. He called for Antelope Dancer to step forward, and slowly, painfully, he and Bear On The Flat moved between the animals inspecting hooves and teeth, stroking legs and ribs, and peering into the packages each of them carried.

At last the two men returned to stand before the lodge and Winter Man waited nervously for the verdict. Bear On The Flat leaned heavily upon his crutch and tried hard to mask his pain. He lifted his head high to speak loudly so that all those watching might hear him.

'Winter Man honours this lodge by the offering of generous gifts. He is courageous in the face of the enemies of the Apsaroke. He will protect my daughter. He is a skilled hunter and is fearless in the buffalo surround. He will bring much meat and many skins to their lodge. She will not know hunger, neither will she fear the cold. He is strong in mind and limb. The children he fathers will be strong, too. I am proud to accept these gifts for my daughter.'

There were shouts of joy and the yipping calls of young unmarried men. Women trilled, and many an older man slapped another on the back as Rain Catcher slipped from the saddle of his mount to tie the lead rein of the bridal horses to one of the tipi staking-pins. Winter Man sat straight and dignified on his roan, his flickering smile betraying no more than the merest suggestion of the depth of his released emotions. He stole a glance at Moon Hawk. Her retiring stance had been forgotten. Almost on tiptoes, her hands clasped before her in her excitement, she was fighting the urge to run across and hug him, it was clear. He smiled at her; he could not stop himself. Messages of love her lips were not allowed to utter shone from her eyes. His smile grew in return, but he found he could not hold her gaze. For some reason he felt embarrassed by her overt show of affection.

Rain Catcher took his mount's jaw-thong in his fingers and led it to one side, waiting for his nephew to join him. Together they rode back through the clustered people, back to Winter Man's family lodge to wait for a response.

Winter Man sat in his father's tipi and smoked with him and the other male relatives who had gathered there. The conversation was light and many jokes were passed back and forth. His mother and sisters brought food and everyone ate, and the talking began again. One of his brothers produced a drum, and songs were sung.

The shadows grew longer. Winter Man had to force himself to be cheery. Bear On The Flat had spoken eloquently outside his lodge, but where were the reciprocal gifts? Where was Moon Hawk? Was he doomed to remain in his father's lodge and not show his face except to the stars?

Painted knuckle-bones were brought out and a game ensued, but Winter Man's usual dexterity was lacking. Each time it was his turn to guess who hid them he misjudged, and those he played against acclaimed their triumph and another tally-stick was added to their pile.

There was a sharp rap on the lodge covering, and all within grew still. They could hear it, too: a singing, coming softly on the breeze from afar, growing louder as it neared.

Winter Man's relief swept through him. He grinned to

hide it as those around him grinned, and when they rose to leave the lodge, he rose, too, on trembling, unsteady legs. He stepped out of himself as he waited to duck through the entrance, and looked at his reactions with wide, uncomprehending eyes. He had waited in the twilight outside many lodges, knew all the quiet words which would light a woman's eyes. He had taken many lovers, and had left each one the happier. Why was he feeling this way? Why was this so different? Not once had he expected the anxiety which haunted his every thought. It was unnerving him.

He stood slightly in front of his relatives, his father at his shoulder, the rhythm of his heartbeat growing faster by the moment. What gifts would be returned? Had he judged wisely in the amount he had offered? It mattered little to him, he would accept whatever was given, but it would matter to Moon Hawk. His gifts would have to be matched if she were to come to him in honour, and if Bear On The Flat's sons had refused to help him gather gifts . . . But Antelope Dancer had been there. Antelope Dancer would have given a horse at least. Or would he? He had not been dressed in his finest clothing, had not worn the happy expression of a brother witnessing his sister's marriage.

The singing grew louder and the bridal procession rounded an obstructing tipi. The turmoil of Winter Man's thoughts flattened like the waters of a lake after a storm. Moon Hawk was sitting astride her father's most prized buffalo-horse, a cougar-skin trimmed with red trade cloth covering the saddle. Behind her, led by Bear On The Flat awkwardly perched on the back of his mount, walked six horses. Winter Man counted them again to make sure he had made no mistake. He had not been wrong. There were seven in all. Moon Hawk had been well honoured by her family, and each of them carried gifts.

The procession halted. Winter Man looked up at Moon Hawk, but she had no eyes for him now. She was nervously staring at some blurred point in her mind, her skin pale beneath the vermilion on her cheeks. Bear On The Flat raised his quirt to catch everyone's attention.

'This is my daughter, Moon Hawk. I give her to this man as his wife.' He pointed first to Winter Man and then to the gifts beside him. 'I give her with honour. May they live happily and at peace.'

As if by common consent, the female relatives of Winter Man moved towards Moon Hawk and bodily lifted her from her horse and ushered her into the lodge. As the men stood patiently, Moon Hawk's female relatives unloaded the bridal horses and set everything out on robes before the lodge. It had been some time since Winter Man had seen so many marriage gifts, and their value over-awed him. There were all types of metal items, knives and awls and kettles, traded from the hairy-faces to the north. There were two thick blankets, one as white as snow with a broad black stripe and the other a vivid scarlet. There were two incised antler riding quirts, a matching pair of parfleches full of dried meat, and saddle-bags containing all manner of smaller items from bracelets and necklaces to wooden bowls and horn spoons. Though some had certainly been gathered from Bear On The Flat's relatives, most, Winter Man realised, had been made with loving care by Moon Hawk's mother. A captured woman who had never had a suitor bring gifts for her, or been honoured by gifts given by her own family, she was ensuring that her eldest daughter lacked no such prestige.

Even though he knew he should not, he raised his eyes to his mother-in-law so that she would know he understood. Little Face was watching him. She caught his look and held it for barely a heartbeat, then drew her robe up to her eyes and looked away. Winter Man, too, averted his eyes as propriety demanded. A mother and her son-in-law could never look at or speak directly to one another, but he would make her something that could pass through Moon Hawk's hands to her, and he smiled as he thought of the brightness it would bring to her eyes.

Full of confidence now, he stepped forward and cast his gaze over the gifts. He lifted his eyes to Bear On The Flat and smiled. 'My heart is full. You honour me by honouring the woman who is my wife. A quarter of each animal I hunt I shall bring to your lodge.'

Bear On The Flat smiled broadly and nodded the once, evidently satisfied with the arrangement. Winter Man turned to his own parents.

'I am your son. Always you have been good to me. You have been mindful of the things I needed to know as I grew into a man. Sometimes I listened and sometimes I did not, but you have always been good to me. These gifts are yours.'

A ripple of appreciation ran through his gathered relatives. All of them would receive gifts in place of those they had donated. A generous man was well thought of by all, and in time of need no one would be reluctant to offer aid to him or his family.

The gifts were distributed and robes were spread upon the ground so that all might sit comfortably. A back-rest was provided for Bear On The Flat, and he and Winter Man's father sat together and talked.

There was movement from the lodge, and the women began to file out. Winter Man felt his heart leap again. He studiously avoided looking at any of his relatives and sat himself on one side of the thick buffalo robe left vacant for him before the fire. A hush crept among those gathered there, and the short hairs on the back of his neck began to rise. Moon Hawk came unseen behind him. A rustle of skins, a chink of elk-teeth, the scent of sweet grass, and she had lowered herself next to him, tucking her legs to one side as a woman should.

Cautiously he turned his eyes to her, not wanting, at that moment, for her to notice his interest. When she had entered his father's lodge, all her clothing had been taken from her. Nothing she wore then did she wear now. She had new leggings and moccasins, rings and bracelets, and tiers of slender white dentalium shells hung from her ears. Most important of all, she wore the elk-tooth dress supplied by his female relatives, visible proof that she had been accepted into their midst. From the little agitated movements she made, he realised that the many elk-teeth on the garment were making it difficult for her to sit comfortably. Apart from round her waist, where a quilled and beaded belt nestled, elk-teeth covered the dress from neck to calf with hardly a space to lay flat a finger between them. The women of his family had done him proud! The elk-teeth alone must have been worth three good horses in barter.

A bowl and spoon were placed in his hands, and a set was offered to Moon Hawk. She took it and smiled, and her head turned quickly towards him. She had noticed him looking at her. Her eyes were bright, but tense. He smiled at her reassuringly.

'You are beautiful,' he whispered.

The flush of colour which swept up her cheeks fired the blood in his veins. She fought with a smile for him, and as he knew she would, she timidly averted her eyes. He lifted his hand and gently placed it on top of hers. She did not draw away from him, but found the confidence to look at him once more. This time her smile held her lips and her eyes shone with love.

Food was offered to them, breaking the enchantment of the moment, and they ate in silence while all those about laughed and joked, and talked. As night closed in, drummers came and songs were sung, and the people rose and danced. Winter Man wrapped Moon Hawk in his war robe and they danced the slow circle dance together, his arm about her shoulders. After a few nervous steps, she slipped her arm round his waist, feeding her hand under his coup shirt and hooking her thumb in his belt by his hip. He pulled her closer to him, feeling her warm body melt against his, and their swaying steps became as one, back and forth, left and right, in time with the beat of the drum, in time with the beat of their hearts.

Couples began to drift into the darkness, and slowly, with hardly a change in their step, Winter Man manoeuvred his bride out of the circle and away into the night.

CHAPTER TEN

MOON HAWK LET herself be guided by the strong arms of her husband. Husband! How often had she dreamed of calling Winter Man her husband? Too many times to contemplate. Now, the reality was with her at last! She leaned her temple against the side of his chest, drinking in the warmth beating through the thickness of his shirt. Each step she took was as if on air. Her happiness was lulling her into a dream-like semi-consciousness, and she willingly abandoned herself to its euphoria.

She felt him touch her hair, the unmistakable impression of a kiss, and she raised her face, wanting his lips to meet her own. He merely smiled at her.

'We are here,' he murmured.

Her gaze followed his. Before her stood a tipi, their tipi, the newly-tanned white skins of its covering looking strangely eerie and forbidding in the darkness.

'Come.'

The pressure of his arm upon her back produced a sudden, agitated quickening of Moon Hawk's pulse. She walked with him to the doorway and watched as he lifted the flap for her to enter. Their eyes met briefly, but she could not read his thoughts and she did not want him to read hers. What was this fear? Why did she not feel excited as she had when he had wrapped her in his robe outside her father's tipi?

She slipped inside the lodge and stood before the dully glowing fire, trying to ease her anxiety by concentrating on what she saw. The lodge was large, far larger than she had expected it to be, but very stark, without the comforts normally found inside a tipi. There was but a single lining-skin hanging from the poles, Winter Man's war record, the stylised forms of horses and men painted in bright colours by his own hand. It hung at the back of the lodge, in the place of honour, keeping the draught from the only bed, a voluminous bed for two.

'Do you like it?'

She turned sharply, but Winter Man was looking about him at the tipi, not at the bed, or at her. She fought for a calm reply.

'Yes. I . . . Its size is beyond my expectations. The women of your family have been very good to us.'

She heard him make a soft, appreciative noise in his throat and he brushed by her to sink to his knees before the fire-pit. He leaned forward and blew gently on the embers, causing them to redden and spark. Cakes of dried buffalo dung were to hand, and he fed the glowing coals until the flames leapt, yellow and blue, to light the lodge with a brightness that was hard on the eyes.

'A paunch full of water, fuel for the fire . . . It is not much, but it is all we shall need for our first night together.'

He spun round on his heel and looked up at her. She tried to smile at him, but her courage failed her and she averted her eyes. Winter Man was on his feet at once, his hands reaching out for her. He clasped her by the shoulders and stood silently until she looked up at him.

'The choice is yours alone, Moon Hawk. There is no reason for you to feel the concern you do, but I respect it, as I should. It will be enough if you will lie in my arms until the dawn.'

Despite her maidenhood, she had not expected him to say those quiet words. They cracked open the shell of fear that had engulfed her heart, releasing a tight knot of emotion that uncurled and grew within her. She reached up and placed her palms flat on his chest, rising to her toes to offer her lips to his.

The moist warmth of his mouth enveloped hers in a caress which was both gentle and tentative. It cut the last restraints binding her spirit to her mortal self, and she leaned into him, slipping her hands round his neck, her fingers seeking the slender braids which fell down his back. His arms tightened about her as his lips swept over hers, and her feet lifted off the ground with the power of their embrace.

Lowering her again, Winter Man withdrew from her arms to hunch his back and pull the heavy coup shirt over

his head. He dropped it where he stood. With a deft flick
and a speed which caught her by surprise, he untied his
leggings and stepped out of both them and his moccasins. He stood before her in his breechclout, the brightness of the fire weaving patterns of light and shadow over
his lithe, sun-bronzed body.

Moon Hawk gathered her wits and reached for the
thonging that held her belt, but his fingers closed over
hers, staying her hand.

'There will be many nights,' he whispered, 'but this
night . . . This night is your night.'

Before she could draw a question from her bewilder-
ment, he kissed her lightly on the forehead and crouched
at her feet to untie her moccasins. She could only rest a
hand on his shoulder and watch in astonishment. Never
had she heard of a man removing a woman's moccasins
before. She had watched her mother remove her father's
when he had returned to the lodge wet and tired after a
day's hunting, but this . . .

She drew a breath and held it as his nimble fingers slid
up past her knees and unfastened the ties that bound her
leggings. Before she knew it, they, too, lay discarded
with his shirt. He reached to untie the belt that kept her
dress tight about her waist, and she shivered a little,
anticipating his next action. In a movement as fluid as
the lifting of an eagle's wings, Winter Man caught the
bottom of her dress in his fingers and stood to raise it
high over her head, leaving her naked and glowing
before him. Without a moment's hesitation, he slipped
one powerful arm behind her shoulders and one behind
her hips, sweeping her up against his chest to hold her
there while he ran an appreciative eye from the tips of
her toes to the ends of her hair.

His roving gaze caught her own and held it fast.
Reflected firelight burned gold in the depths of his
dark, unblinking eyes, and she felt herself being drawn
irretrievably towards the seething force within.

'Give yourself to me, Moon Hawk, and I shall take
you to the stars and back.'

She thrilled to the passion barely curbed in his voice,
to the indisputable belief in the measure of his own

virility. If anyone could take her to the stars, it was Winter Man. In his arms he could take her anywhere.

He crossed to their bed and lowered her on to the heaped woolly buffalo robes. She reached for him as he loosened his clasp and he kissed her again, on the lips, on the eyes, on her cheek and her chin, lightly and quickly, making her senses dance and her flesh quiver. He began to stroke her neck and her shoulders with long, tender passes of his fingers. He was holding something, she realised; leaves, soft and pliant. The heady scent of mint filled her nostrils. He was rubbing her with mint: her arms, her breasts, her ribs, her stomach, down past her hips and thighs, down to her feet. She draped an arm across his shoulders as his head turned from hers, and relaxed back into the robes to breathe deeply of the herb and luxuriate in the delights his sensuous touch could evoke.

Winter Man coaxed her to turn and lie on her stomach. He massaged the soles of her feet and the backs of her calves, working slowly, inexorably, over every part of her, out to the very tips of her fingers.

Moon Hawk had never known such pleasure. It seemed that her heartbeat was slowing, her breathing, too; but her skin . . . Her skin tingled and prickled and quivered beneath his subtle touch. It was so . . . *alive*.

Without warning the sensation roared with new intensity. Her eyes sprang open and her lips parted in a silent gasp as she tensed, momentarily, beneath the onslaught of his teeth and his tongue and the gentle raking of his nails. She could not bear it! She could not cope with the response erupting within herself! She needed to hold him, to feel his strong, still arms calmly about her. She forced herself on to her elbows as his teeth ravished the base of her spine. In a whirl of delight he turned her to him and locked his mouth on hers. Like a licking flame his tongue darted about her own, as the force of his kisses let loose her passion and fired a need deep in the hollow of her belly.

He released her lips and she breathed again, short and sharp and tremulous. She spread her hands across the glistening, knotted muscles of his shoulders, pushing her finger-tips deep into his flesh as her ardour lit and burned. His hands cupped the swelling of her breasts as the moist heat of his mouth enveloped them and Moon Hawk forced her rigid fingers through his long, thick hair, stretching the sinews in her arms until she felt they would snap. He teased at her nipples with his teeth, and she arched her back for him and for herself as his exploring fingers snaked across her stomach in search of her thighs. Her craving grew, and her body moved beneath his with the instincts of the wild.

Winter Man made his thrust—once, twice—penetrating deep inside the quivering body which opened to him. Moon Hawk cried out in her pain and her pleasure, and she clung to him as he rekindled her ecstasy and incited her desire. They moved as one; arched and rose, seethed and goaded. He wrapped his arms round her, binding her body to his, and rolled over on his back, taking her with him. Freed from his weight, she found new will, new command, and let loose the final rein on her soul. She kissed and caressed him, massaged and clawed him. She tasted the salt of his skin until the strain of her unsatisfied passion built to an agony which threatened to overflow and drown her. At the peak of the flood, as her screaming senses overwhelmed her, Winter Man broke and satiated them both.

Moon Hawk lay limply across him, whimpering softly as her spent body quivered with release. Winter Man curled an arm about her back and gently stroked his fingers down her spine as he relaxed into the buffalo robes and waited for his own tormented passions to subside.

From deep within, a sigh rose up his throat to escape in a tremulous breath. He opened his eyes and smiled. The fire had died in the central pit and the only light in the tipi came from the stars peeking through the open smoke-flaps above. The dark lines of the lodge poles were clearly visible against the lighter cover, if wavering slightly in the gloom. They spread out from their cluster at the smoke-hole like the supporting radials of a spider's web, stretching before and behind, in a snug, comforting circle all around them.

He eased himself as best he could, not wanting to disturb Moon Hawk, and angled his head so he could see her face. He smiled again, laughed almost. Her tousled hair had settled across her eyes like the untidy mane of a horse. He ran his nails lightly over her brow, hooking up each damp lock and lifting it away. She hardly murmured, and she did not offer to move. He kissed her gently on the cheek and lay back self-satisfied.

It had been better than he had expected. Moon Hawk had been better than he had dared to hope. The storm he had unleashed! The frenzy with which, at the last, *she* had taken *him!*

A shiver zig-zagged through his flesh with the potency of the recent memory. He filled his lungs with the crisp night air and let out the breath in one slow, unfaltering stream. He had judged it to perfection; he could say no more. Beneath his subtle guidance she would blossom and flower and be everything he wanted in a lover—and she would not even know that he was tutoring her. He smiled again, and drew his fingers idly up her spine. Her damp skin was chilling; his, too. He pulled the edge of a woolly robe over her back, and she started from her doze with a violent shudder. Clamping his arm across her shoulderblades, he held her fast.

'It is well. You lie safe in my arms.'

He felt the rapid flicking of her eyelashes upon his chest, and her tension seeped away. He relaxed his grip on her, and she nestled herself into the curve of his body. The shuddering sigh which left her was gratifying to hear, and he stroked her hair as she slipped an arm comfortably round him.

'I love you, Winter Man.'

He smiled, nuzzling tenderly at her cheek.

'I know,' he whispered. 'I know.'

A shaft of yellow sunlight streaked diagonally through the smoke-flaps as if through a chink in a cloud. Noises of the waking village filtered through the tipi covering, and Winter Man could clearly hear snippets of conversation as people walked by. If he and Moon Hawk did not make an appearance soon, the lewd banter that would greet them would last all day. He anticipated the teasing with some glee, but he doubted that Moon Hawk would find it amusing. He raised himself on an elbow and blew gently on her face until her eyelids began to flicker. He was waiting with a smile as she drew her vision into focus.

'Welcome, wife, to the new day.'

Her smiling response gladdened his heart. She reached up to stroke his cheek, and he bent and kissed her softly on the lips. They sat quietly together in the warm pool of sunlight enjoying each other's nearness. Moon Hawk raised a hand to her breast, an unconscious movement Winter Man did not fail to notice. He had been most careful not to hurt her; at least, he thought he had.

'Are you sore?'

She looked at him obliquely, then shook her head. 'Not as much as I expected.'

He smiled in his relief. They were not talking about the same thing, he was certain.

Her contentment suddenly flew. 'Did—did I do that?' Her hand reached out to touch his chest, but she withdrew her fingers before making contact with his skin. Her horrified reaction to the scratches she saw made him chuckle. 'Did I hurt your shoulder, too? I did not think. I . . .'

'No, no.' It had been the throbbing of his injured shoulder which had woken him, but he was not going to tell her that.

She shrugged, a blush beginning to rise up her cheeks. 'Your touch excited me.'

Winter Man reeled back as if affronted. 'Of course my touch excited you! What sort of a man would I be if my touch could not excite you?'

Moon Hawk giggled and sought his arms again.

The tipi shuddered beneath the heavy whack of a riding quirt, and children's laughter erupted close by. Moon Hawk looked first at the lodge covering and then up at the shaft of sunlight falling through the smoke-hole, her eyes growing wider by the moment.

'Oh, no! We shall never hear the end of this!'

She tore herself from him and scrambled into her dress, the elk-teeth chinking together in her haste.

The tipi was assaulted again, the laughter of the children frenzied. Some sly adult was encouraging them.

'Lakota! Lakota!' Winter Man responded in a loud, terrified voice. 'My lodge is being attacked by Lakota!'

Outside, the children shrieked with excitement and answered him with Lakota war-cries and more thumps on the cover.

'No! No! I am wrong!' Winter Man called out to them. 'It is a bear! A bear is trying to get into my tipi!'

Again the uproarious laughter, this time accompanied by much growling and scratching at the lodge.

'Stop playing with the children and let us go!' Moon Hawk begged him in an urgent whisper.

Winter Man tapped her on the nose with his finger, his face alight with mischief. 'Not married to you a day, and already you are nagging me!'

He clothed himself in his breechclout and draped his leggings over his shoulder. 'I have my gun!' he cried out. 'I am going hunting *bear!*'

The ensuing cries of panic brought a smile to Moon Hawk's lips. Winter Man waited by the doorway for the scurrying of tiny feet to subside and then he whipped back the flap and stepped out. Hunching himself up as if he was tracking, he stretched out his arms to hold a make-believe gun. All around, adults were standing watching, but he had eyes only for the small faces peering from behind neighbouring tipis, or their mothers' legs.

'I shall skin a bear today!' He took three very heavy steps in the direction of a group of sheltering children, and they screamed and fled for a new hiding-place.

He straightened, and shot out a hand towards another group of sheltering children, transfixing them to the spot with an angry eye.

'Come out! Come out! Stand in a line!'

Slowly, anxiously, not quite knowing what to expect, the children filed out one behind the other. Winter Man caught his hands behind his back and inspected them, inspiring both dread and mirth from the advantage of his towering height.

'A Lakota struck my lodge,' he said to a six-year-old boy. 'Did you see him?'

The boy could only shake his head, his cheeks looking fit to burst with the laughter held back in them.

'Did you?' Winter Man asked another. Again the same reply. He walked to the end of the line and spun on his heel, making the children shudder. 'Was it a *bear*?'

Despite hands clamped over mouths, the laughter could not be held at bay. Winter Man played to them, spreading his arms expansively and widening his eyes in mock astonishment.

'Was it a *Lakota* bear?'

Not one of the children could stand up straight, and many of the watching adults, too, were laughing. Winter Man found difficulty in making himself heard.

'I know who it was! It was *you*!'

With all the grace of a three-legged buffalo, he lumbered after them, his rigid arms somehow continually missing the small agile bodies. He even managed to trip over one little girl, falling flat on his face and causing many a guffaw from the adults and shrieks of merriment from the escaping children.

At last all the youngsters had fled, and he sat alone on the ground. A shadow crossed his eyes and he looked up at Moon Hawk. She smiled and offered him her hand.

'You do realise,' she told him as she helped him up, 'that every child in the village will be striking the outside of our lodge each morning for the next month?'

He shrugged affably and slipped an arm round her shoulders. 'Complaints! Complaints! It has stopped the singing of bawdy songs. What more do you want?'

He drew her into his side and they began walking towards the creek for the day's ablutions.

A distance away, watching between the heads of others, two men stood together, their eyes full of scorn.

'Your brother-in-law would make a good clown,' Skins The Wolf said.

Runs His Horse turned away in disgust. 'He is a clown!'

'Be patient, my friend. The dishonour he brought you will be returned ten-fold, I swear.'

Moon Hawk's brother shook off the comforting hand from his shoulder and he walked away between the lodges. Skins The Wolf curled a sneering lip in the direction of his back and returned his attention to the disappearing figure of Winter Man.

'Enjoy,' he murmured beneath his breath. 'You will be blind to the arrow which takes out your heart.'

The cold water of the creek had been unusually invigorating. Perhaps it had merely been the company and the circumstance; Moon Hawk believed so, but it seemed imprudent to delve too deeply into the reasons for her intensified senses. She walked at Winter Man's side seeing new colours in the dry, over-grazed pasture they trod, a different beauty in the cloud formations above their heads. The air seemed never to have smelled so sweet, or the breeze to have felt so vital. She locked her arm about her husband's for the sheer enjoyment of his touch, and listened to him laugh and joke with the young men who constantly called out to him.

Meat was waiting outside their tipi, a kettleful already cooked. It steamed busily when she removed the lid.

'I think we are about to entertain guests,' Winter Man mused, raising a jocular eyebrow.

Moon Hawk lifted the kettle into the lodge and lost no time in preparing a fire for it to sit over. She brushed Winter Man's hair as a wife should, and painted his face as he directed. Then she sat and let him brush her hair and let him paint her face. She felt as proud as any married woman ever could. It was a husband's act of love and devotion that everyone in the village could see.

When the stew bubbled noisily, she tied up the door-flap and took her place beside Winter Man at the rear of the lodge. They did not have to wait long. His female relatives were the first to come, bringing furnishings for the tipi. Each was offered food and each provided a bowl to eat from. Winter Man's brothers and uncles came, too. One led two of his horses: the roan with the short line around its neck, which was picketed to a tipi-pin, and one of his buffalo-horses packed with his personal possessions.

Winter Man unloaded it with dignity and care. Various pad and antler saddles he left outside the doorway. Bags containing clothing, paint powders and tools, he let Moon Hawk arrange as she wished. A bundle of seasoning arrow-shafts he hoisted high into the apex of the tipi. His gun and his bow-case he tied to the lodge poles above the bed, but his shield, a man's most valued possession next to his Medicine, he entrusted to the hands of Moon Hawk. As his wife, it was both her duty and her privilege to keep its face, and the face of its cover, turned forever to the sun as it travelled slowly across the sky. The mystical properties imbued in the shield during its creation were nourished by the direct light of the sun. A sunned shield would never betray its owner's trust, and would deflect every arrow-head, axe-blow and musket-ball it encountered. Moon Hawk felt her world was complete.

Visitors kept arriving all through the day. Each brought a gift—a blessing for the tipi from an aged grandfather, or a bundle of firewood from Moon Hawk's young sister, Turtle. When everyone had gone, and the night was nearly upon them, another shook the deer-hoof rattle and announced himself.

'Ho! It is Antelope Dancer.'

Moon Hawk's happiness died in her breast as the acrimonious exchanges of the day before rose unbidden and sour in her mind. Like Runs His Horse, her eldest brother had wanted nothing to do with her marriage, or the exchange of gifts. He had relented only after Little Face had shamed him into helping Bear On The Flat in his infirmity. Even then there had been an atmosphere between father and son which had threatened to ruin the joy of the occasion for her. What could he want?

Winter Man bade him enter and indicated a seat by his side, but Antelope Dancer refused to sit until he had said what he wanted.

'There was a time when we spoke well together, and then that time passed. I believe we should speak well together again.'

He extended his arm, a twist of tobacco in his hand. Winter Man took it and lifted his pipe-bag from its rest. The two men sat and smoked. When they had finished, their eyes smiled and merriment filled their faces. Moon Hawk could only look at them with eyes which brimmed with unshed tears of happiness.

'Come, wife! My brother-in-law sits here dying of hunger!'

Antelope Dancer laughed, and pronounced the food she gave him as better than anything she had ever cooked in her father's lodge. She did not reply, seeing no point in telling him that it had not been her hand that had prepared it.

'Perhaps . . .' Winter Man began, as the other was about to leave. 'Perhaps the next time you sit here, Runs His Horse will sit with you.'

Antelope Dancer gazed at him a moment before lowering his eyes. 'I shall talk with him,' he said, but from the tone he used Moon Hawk knew he held little optimism.

One day drifted into another. Always the couple were happy. Winter Man entered his roan in a horse-race, and Moon Hawk watched him win it. He brought a great pile of wagered items to the lodge, but for Moon Hawk the pleasure had been in the way he had ridden and the laughter in his face. Their evenings were filled with singing and dancing at other lodges, their nights with the heady passions of new lovers.

The only cloud on the horizon of their contentment was the gnawing ache in Winter Man's shoulder. There were days when Moon Hawk knew instinctively that it was paining him, others when he laughed too much for anything to hurt him, but in the dark corners of her mind the same fear always lurked: his shoulder was taking too long to mend. If she questioned him about it, he would not be drawn, uttering no more than meaningless replies to soothe her anxiety. She heard from another that he was offering gifts to Star Ghost in return for curing rites. To know that he was unwilling to discuss it with her was like living with a festering wound. Out of desperation she went to see Star Ghost herself.

'If he had broken his arm, he would be patient waiting for it to mend,' the crippled healer told her. 'A broken arm can be seen with anyone's eyes, but it is not a bone that is broken in Winter Man's shoulder; it is sinews which have been stretched and torn.'

Moon Hawk knew the strength of sinews. She had seen them in the animals she had butchered. Nevertheless, Star Ghost insisted on showing her a length of buffalo-hair rope, pointing to the individual strands which made up the whole. Many were tufted where they had snapped.

'An old man's sinews look like this—my sinews.' He jerked hard on the rope, and the strands gave a little more. 'This rope is a dead thing and it cannot heal. Winter Man is not a dead thing. He is alive. He is young and he is strong. His shoulder will heal. It will take time, but it will heal.'

Star Ghost rested his hands on his knees and straightened his back. He peered at her haughtily, daring her to question his judgement. She felt keenly ill at ease.

'I—I understand that. It is my husband's attitude which worries me.'

'His fears will not allow him patience.'

'Fears?' Moon Hawk had never thought of Winter Man having any fears. He rode like the wind, and had always been one of the first to mount his horse in defence of the village. He was a Good Young Man with coups to his name. How could he possibly have fears?

Star Ghost lowered his eyes in thought, then raised them again and looked her straight in the eye.

'You are married now.' He circled his hand about her face as though he were trying to mesmerise her. 'The seasons have turned one into another and the Moon of the Falling Leaves is here once more, but there is no child growing in your belly. How do you feel?'

Images of Jay shot through her mind. She and Hillside had been married a full turning of the seasons, and there was no child growing in her belly. The women of the village talked in low tones about her: some said it was a judgement, some a curse, but they all said she was barren.

Moon Hawk, herself, had seen her walk into the women's willow lodge in tears. Even though she had never said so, Jay thought herself barren, too.

Moon Hawk shuddered, dreading anything so dire happening to her. But what was the connection with Winter Man?

'A woman who cannot bear children is not truly a woman. She is like a *berdache*, a man-woman. A man who, through a weakness of his body, cannot hunt and cannot fight, is not truly a man. He is . . .' The healer opened his arms in explanation, but the words he sought would not come to him. He rested his hands back on his knees and hung his head. 'He is like a dead thing which has not died.'

Moon Hawk could not help herself. She let her gaze drop to the old man's leggings, to the thin, deformed legs which they hid. Was that how Star Ghost thought of himself? As a dead thing which had not died? His knowledge had helped so many. She wanted to reach out and touch his hand, show him that she did not think of him in that way, but she knew it would be unseemly, and a man such as Star Ghost would not graciously have accepted it. She forced her concentration back on to Winter Man, and slowly, like the waking of a frosty day, she became aware of what was simmering in his mind. It was not the injury that caused him the pain, but the fear of losing strength in the limb.

'What can I do?' she asked.

'You must show him the patience he cannot find in himself.'

Moon Hawk tried. She tried very hard, but the knowledge Star Ghost had passed on to her made her see Winter Man in a different light. She saw the still times when he sat, his brow furrowed, seeing nothing. She heard the irritated rasping of his breath when he was using his hands to mend a saddle, and the muscles in his shoulder refused to give him the power he demanded. She saw him dress less often in his bright clothing and talk less to the other Good Young Men. Hillside, his brother-friend for many years, took to coming more frequently to the lodge. Moon Hawk knew that he, too, had noticed the change in Winter Man, but she never spoke of it with him. She left the two men to smoke or to talk, or simply to sit together, and she prayed to First Maker.

When the Crier beat his drum and called for the village to be made ready for the final move before the snows, Winter Man leaped with renewed vitality. Moon Hawk knew that it was because he had something to occupy his thoughts at last, but, seeing the change in him, breathed relief at every step. She was mindful of her prayers and, when he was not close to see her, she walked along the creek to the marshy place and tied a strip of red cloth to one of the stunted oaks as an offering of thanks to First Maker.

She had helped her mother to move their family tipi many times each year. It was something she had practised since girlhood, when Little Face had made her a play-tipi of her own, just like the one Turtle now owned. There was a sort of unspoken competition between the women as to who could strike her lodge and pack it and all its contents on the horses in the shortest time. Every item, however small, had a travelling-bag of its own, and things not needed on the morning of the move were packed away the night before.

The evening was as no other evening could have been. By the light of fires, women and girls hurried between the lodges of their kin with heavy loads tied in rawhide. Others were reinforcing the lashings of horse travois ready to take the burdens with the coming of the dawn. Men and boys were bringing strings of horses in from the surrounding hills and picketing them close to the tipis. Even the younger children were busy, struggling with dogs unused to being leashed. Amid all, puppies barked and scampered back and forth, excited by all the bustle.

Winter Man picketed his horses outside their lodge, allocating which could be used for burdens and which for riding. With some apologies, he offered Moon Hawk a notched-eared skewbald to ride.

'I wish you to hold your head high when you ride with the other brides, but I cannot give you one of my best buffalo-horses.'

'I would not expect it,' she answered. 'To carry me and the weight of a tipi would ruin it for hunting.'

He smiled a little, relieved that she understood. 'I had hoped the skewbald would be a sound buffalo-horse. Its wind is good, its legs strong, but it is not as quick witted as is needed. The black was quick witted, but it still died in the crush of the wash. I am left with only two trained horses.'

Moon Hawk nodded her understanding. 'I shall be proud to ride the skewbald among the other brides.'

As the first streak of yellowing light filtered through the clouds in the eastern sky, horses were standing patiently saddled or harnessed, awaiting their loads. There was surprisingly little noise considering the concentrated industry, but every woman knew the tasks awaiting her, and the men gave them room to do them. Smaller children slept blissfully on, unaware that lodge covers were being rolled back above their heads.

Moon Hawk knelt on the damp grass in her elk-tooth dress, folding and packing her lodge covering to fit into the space between the high pommel and cantle of her antler saddle. She paused a moment, wondering if Little Face was coping with the packing of the family tipi. Being a captured woman meant that there were no sisters or female cousins to help her. A grandmother would, surely—yes, a grandmother had often helped when there had been the two of them.

With a heave, she picked up the rectangular package and slipped it over the open saddle-frame, adjusting the length of the wide stirrup-thong so that it hung down the same amount on either side of the skewbald's ribs, before tying the cover solidly into position. A folded buffalo robe set on the top made a comfortable seat for her, and she proceeded to tie Winter Man's shield and lance to the cantle so that they stood decoratively for all to see. Two of her unmarried sisters-in-law helped to take the tipi poles down and harness them to waiting horses, and the back-rests and the smaller baggage were loaded on to a horse-travois. By the time the sun had risen one finger above the horizon, Moon Hawk was sat upon her skewbald, manoeuvring her horses into the line as the village left their autumn site.

She lifted herself in her stirrups, looking for Little Face, but there was too much movement, too many milling faces. For the next few months, whenever the village moved, her place in the column would be with the other brides, not with her family. She had not expected to feel sad for that, but she did. Her eyes swept the village site for the last time. It had meant more to her than any other. She and Winter Man had courted there, married there, loved there, and only the worn earth and a myriad of cold fire-pits showed that a village had stood there at all.

She watched as dogs sniffed among the remains, hoping to find some discarded food. Most returned to the line unrewarded. The wind was blowing cold from the Shining Mountains. She pulled her robe more tightly round her shoulders and turned her eyes ahead. Life, for her, would never quite be the same again.

CHAPTER ELEVEN

THE MORNING WAS full of changes. The sky cleared for a while and was as blue as a kingfisher's wing. The peaks of the Shining Mountains seemed unusually close, and looked, at times, as if they were dancing with white flames; snow, Winter Man knew, being whipped from the high ridges by gales too harsh to contemplate—storm winds. The air suddenly chilled, and thick grey clouds reared above the peaks to scud across to the further horizon like dirty cottonwood seeds blowing before the wind. The streams began to rise, telling of unseen cloudbursts in the higher reaches.

As an outrider, Winter Man rode to and fro beyond the slowly moving column or sat astride his fast, un-burdened roan, his keen eyes directed to the deeply folding land either side of the sprawling line, but of the foes he watched for there was no sign.

The land was chànging as they pushed south. Pockets of berry-bushes were becoming more numerous and scattered, not merely cleaving to the edges of creeks where the water was. The grass, too, was more lush, and of a finer quality. Birch and ash and oak thickets flourished in sheltered delves.

He turned his eyes to the column meandering along the lowlands below. It was a sight which never tired him. So many people . . . So many horses . . . Their noise and colour filled his senses. Who would have thought, during the same journey a year ago, that he would have a wife riding there below him now? He shook his head and chuckled loudly. Not he! A complete man—that was what Hillside called him. Strangely enough, that was how he felt. He had expected marriage to feel no different from the taking of a new lover, but it did, though he was still uncertain why. Hillside had laughed, and told him to enjoy and not complain. At the time he had chuckled and nodded his agreement, but Winter

Man knew only too well the truth hidden in those words. His contentment with any one woman had never lasted. Despite their marriage, he knew it would not last with Moon Hawk, either. It was the way of things, something he accepted. Better that he made the most of what he had while it was there to savour.

He flicked his quirt towards his roan's thigh, and it obediently began to descend the ridge. Boys were hunting jack-rabbits further down the slope, though by the look of it, more arrows had been broken than rabbits killed. Two dogs were busily enlarging the animals' holes, but he decided that the rabbits had little cause for concern.

He altered the weight of the shortened musket cradled in his arms and heeled the roan sharply in the ribs to quicken its gait. The middle of the day had come and gone. A man was laughed at if his mind dwelled on hunger after travelling for so short a time, but it would be an excuse to visit the column and seek out Moon Hawk. He had ridden by her position twice just to look at her, though he did not think she had seen him. Perhaps she would enjoy a quiet word, a joke, maybe. It would be something for the other brides to tease her about—a doting husband full of concern for the well-being of his wife. She would blush. He liked to see her blush. He had never known any woman blush as easily as Moon Hawk.

He cantered on to the flatter land, moving parallel and slightly faster than the wide, untidy line. Moon Hawk turned and smiled at his approach, though he knew she could not possibly have heard him. A secret sense, perhaps? A woman's intuition?

'How goes your ride? Have you lost any of our belongings yet?'

Her face was a study of affronted pride. 'Of course not!'

He laughed, and she realised he had only been joking. She smiled coyly, trying to hide the reddening of her cheeks.

'Is there food for a hungry husband?'

She unhooked a long, fringed bag from the pommel of

her saddle and offered it to him. 'I packed it especially for you.' She pointed to her own, hanging down the other side of the skewbald's neck. 'Is there sight of much game?'

'There is little sight of anything. It is as though the animals sense a wrongness in the air.'

Her smile faded and her tone become serious. 'There is talk of a coming storm. The river cannot be crossed in a flood.'

Winter Man turned his eyes to hers, but she would not hold his gaze. Was she frightened of the crossing?

'You can swim?' It was half a question, half a statement.

Her eyes swept over him in such a deprecating manner that it brought memories of their first meeting to his mind. 'I can swim in fast water, but no one can swim in a flood. My father's leg is broken, and my mother has few horses to carry their belongings.'

Of course! How foolish of him not to realise. She feared for her family.

'We shall help them. My horses are strong and can make the crossing many times without exhaustion. And you—you I shall hold in my arms and show you why my other name is Fish.'

He stood in his stirrups and leaned sideways to plant a kiss on her forehead before she realised what was happening. She giggled and smiled happily at him, and blushed to the roots of her hair when the young women round her began to taunt her with lovers' songs. Winter Man slapped the quirt down on the roan's hindquarters and galloped back up to his vantage-point.

Despite so casually countering her worries about the river crossing, Winter Man knew that she was right, and he knew, too, that she was not the only one seeing cause for concern. Beyond the sight of the column, mystics knowledgeable in Weather Medicine were consulting with their spirit-helpers.

The clouds grew darker, and heavier, and descended to curtain the Shining Mountains from the people's eyes. Occasionally it would drizzle. Once there was a sudden shower of stinging hail.

Turtle rode up the line on an old mare trailing a loaded travois. She hit the tired animal repeatedly with her quirt until she had drawn level with her sister.

'Can I ride with you? Mother told me not to come, that it was not my place, but you will let me ride with you?'

Her plea was so woeful that Moon Hawk had not the heart to send her back, and the girl rode quite happily with the brides as though she were one herself. One of the young women asked her who her sweetheart was. To Moon Hawk's embarrassment, Turtle told them all about Snow Rattle and how good a provider he would become when he grew older.

The village reached the river as the daylight was fading. A heavy silence slipped down the column as each family group came close enough to observe its brown, undulating back. The clouds that had threatened to loosen their rains had done so further up the forested slopes. The river was in flood. No crossing would be attempted before the dawn, at the very earliest.

Moon Hawk lay comfortably in Winter Man's arms, sharing their woolly buffalo robes for added warmth. There were no stars, and even the dull, reflected light from the peaks of the mountains could not be seen for the thickness of the cloud. It was very dark. The people had wrapped themselves for sleep long before, but there was still much movement to be heard. There was coughing from a sick person, and the fretful whimpering of a young child. A grandmother sang to comfort it, and those who listened added their voices softly to hers. The horses snorted and stamped. The dogs barked at nothing and themselves, and at a distant, single wolf which scented them. Above everything, with the hissing of a giant serpent, the river surged relentlessly by.

'Have you vermilion to paint your wrists and ankles?' Moon Hawk whispered. She felt her husband chuckle. 'Do not laugh! The water monsters will remember and seek you out.'

'I have crossed wider rivers than this, and I have never needed to paint red stripes about my wrists to protect me from water monsters!'

'Then your Medicine must be very strong. Twice I have mourned relatives who were killed by them.'

A kiss brushed her lightly on the cheek, and his voice became more tolerant. 'If it will make you happy, you can paint me with the protection in the morning.'

She smiled, seeking his lips with her own. He could laugh at her, she did not mind, just as long as he was safe.

It rained during the night and the clouds descended even further. The Apsaroke rose to a world of moist, grey mist, reminiscent of a fear-dream. There was wailing to be heard in some quarters and chanted incantations to sacred beings. Winter Man left Moon Hawk to sit in circles with the men. He looked happier when he returned.

'The mystics are making Weather Medicine.'

Moon Hawk tried not to look dubious. Rumour was that the mystics had sat the day before, too. 'Are they being heard?'

'Yes. The first man will cross before noon. You had better start making a raft for our possessions.'

Moon Hawk watched him take six paces and disappear into the murk. Noon. She shook her head. It seemed far too short a time to her.

As did the other women around her, Moon Hawk began the task of untying the lodge poles and lashing them in triangles to form the basis of a raft. Moving about became more and more difficult. With the rain of the night and the constant milling of the horses, the ground was being churned like a buffalo's mud-wallow. People slipped and slithered and many fell, the dark mud sticking to their clothing like boiled glue, but as tempers frayed, smiles grew. It struck a balance everyone was grateful for.

One moment the light was grey and dull like the onset of twilight, the next it was as if a giant fire had been lit all round them. There was a hush among the Aparoke as eyes were turned skywards; then laughter and cheering broke out up and down the line. The mist was lifting, disappearing as the people watched.

The women worked with a new will, singing songs and chattering gaily. The sun was shining now, and there were no clouds at all. Boys kept riding up and down the column giving out the news: the level of the river was down; a catch-line had been made fast from bank to bank; the first horses had reached the other side.

Turtle came and sat herself heavily on the edge of Moon Hawk's raft, her face puckered and stern.

'Why are you not helping our mother?' Moon Hawk asked.

The girl made a sullen face. 'She says I am no use to her. Is it *my* fault that Bobtailed Cat keeps running away?'

Moon Hawk smiled, remembering similar grievances of her own when it had been Turtle who had been the youngest and had refused to sit still.

'And she will not let me take my own lodge across the water,' the girl added.

'It runs too swiftly, and your horse is not strong.'

Turtle stamped her foot in the mud, splattering it in all directions. 'That old mare is not my horse! My horse was stolen by the Shoshone!'

Moon Hawk laughed at her sister's fit of indignation, which only incensed Turtle the more. The girl picked up a discarded stick and strutted off towards the nearby thicket, muttering to herself and striking out at any tuft of greenery which dared to stand above the mud. Moon Hawk shook her head and went back to her work.

A muffled cry caught her attention, and the flesh of her neck crawled with a sudden dread. Someone had been swept downstream, she was sure—and she had not painted the red stripes on Winter Man's wrists! Oh, let it not be he, she begged.

The cry was not a single shout. It was being taken up by others, building to an uproar. Work stopped as the women raised their heads to look and listen. The noise was not coming from the crossing-point, that was clear, but from further along the column. The dull boom of a powder gun made everyone jump, and a woman close to Moon Hawk screamed. There was a sudden flurry of confusion as the people caught and remounted startled horses, beating their quirts down upon their animals, desperate to find a place of safety. There was no doubt, now. The Apsaroke were being attacked!

He came through the crowd at a gallop, oblivious to the panic around him—a man on a painted grey, its tail tied up for war. Moon Hawk felt her jaw go slack at the sight of him. He wore no shirt, only leggings and a breechclout, but no Apsaroke dressed his hair in that way, totally braided and with a side parting. Already the cry was going up, 'Piegan! Piegan!'

Fresh hoofbeats caused the women to cower, but it was an Apsaroke this time, Hillside. The women stood and trilled for him as he whipped his horse faster to ride the enemy down, but as Moon Hawk watched, the Piegan turned in his saddle, a powder gun in his hand. She saw the smoke issue from the barrel before she heard the boom of the shot. Hillside slumped to one side and then sat straight again. The pair of them disappeared into the thicket, one after the other, before she could grasp whether he had been struck by the ball.

Her heart rose into her throat as she stared in horror at the dense shrubbery. *'Turtle!'*

Moon Hawk was running in the wake of the riders before anyone could stop her, out of the safety of the group, across the open ground towards the trees. Her mud-plastered moccasins bit into the deep hoofprints the horses had left, but the space seemed forever, and her momentum a snail's. And then she saw her sister, on her knees, peering from behind the stubby trunk of an gnarled ash.

'Turtle!'

The girl sprinted towards her, covered half the distance and drew abruptly to a slithering halt. Her eyes widened and she began to point, but Moon Hawk had already sensed the Piegan's approach. Her hand sought the knife-sheath at her back as she turned, but he was closer than she had anticipated. A cry of fear rose from her lungs. It seemed to catch in her throat, for although she opened her mouth, she never heard it leave. She could hear nothing, nothing at all, not even the beat of the hooves as the horse bore down on her. Her sight was her only sense which mattered, her only sense which worked.

His horse was a pinto, dappled grey and white about its muzzle. Foam covered its bared teeth, and from its jaw-thong hung a single eagle-feather with two red spots daubed below the curving black tip. He was young, the Piegan, as young as herself, painted in the colours of his warrior society. His thin lips looked almost black, drawn so tightly across his gritted teeth, but his eyes were large, larger than the pinto's, and the white shone all round the dark iris.

Horse and rider dipped and leapt towards her, so slowly, but always, inevitably, towards her. She saw the muscles spring in the Piegan's thin arm as he tightened his grip on the club in his hand and raised it for the strike. Her own arm was lifting in her defence. She felt the power building in her legs to propel herself aside, but there was no time, she knew; there was no time.

The pinto's breath was hot and foul on her face. Horse and man filled her vision. And then his arm fell back; his head rocked on his neck. The horse swerved, knocking Moon Hawk off her feet with a glancing blow from its powerful shoulder. Dim and muffled, the low boom of a powder gun penetrated her dulled hearing, and sky and earth turned about one another. She hit the ground with such force that she felt the mud splatter and spread beneath her back. She screamed as she saw the Piegan fling himself towards her. He landed askew, across her hips. Her own knife was still in her hand, and she drove the blade again and again into his shoulders and neck, into anything she could reach in a frenzied attempt to kill him before he killed her.

'Moon Hawk! Moon Hawk!' A strong hand clamped about her wrist, holding the bloody knife motionless in the air. 'He is dead, Moon Hawk!'

She raised her eyes to the figure above her and found Hillside standing there, a little awkwardly, breathing hard.

'He was dead before he left his saddle.'

Dead? Her muscles still tensed in disbelief; she looked at the man across her legs. He lay quite motionless, his face hidden in the mud, his naked back a mass of bloody gashes. She shut her eyes against the sight and bit back her revulsion. Hillside loosened her wrist and bent to haul the Piegan from her.

'Turtle!' Moon Hawk almost screamed her sister's name, twisting this way and that, searching the faces for whoever held her safely.

'Moon Hawk! Moon Hawk!' Again, Hillside's strident voice, again his clasping hand. She turned to him, knowing, even before he spoke the dreaded words.

'She was taken.' He caught her to him as she struggled to free herself from his grasp. 'No! The men will ride. They will bring her back.'

The terror she had endured, the suddenness of the raid, her inability to help Turtle, it all bubbled up inside her and spilled over in trembling sobs as she leaned her weight against him. She felt his arm slip about her shoulder, his cheek rest on her hair, and she gave her helplessness its rein, and she cried.

Winter Man saw the couple entwined in each other's arms and pulled hard on the jaw-thong of his roan, almost causing it to fall as it slid to a halt. Hillside he recognised at once. The mud-caked woman he would have sworn was his wife, Jay, if further back along the column she had not run to his side, begging news of her husband. The mud-caked woman was Moon Hawk.

Hillside was the first to raise his eyes and see him. 'They have taken Turtle,' he called.

Winter Man nudged the roan with his knees, and it walked forward on his command. The milling women parted for him to pass, and he gave the dead Piegan a cursory glance.

'Winter Man!'

Moon Hawk's voice, so shrill and demanding, caught him like an unexpected blow. He watched her reach out a hand to him, saw the other still firmly clasping Hillside's shoulder. She seemed to need such an effort to peel herself away. His eyes swept the filthy bridal dress, her daubed hair, her muddied face, but he could not look her in the eye as she approached his roan, could not bear the thought of her touching him.

'Get my shield!'

His snapped command stopped her in mid-stride.

Though he set his eyes on Hillside, the man's image was a blur. Moon Hawk he could see clearly through his side vision. He saw her hesitate. He saw her turn away. It felt as if she was ripping something from inside him.

'I cannot go with you,' Hillside told him.

Winter Man pulled his sight fully into focus and knew with sickening certainty that his disquiet had been entirely without cause. Hillside was wilting like a tobacco-plant in a drought, using his gun to support himself as an old man used a stick.

'Where are you hit?'

'In my side. The one who did it I let escape.'

Hillside bared his teeth in a tight grimace, partly to curse the Piegan who had wounded him, partly to hide his pain. Winter Man felt he should say something encouraging, but the only words that came to mind were mumblings of insincerity.

Moon Hawk ran across with the shield. Winter Man took it from her hands and looped the wide strap over his chest so that the heavy rawhide circle sat comfortably on his back on top of his bow-case.

'Have you enough powder? Enough shot? Do you want your lance?'

He waved her questions aside, not quite knowing what to say to her. His eyes had played tricks on him, his eyes and his mind. He knew he had been wrong, yet he still felt the need to avoid her gaze. He did not know why, and not knowing disturbed him.

'Hillside! Are you hurt? Why did you not say something?'

In two strides Moon Hawk was by the injured man's side. Winter Man watched as she fed her neck beneath his arm and her hand behind his back to take Hillside's weight, and Winter Man tasted the bitterness of jealousy.

Reaching for the quirt dangling at his wrist, he clasped it tightly enough to crush the antler handle in his fist and lashed down on his horse's rump. The roan jumped forward on all four hooves in its surprise before breaking away. Winter Man heard Moon Hawk call his name, but he did not look back at her. He rode with all the speed the roan could muster, back along the column, out towards where the Piegan would be gathering before beginning the return journey to their own lands. He rode on a warrior's instinct, barely noting the other armed men heading in the same direction, hardly hearing the trilling of the women as he sped past them. The stream of air was cold in his face. He wished it colder, numbingly cold. He did not want to think, or see, or feel.

The roan was tiring beneath him, and he let it slow of its own accord. It fell into a walk and stopped altogether. Winter Man patted its sweating shoulder as it lowered its head. It was puffing hard. He had ridden it foolishly. If he came upon the Piegan unawares, the animal would not have the strength to carry him to safety.

He slipped from the saddle and walked the horse awhile, surveying the land about him. The Shining Mountains were on his left, their snowy peaks too dazzling for his eyes to hold for very long. Below them, clothing their base like a woolly robe, the varied greens of pine trees swept down towards him, turning into oak and ash, elder and choke-cherry before dwindling into thickets and single bushes, and finally into the horizon-filling vista of unbroken grass; except that it was not unbroken.

The continuous, undulating expanse of parched grass-land was an illusion of distance and sight that Winter Man well understood. There were washes and gulleys, hollows and cut-backs, and in some places even the sheer drop of a cliff; more places for raiders to hide than a man could possibly count. Having lost sight of the Piegan, his chances of coming across their trail by accident were slight. Better he should look for other Apsaroke and add to their stength. A man alone was nothing.

From the advantage of a height, he saw them: six men and six horses. The horses were grouped together, a little distance away. If another man sat in their midst holding their jaw-thongs, Winter Man could not see him. In truth, he could see very little. The sun, so slow to penetrate the mist and cloud of the morning, was on the wane, but its late autumn heat had been enough to create a shimmering haze that distorted faraway objects. Were they Apsaroke or Piegan? Could they be of some other people—Bannock or Shoshone—who were ignorant of what had occurred to the south of them? They acted as though they were unaware. No raiding party Winter Man had ever been a member of sat so openly for all to see. And they were sitting, of that he was sure. But doing what? Smoking? Making Medicine? Waiting for a report from their wolves?

Tension gripped his scalp and shivered down his neck. He looked behind him, but there was nothing, nothing at all.

Decisions. To go down among them—or not?

He had seen no sign of any Apsaroke since his roan had outrun those leaving the column. It seemed inconceivable that there was not a group of Good Young Man in the vicinity, and he would look a clown if he were caught spying on his own people! Yet, if he went down and they were Piegan, or Shoshone, or any other enemy, he would be killed. Where was his strong heart? Where was the fearlessness his grandfather had praised when he had gained his hair-pendant shirt? He was a Good Young Man with coups to his name, and Good Young Men did not hide behind the brow of a hill!

He slithered backwards, out of sight of the sitting men, to where his horse was tethered. He spoke softly to it, telling it what he was about, while he strung his bow and checked the powder in his gun. When he was ready, his roan was ready, too, its ears pricked and twitching. Man and horse cantered round the base of the mound and over the saddle between two others, directly into the group's line of vision. Not one of the men moved. No one had seen him. He was breathing harder than the roan now, nervous perspiration oozing down his spine. He shifted the weight of the powder gun in his right hand, resting the curved butt on his thigh. It would be his weapon of first use, then it would have to be discarded. He could loose six arrows in the time it took to reload it—if he were given the time to loose six before he was plunged into the midst of hand-to-hand fighting—if he were allowed to get that close . . .

He had been seen! A man was standing, stringing his bow, reaching for an arrow.

Winter Man felt the power of his Medicine fill his chest. He cocked the heavy powder gun and sent the roan into a gallop. Keeping low behind its neck, he levelled the weapon and sighted his target down the barrel.

Frost! It was Frost! The men were Apsaroke!

He swung the gun high above his head in a salute, and sat tall in the saddle as he rode towards them. For one heart-rending moment it looked as though Frost was not going to lay down his bow, but he did—finally. He took a few steps forward as Winter Man drew up the roan in front of him.

'You should be grateful for my keen eyes!' Frost snapped, tapping him sharply on the arm with his bow as if taking a coup. 'Riding out of the sun like that . . . I could have shot you from your horse!'

Winter Man grinned at him. Their near mistake had shaken them both, it was clear. He raised his eyes to look at the men hanging back, and his feeling of well-being rapidly left him. His brother-in-law, Runs His Horse, gazed at him with undisguised contempt. By his side stood Skins The Wolf, an elaborately quilled pipe-bag caught in his fingers. Flanking them were three other Lumpwoods, untested young men without war honours.

Skins The Wolf swaggered forward, an easy smile lighting his face. 'The crippled Fox joins us! Now we are seven.'

Winter Man bristled with irritation. 'I am not crippled.'

'Then you will not decline the honour of leading the feinted attack, will you?'

The question was issued like a dare. Winter Man tried to remain aloof. 'What feinted attack?'

Frost was more than willing to impart the information. 'We have sighted the Piegan. They . . .'

'How many?'

'Ten or twelve.'

Not *the* Piegan, then; *some* Piegan. Winter Man knew

the raiders had been at least thirty strong when they had hit the Apsaroke column.

'They are in a cut-back at the edge of a wash east of here. They have two of our children with them, a boy of three or four and an older girl.'

'Turtle?'

'Turtle!' Runs His Horse looked aghast, but his ignorance was only to be expected. In the turmoil of a raid, few, other than those close at hand, knew who had been taken and who wounded or killed. Runs His Horse turned forcefully to the man by his side. 'Was it Turtle?' The man shrugged. Runs His Horse kept at him. 'You know my sister! Was she the girl?' The scout would not look him in the eye.

Winter Man sat in his saddle watching the exchange with mounting unease. Who would have given the status of wolf to a man whose testimony could not be trusted?

The fragments began to fall into place with repelling clarity. When he had first seen the group, he had thought they had been smoking. He had not been wrong. They had been giving their allegiance to a pipe-carrier—a leader. They had been giving their allegiance to Skins The Wolf. Instinctively each knew the other's thoughts. Winter Man felt his rancour growing, and fought to keep his voice steady.

'You do not have the honours to elevate yourself to be a Good Man.'

Skins The Wolf curled his lip in a snarl. 'I am the senior here through virtue of my coups. I am senior to you.'

It was something Winter Man could not deny, though it left him with a very bitter taste. Had it not been for the children, he would have left Skins The Wolf to his newly-acquired authority and ridden away.

'There is no time for argument about who carries the pipe and who does not,' Runs His Horse insisted. 'If we do not get the children back before the onset of night, we may lose them for good!'

'Then let us be gone!' Skins The Wolf roared at him.

The others mounted their horses as Winter Man looked on incredulously.

'What is the layout of this cut-back? Why have the Piegan stopped there? What plan are we working to? We cannot simply ride into their arms!'

Skins The Wolf wheeled his horse about, making it skitter back on its hind legs. 'Why not?' he called. 'Has your courage deserted you, cripple?'

His vociferous laughter, his shining eyes, brought previous taunts and sneering sarcasm back to Winter Man's mind. They had been friends, friends since childhood when Skins The Wolf had been his constant shadow. What had happened to change that? What had he done to deserve such contempt?

The self-appointed pipe-carrier gave his orders while they rode. Winter Man was to lead a diversionary assault on the Piegan from the place the scout had used to spy on them, while Skins The Wolf would lead the rest in along the wash in a frontal attack. Who would take the children would depend on where they were being kept. It seemed pure foolishness to split such small a group in the face of ten adversaries, but Winter Man knew that to offer his opinion would change nothing.

'Who will ride with me?' he enquired of their leader.

'You can take my wolf if you want. He has seen the cut-back.'

. . . if you want? What sort of a plan was this? Winter Man glanced at the scout and shook his head. The last person he needed to guard his back was a man who could not recognise a girl he had seen once a day for the last year.

'I shall take Frost.'

'You had better take your brother-in-law, too. He is so agitated over the loss of his sister that he will be of no use to me.'

Runs His Horse was not over-pleased to find whom he was riding with, and let both Winter Man and Skins The Wolf know it. Skins The Wolf quietened him with an authoritative rebuke, and the small party split to go their different ways.

Winter Man pulled the two men up at the edge of a small, shrub-covered delve.

'We shall leave the horses hidden here and go the rest of the way on foot.'

'Foolishness! We are supposed to be mounting a feinted attack to cover Skins The Wolf. How are we supposed to do that on foot?'

Winter Man rounded on his brother-in-law. 'We do not know what we are riding into, or where the children are. Do you want to take your sister back alive, or do you want her scalped?'

Runs His Horse relented, and the three men walked a little further before going on to their hands and knees, and then on to their bellies.

The silence of sign-language took over from the whisperings of speech as Winter Man gave his directions. He needed to know where the Piegan were, their exact number, their strengths and weaknesses, the lie of the land they had chosen to hide in. Above all, he needed to know why they had chosen to hide instead of swiftly making their escape as raiders normally would.

This taste of leadership was a far different challenge from that Winter Man had faced at the Shoshone village when he had taken the roan. Not only did the lives of his two men depend upon his judgment, but the lives of the captured children did, too; yet he was surprised to find that the responsibility held no awe for him this time.

His two men reported back. Runs His Horse had seen the Piegans' mounts. He had counted twenty-three, though seven were unsaddled pack animals captured from their own people. They had two guards. The land looked less like a wash and more like the opening of a steep coulee. He did not look happy. When Winter Man asked for Frost's testimony, the young man hung his head and raised guarded eyes to his.

'They are there, but you will not like it.'

Winter Man's heart sank, but did not let his feelings show in his face. He decided to see for himself, and Frost led the way.

Frost had been right. He did not like it. It was even worse than he had expected. The Piegan numbered seventeen, not ten or twelve. Three were wounded in a limb, but still able to fight. One man, a pipe-carrier of renown by the headdress of eagle feathers beside him, was laid immobile on the ground. Turtle was sitting half-hidden in some bushes at the bottom of an incline, her arms comfortingly round the boy as though she were his mother. At least they had not been harmed—yet.

The cut-back was the steepest Winter Man had ever seen, and if he had been asked he would have called it cliff-faced. The Piegan horses had been picketed at its opening from the wash, effectively creating a barrier against a mounted attack from that direction. At the rear of the cut-back, a defile crept between two walls of rock, giving a route one man could hold alone while the others made their escape. For Winter Man to attempt an attack—however feinted—would be casting all their lives to the wind.

He indicated that they should withdraw, and the three lay prone in the grass to exchange a whispered word. There seemed little to say. Both his men had earned coups and knew the futility of what Skins The Wolf had asked of them. Even Runs His Horse was appalled.

'How could he say that his intention was to rescue the children? It is impossible. As soon as Skins The Wolf rides down the wash, the Piegan will . . . Winter Man! Turtle is going to be killed!'

CHAPTER TWELVE

WINTER MAN LAY in the grass, weighing his options. To attempt any sort of diversionary attack against the Piegan would be tantamount to killing the children by his own hand; yet if he did nothing they would still die. Skins The Wolf would grow tired of waiting and lead his men in from the wash, but they would become tangled among the picketed horses and be cut down. The Piegan would kill the children before they realised the attackers were only four.

'We cannot sit here for ever!' Runs His Horse had overcome his dismay and was eager to act.

'What do you suggest?' Frost hissed at him. 'As soon as we push our noses over the ridge, every Piegan in that cut-back will fire at us. Are you as blind as that scout Skins The Wolf sent to spy on them? Did you not count how many guns they hold? There will not be enough left of us for our families to recognise!'

Winter Man reached out and rested a hand casually on the young man's forearm, and Frost became silent. He was frightened, Winter Man knew. To die valiantly in battle was the hope of every man, bred into them from birth; but there was courage, and there was virtual suicide.

There was also such a thing as sacrifice.

A man might sacrifice his own life to save his friend's, a father to save his children, but would one man sacrifice others in order to gain a prestigious war honour? Skins The Wolf had done just that in the Shoshone village when Winter Man had been capturing the roan. He had taken himself a grand coup, and . . . and he had *run*. There was no other way it could be told. At the time, Hillside had seen the action for what it was. Winter Man had refused to accept that any Apsaroke could be so dishonourable, but he knew that he had been wrong. Such men had lived before. During the long, snow-

bound days the old people told warning-stories of their
contemptuous exploits, striking horror and shame into
the hearts of their grandchildren. Winter Man had
listened to the stories often enough, but he had never
expected to be faced with a similar situation.

In his fear, Frost had been the one to take the blind-
fold from Winter Man's eyes. The Piegan would shoot at
them in alarm as soon as they appeared over the ridge,
believing that there were more than three of them. Their
guns would be discharged. Skins The Wolf would lead
his men into the cut-back, creating more panic. In the
narrow confines of the gulley a bow would be almost
useless; the Piegan would rely on hand-to-hand fighting.
Skins The Wolf was an accomplished warrior who would
keep his head in the fray, dipping in and out to gain the
coups he wanted. Those who rode with him were untried
and liable to lose their nerve in the face of such over-
whelming odds. Like as not, he would be the only
Apsaroke to ride out alive, and with the three of them
lying dead on the ridge, he could wail his grief with
impunity. There would be no witnesses to speak against
his foolishness.

Winter Man eyed his younger companions. He could
not share the burden of his knowledge with them. As he
had once not believed it possible, they would not believe
him now. Even if they did, what good would it serve? If a
man must die, let him die knowing his true worth, not
the little another places upon his life.

Winter Man's responsibilities were growing, he realised. Not only did he have these two men to consider,
but also the children and the three untested youths who
rode with Skins The Wolf. He could not look after them
all, it was beyond his capabilities; yet if he did not try, he
would be failing himself. A pipe-carrier did not abandon
his men when the flow of battle turned against him, and
if Skins The Wolf had abrogated his obligations as a
leader, Winter Man had no alternative but to take on the
role.

'Well?'

He looked into the fierce eyes of Runs His Horse and
stifled a pang of resentment. He had not had their names

called by the Crier; they had never given their allegiance
to him. He could not expect them to accord him the
deference they would to a Good Man. To them he was
just one of their number, a man of slightly senior standing due to the extra war honours he had gained. If ever
he had wished he had done as his mentors had urged him
and deliberately set out to acquire the coups he needed
to lift himself above his contemporaries, this was the
time!

'The safety of the children is paramount,' he stated
stiffly. 'It is they we are rescuing. The diversion for Skins
The Wolf and his men is secondary.'

Runs His Horse opened his mouth to object, but
Winter Man silenced him with an intimidating glare.

'Frost and I shall creep over the ridge and down the
slope to a position behind where the children are sitting.
You will force one of our animals over the edge of the
cliff above the Piegan horses. The Piegan will, I hope,
believe it is a stray they ran off from our line and will not
believe they are under attack. While their attention is
turned, Frost and I shall snatch the children and make
our escape the way we went down.'

'And whose horse are we going to kill?' his brother-in-
law snarled.

'Mine.'

The younger man's eyes widened in surprise, and
Winter Man felt an intense satisfaction in being able to
render him speechless at last.

'Better the horse be mine,' Frost offered. 'The roan is
the fastest of the three we have. Even if we get the
children up here unharmed they still have to be returned
to the safety of the village, and these Piegan are not the
only ones within striking distance.'

Frost was offering more than his mount. He was
saying that he did not expect to return to use it. Runs His
Horse looked suitably contrite and cleared his throat to
speak.

'If the horse is to be Frost's, then it will be I who go
down into the cut-back. Turtle is my sister.'

Despite Frost's objections, Winter Man agreed with
Runs His Horse. 'You will be the one to take the

children. I shall cover your escape. Leave your bow-case
here and give Frost your gun and powder. If we are
discovered, he will cover us both.'

Winter Man waited, half-expecting some show of
dissent from his brother-in-law, but he was already
divesting himself of his weapons and removing the gaudy
jewellery and hair ornaments so beloved by the younger
men. For the time being, at least, he seemed to have
accepted Winter Man's authority.

The sun was tipping the peaks of the mountains when
the two men slipped over the edge of the ridge. Most of
the initial slope was already in heavy shadow, which
helped to cover their movement between the sparse
bushes. Winter Man had expected to be able to see
Turtle's head, but the shelving face of the cut-back was
so ridged that it was impossible to see the floor of the
gulley. He only hoped that he was not slithering past
where she was sitting. By the time they had reached
half-way down the slope he could hear the Piegan quite
clearly, though not speaking the language, he could not
understand what was being said.

A little further down he picked up the strains of
someone singing. He could have been wrong, but it
sounded like a death-song. The pipe-carrier, who had
gained so many coup feathers as to be able to make a
distinctive headdress of them, had been lying prone
surrounded by his followers. The voice did not sound
like that of a dying man. Perhaps someone was singing
the song on his behalf. Perhaps he was held in such high
regard that no one wanted to leave his side until he had
breathed his last. Enemy or not, Winter Man held
admiration for a man who could command that sort of
respect, and he vowed, then and there, that if First
Maker allowed him to see the following dawn, he would
strive to be just such a man.

He and Runs His Horse gained the positions they
wanted above Turtle. The boy in her arms was whimpering quietly, but from her back Turtle looked as if she was
being as bravely stoic as any woman twice her age. She
had one guard. He had been watching her and the boy
for some time, for his vigilance had dulled and he gave

them only an occasional glance as he leaned his weight on his feathered lance.

Winter Man eased his sweating palms down his leggings and waited. He did not see Frost's horse go over the ridge, but he heard it scream as it lost its footing on the steep incline, and he heard the panic of the mounts caught in its path below. To a man, the Piegan stood clutching their guns, their eyes searching the tufted ridges about the cut-back for a sign of attackers. No one fired his weapon. The boom of a powder gun was as loud as a crack of thunder overhead, and they were too well disciplined to give their position away unnecessarily, but they watched for movement with the keen sight of hawks.

Winter Man flattened himself into the dusty slope and hoped Frost and Runs His Horse had had the sense to do the same. Three of the picketed horses galloped in terror into the midst of the Piegan, causing some harsh words to be uttered. Softer words followed, a quick discussion, Winter Man reasoned, and he raised his eyes enough to watch a number of the Piegan jog towards the mouth of the cut-back. It was as he had hoped. They were splitting their force in an effort to stop the frightened horses fleeing along the wash and escaping up on to the open plain; but to Winter Man's consternation the children's guard, now fully alert, remained where he was.

The reverberating boom of muskets caught everyone by surprise. Even Winter Man shuddered. Skins The Wolf was making his attack, right into the teeth of the armed Piegan chasing their horses. The guard with the lance jumped forward and began to run towards the confusion, but he caught his step and turned towards the children. Winter Man did not wait to see what he intended to do. He leapt up, levelled his own musket and fired.

Turtle screamed just below him, but he paid her no attention. He dropped his gun and pulled a handful of arrows from his quiver. As fast as he could notch them in the string, he fired at the nearest Piegan, in the back or in the chest mattered little, so long as they had no chance to raise their guns to him or to Runs His Horse, who was hustling Turtle up the steep slope behind him, the terrified boy clasped tightly under his arm.

For a while the advantage was Winter Man's through surprise, but it was not without effort. The bow was made from elk-antler and needed a man's strength to draw it. Each time he did, the pressure on his injured shoulder increased until he was gritting his teeth against the pain.

A musket-ball shattered a woody stem of the bush he stood beside, and Winter Man knew it could easily have been one of his bones. He loosed another arrow, and turned to climb the slope in the wake of the others. To his horror he saw a Piegan, a brass-headed axe glinting in his hand, scrambling up the rise in pursuit of Runs His Horse. Winter Man reached for another arrow, but a flame seared along his right arm. Instinctively he pulled it into his body. He was covered in blood from wrist to elbow, his fingers standing out rigid from his hand like the claws of a dead buzzard. No matter how he tried, they refused to flex. He could not notch an arrow. He could not draw the bow. There was nothing else to do. He forced himself up the incline, ignoring the hollow thumps as musket-balls buried themselves in the earth about him. An arrow zipped under his arm and embedded itself in the ground by his face. Its fletching teased at Winter Man's cheek as the shaft juddered with the impact. He put his foot on it and climbed.

Runs His Horse had not looked back, not once, and knew nothing of the Piegan behind him, Winter Man was certain. Two more steps, and he would feel the axe blade shattering his spine, then the children would be cut down and . . .

With a huge effort, Winter Man launched himself upwards, reaching out with his bow, his eyes fixed on the Piegan's trailing foot. There was a sudden jarring of his arm, and his weakened shoulder bulged as muscles and sinews were stretched and torn anew. The pain threatened to overwhelm him, but he refused to let the bow slip from his grasp, and then he was falling – and the Piegan was falling with him.

There was dust and light and coarse-leafed bushes

tearing at his flesh. He was fighting for breath, and coughing, and trying to blink the debris from his eyes.

Get up! he told himself. Get on your feet! Do you want to be skewered like a wounded buffalo?

But he could not get up. He lay on his back, head-first in a bush, his legs reaching up the slope. His left arm was trapped beneath him, his bloodied right lay uselessly by his side. He could hear horses whinnying, their hooves thundering by him as they galloped round the cut-back seeking an escape. Why had the Piegan not caught them? There were calls and cries and more musket-fire than he would have believed possible. Had Skins The Wolf made it into the cut-back? Were all his men still alive?

He filled his lungs with air, braced himself, and rolled. The restraining bush gave under his weight and he fell on to the gulley floor where Turtle and the boy had been made to sit. His powder gun slithered down the last of the slope and landed on his legs. Instinctively he picked it up, and stood—and parried a thrust from a Piegan lance.

Attack! Attack!

He swung the musket like a club, crashing it down on the Piegan's arm. An upper-cut caught the man on the jaw and sent him reeling backwards. Another Piegan appeared in his place. Winter Man screamed his Fox battle-cry and launched himself forward. Somewhere in the depths of his raging mind a calm voice was suggesting he sing his death-song so that the Ones Above would be ready for his coming, but there seemed no time for him even to take a conscious breath. A figure flitted in and out of his side-vision. He whirled about to face it, the musket raised for another strike.

'Winter Man!'

He paused for a moment, for a heart's beat, for the time it took the killer to become the killed; but the man did not attack him, did not move from where he stood.

Frost.

The pain in Winter Man's shoulder gnawed into the bone where no pain had been before. The musket seemed as heavy as a tree in his hand.

Frost. No—his sight was deceiving him. It could not be Frost. Frost was on the height. He was with the roan, taking the children to safety. *The children* . . .

A rage exploded in his heart to fire his strength. 'The children! You have left the children!'

A bloodied lance was planted in his path. Its otter-skin-wrapped shaft swung back and forth before his eyes. A bay horse skitted close by. A man's voice boomed out.

'Frost! You know better than to touch a man whose shadow has left his body!'

Running Fisher sat astride the bay. Winter Man blinked, but would not believe what he was seeing. The image was in his mind. It could not be flesh, but it was the pipe-carrier, and the older man was looking down at him, his lined features heavy with concern.

A cool wind chilled Winter Man's body. He shuddered a little. His right arm, the arm which had hung so uselessly, was raised now. He could flex his fingers—if painfully. He had almost shot Frost earlier. Had he been going to attack him again? He swallowed down his rising guilt and lowered his arm. 'The shadow has not left my body,' he said.

Running Fisher slipped from his saddle and took a step towards him. 'You mean it has returned. You stagger, Winter Man. Where are you injured? Which blood is yours and which our enemies'?'

Winter Man did feel frail. He was trembling, as if in a fever, yet he felt cold. Lying at his feet were the bodies of four Piegan. He could only remember killing two. This was foolishness. He had never been like this before. Think! Think!

'Are the children safe?' he asked.

'Yes.'

'Have the Piegan been routed?'

'Most are dead. Some fled, but they will take back fearful stories of the warriors of the Apsaroke.'

Winter Man nodded, though he had little understanding. There were men in the cut-back, stripping the dead, gathering the Piegan horses. 'What brought you?'

'I did!' Frost's eyes were bright, his face one grin from

ear to ear. 'I saw them in the distance—before I sent my horse over the ridge—I made them see me, and they came.' The grin faded, the bright eyes dulled. His face became almost pinched with hurt pride. 'I did not desert my given duty, Winter Man. When Runs His Horse delivered the children to me, I made sure they were safe.'

Winter Man reached out and laid a hand on his shoulder. 'I am proud of you. You will be a Good Man one day.'

'Good Man!' Frost laughed. 'It is you who will be the Good Man.' He became more serious. 'When you are, if you think me worthy and you have the Crier call my name, I shall smoke your pipe and follow you.'

It was something said often between young men, but never in the hearing of a respected pipe-carrier. Both men glanced shame-faced towards the one who stood with them, but Running Fisher acted as if he had not heard a word.

Winter Man tried not to smile too much, but it was difficult. The shaking frailty was leaving him. His blood pulsed with the power he knew was his. His Medicine was strong. He would be a Good Man and men would follow him. It *was* within his grasp; it always had been. He had simply never reached.

Frost began to turn away, but Winter Man pulled him back. There was one more question he had to ask.

'The others? Those who rode?'

Frost spoke more quietly now, less easily. 'Storm took an arrow in the chest. It pierced a lung. He was still alive when I saw him. Bull Neck is wounded in the thigh. Bluebird is unharmed.' He shook his head and chuckled. 'Skins The Wolf—as you might have guessed—counted a coup! He has captured the most elaborate bonnet of honour feathers a man could . . .'

Winter Man felt something snap inside him. 'What! How can you stand there and laugh? He would have killed us all!'

He pushed past him, and catching hold of the jaw-thong of a riderless horse, pulled himself into the saddle.

'Winter Man! You are behaving the way Hillside did after the raid on the Shoshone.'

He had meant to ignore Running Fisher's call, but the memory of that night, of the guilt he had felt afterwards, it all came streaming back into his mind. He jerked the horse round while his feet fought for the stirrups.

'I act as Hillside did because I now see with the clarity of Hillside's sight. It is Frost who is as blind as I was then!'

He took the horse along the cut-back towards the mouth of the wash, searching every face for Skins The Wolf. There was no sign of him, not even in the wash, and he urged the horse up the steep hill which led to the flatter land above. Travois were being constructed to take the wounded. Turtle and the boy were locked in the reassuring arms of one of the older men. Captured shields and weapons of all kinds were being distributed. To one side, away from the bustle, Skins The Wolf was parading himself before his admirers, the captured coup bonnet sitting on his head. Winter Man rode up to them and slipped from the saddle.

Skins The Wolf saw him and flourished a hand in the air. 'The cripple lives!'

'Do I disappoint you?'

Skins The Wolf cocked his head a little to one side. 'You sound annoyed. Did you not gain a coup?'

'I was too busy rescuing the children to think of such things.'

'I heard you had taken them. My plan worked well.'

'Worked well! The only reason we are all alive is because of Running Fisher's intervention.' He shrugged back his shoulders and swept his eyes up the man in the same condescending manner Skins The Wolf usually used to such good effect. 'For a pipe-carrier, you seem very eager to flaunt your spoils. How are your wounded men? I would have thought you would have been with them.'

'I am no healer,' Skins The Wolf retorted. 'I am a warrior, a gainer of coups.' He tossed his head, and the white breath feathers at the base of the eagle plumes eddied and swam like spring grass in the wind. The bonnet was a magnificent piece of workmanship. Twenty-eight eagle tail feathers set upright on a breath-feathered cap, the ermine pendants so many as almost to hide the darkness of his hair. 'I counted a grand coup on the owner of this, killed him and took it from his head!'

Winter Man raised a disparaging eyebrow. 'Even you cannot count a grand coup on a dead man.'

The silence was awesome. Skins The Wolf seemed to grow before his eyes. His look of defiance had altered to one of stone-masked hatred, his dark eyes as cold as a dead man's. If they had not both been Apsaroke, Winter Man felt sure a knife would have been plunged into his heart.

'What is this?' Running Fisher demanded, pushing his way through the gathered throng.

'Skins The Wolf took a grand coup and captured the Piegan's coup bonnet,' someone offered. The man's tone lowered in disgust. 'Winter Man speaks against him.'

'Why?'

Winter Man turned his eyes away from his adversary and met Running Fisher's authoritive gaze. 'The man was dead, or dying, prone on the ground, incapable of movement. His condition was the reason the Piegan had stopped in the cut-back and not ridden on. He was a respected war leader—he must have been; his men refused to leave him while he still lived. They were singing his death-song.'

Skins The Wolf cut into his explanation with a scoffing grunt. 'They spoke to you, did they, and told you all this to your face?'

Winter Man rounded on him. 'I saw it with my eyes.' He looked back at Running Fisher. 'Call Runs His Horse and Frost. They saw it, too.'

Running Fisher frowned, and for a moment did nothing, but the two men were eventually called as witnesses. When they came, Winter Man did not wait for the pipe-carrier to question them; he did it himself.

'When we looked over the ridge into the cut-back, did

you see that bonnet?' He pointed to the head of Skins The Wolf.'

Runs His Horse answered immediately. 'Yes.' Frost nodded.

'Where was it?'

Both men looked questioningly at Winter Man, and then at the bonnet, and finally at Skins The Wolf.

'Where was the bonnet?' Winter Man repeated. A simple answer; that was all he wanted.

Frost shrugged. 'On the ground.'

'Where on the ground?' This was becoming more difficult than he had anticipated. Surely they could not have been as blind as the scout!

Runs His Horse shook his head, not understanding what detail was being asked of him. 'Just on the ground.'

'Who was it standing beside?'

Running Fisher intervened. 'Winter Man believes it belonged to a dying man. Was it standing beside such a man?'

'Yes, but there were five or six other men there who were as close to it. I could not say who it belonged to.'

'It belonged to the man I counted coup against; the man I killed.' Skins The Wolf held up the stained head of his stone club and looked each man in the eye, daring them to dispute the fact.

No one did. Winter Man stood alone, and he knew it. The coup would stand. The prestige would belong to Skins The Wolf, even if no man could be found who actually saw him take either coup or bonnet. In the heat of frenzied battle it was sometimes so. A warrior's oath was always believed. An Apsaroke never lied.

'Winter Man killed four Piegan,' Frost ventured, trying to lighten the heavy atmosphere. If anything, his words only made it worse.

Winter Man turned away from the group. He had no wish to hear Running Fisher's verdict, or the congratulations of the other men. What he did hear was the voice of Skins The Wolf, loud and biting, aimed at his back.

'He may have killed four Piegan, but he counted no coup!'

He even heard the ripple of laughter that followed it. To his annoyance, Frost ran hot on his heels.

'I told what I saw. I could do no more.'

Winter Man did not look at him; he did not speak. Frost kept his pace like a devoted puppy.

'I only told what I saw. What else could I do?'

Winter Man stopped. He was being too hard on the young man, taking the anger he felt for Skins The Wolf out on him. Had he thought on it, he would have realised that neither of his companions would have seen with his eyes what lay below that ridge, or would have interpreted what they had seen with his mind. Show four men the same object and each will tell something different about it; it was well known.

He touched Frost lightly on the arm and smiled at him. 'You could have done nothing. You spoke the truth. You spoke well. I asked no more of you.'

Frost did not seem reassured. Winter Man looked about him, wanting to alter the course of the conversation. 'What happened to my roan?'

Frost showed him, and went in search of a horse for himself, leaving Winter Man gratefully alone. When the men left the wash for the open plain, he rode a little distance from them; by their design or his, he was not certain, and he did not care.

He only had one visitor, Running Fisher. Like a Good Man should, he was seeing each of his men in turn, ensuring the comfort of the wounded. They rode together for some distance before he spoke.

'Skins The Wolf will not forget that you stood against him in the witnessing.'

Winter Man turned and looked the pipe-carrier directly in the eye. 'And I shall not forget that he took a coup bonnet from a dead man.'

'That is not the way it will be told.'

'No,' Winter Man agreed. 'But that was the way it happened.'

CHAPTER THIRTEEN

THE SUN STOOD two fingers above the undulating horizon, a muted yellow ball casting light between the shortening shadows.

Moon Hawk looked out over the flowing river, her eyes searching each rise and delve in the land beyond its banks. Every spare moment had been spent there since the dawn. Other women had come, to look and to wait. Not one of them had spoken. Not one had stayed as long as Moon Hawk.

'The people move, daughter. It is time to leave.'

Leave? How could she leave? Winter Man was out there. Turtle was out there, somewhere. Dead, perhaps.

The stinging tears rose once more. She bit them back. A woman cried when there was no hope; she wailed her grief and cut her hair and gashed her legs. She was strong until then. She believed. Moon Hawk made herself believe.

Why had she called to Turtle? If she had not called, her sister would have remained hidden in the thicket. She would never have been taken.

Five children had been taken in all. Three had been reunited with their families before half the people had crossed the river. Little Face had run so hard then, run to the men who had brought them back, run to each one begging for news of Turtle. She had received only shaken heads and words of encouragement that she had not heard. So pale she had looked, still looked, so stricken.

How cruel that the captors should be Piegan, the people of her birth. Little Face had been snatched from her family by the Apsaroke, and now her Apsaroke daughter had been snatched by the Piegan. What memories she must be reliving, what terrors!

'The level has dropped in the night, Moon Hawk. See, the river no longer tumbles as it did when we crossed. When Winter Man reaches it, the roan will swim it easily. Turtle will be held safe in his arms.'

She turned her eyes to her father. He altered his weight between his one good leg and the crutch beneath his arm. His steady gaze did not leave her. He believed, she knew he did. Why could she not have his faith?

He touched her arm and peered deep into her eyes. 'We must leave.'

She took a deep, shaking breath and nodded.

The column moved on with hardly a space for a dog to pass between one rider and the next. There was no happy singing, no excited conversation. No woman rode to visit another further up the line. The raiders had come too quickly, come out of the mist under the eyes of the vigilant outriders to steal and kill and take captives. They might come again.

Antelope Dancer drew his horse up among the family group. He looked at them as they all looked at him, but they knew he had no news. None the less, Little Face had to ask.

'My son?'

'Mother, Runs His Horse is riding with the men. I have spoken with those who saw him leave. He does not ride alone. He is not lost. There are many who have not returned yet. Two pipe-carriers have not returned yet. He will have joined one of them, I am sure. He will be searching for Turtle.'

Little Face straightened her back and lifted her chin. Despite the unshed tears held bright in her eyes, her mother was making herself believe, Moon Hawk could see. She only wished her brother's castigating tone would show a little more sympathy. Could he not understand how their mother felt? Two of her children were missing!

'Why are you here?' he snapped. 'You should be riding with the brides.'

Moon Hawk stared at him in astonishment.

'She is better here,' their father answered simply, but Antelope Dancer snapped at him, too.

'If Winter Man returns and finds her not where she should be, he will think she was been taken.'

Bear On The Flat remained very calm. 'My son, you were not to know that Turtle had been captured. If every man had ridden after the Piegan, who would there be to guard those who cannot guard themselves?' He indicated the people ahead in the column.

Antelope Dancer hung his head, and finally nodded his acceptance of his role. 'I shall bring word as soon as it reaches me.' He slapped his quirt down on his horse's back and rode away again.

News came not through Antelope Dancer, but through the bustle and excitement of the returning men. They poured over the ridge, whooping their society battle-cries, as if to attack the column themselves, and proceeded to gallop up and down the line, brandishing scalps and banners and captured shields. The battle had been furious, the victory theirs. Runs His Horse rode up to the family group and placed a bright-eyed Turtle in their mother's eagerly opened arms. Moon Hawk had never seen her cry so much, or hug her daughter so hard. Moon Hawk hugged her sister, too, and she cried; she could not help herself.

Slower mounts neared the column: horses pulling wounded men on travois. The exuberance, the chatter, it was cut at a stroke as anxious faces gathered to look for missing relatives. Moon Hawk lifted herself in her stirrups, a sickening uncertainty biting deep into her fears. Where was Winter Man? Where was his roan?

She felt a tap on her shoulder and turned.

'Winter M——!' Her voice failed her as her eyes swept over his muscular frame. He looked as if a hundred crows had raked him with their claws. His left arm was dangling heavily by his side; his right forearm was bound in a strip of his legging. His lower lip was split in two places, and one eye was partly closed through the weight of bruising to his temple. He sat there and grinned at her.

'Winter Man!' She leaned out from her saddle, reaching for him with her hands, wanting to hug him to her, but she dared not touch him.

He laughed. 'It is nothing! I fell down a bank and had a fight with a thorn-bush.'

'Huh! Do not believe him!' Runs His Horse countered. 'He killed four Piegan with his bare hands. You should have seen him before he washed himself in the river. Anyone would have thought he had painted himself in blood!'

Moon Hawk's stomach knotted. Her hand rose to her lips in her anguish and fear as she looked at her husband. How close to death had he been? How could men make so little of it?

Winter Man smiled softly at her. 'Your brother exaggerates.'

'Exaggerate, do I? He saw his reflection in the water and fell off his horse with the shock!'

'Your brother *exaggerates*,' Winter Man repeated in a louder voice, his laughing eyes flicking across to him.

Moon Hawk looked from the one to the other of them and brought her fist down hard on her thigh. 'You men! You would make believe an arrow through a lung was no more than a scratch!'

It was as if she had struck them both down. She knew she had said something distressing. Winter Man's shoulders slumped. His head fell. All at once he looked very tired.

'Storm has an arrow through a lung,' he said.

'How is he?' Bear On The Flat enquired.

'Unconscious most of the time.'

He drew his roan about and began to walk it up the line. Moon Hawk pulled her horse from its position and followed him.

The column moved no further that day. There were injured to be tended, dead to grieve for, honours to be recognised. Moon Hawk washed and dressed her husband's injuries. She wanted Star Ghost to take a look at him, but Winter Man would not hear of it.

'There are many worse than I,' he told her. 'My body will heal itself. A salve will help.'

So she smeared his wounds, and he groaned and grimaced at her every touch until she laughed at him.

'Some strong-hearted warrior are you! I wager you would not have made this fuss if the Piegan had taken you alive and tortured you!'

In a movement so swift that she never saw it coming, Winter Man pushed her off balance and rolled with her on the ground, trapping her in his arms. His laughing eyes were full of mischief.

'Speaking of tortures . . .' He kissed her lightly on the lips. 'What sorts of *tortures* . . .' Again his lips brushed hers. ' . . . did you have in mind?'

Moon Hawk could feel the fire kindle within her. How easily he could arouse her . . . If only she could free her arms!

She fought to subdue the smile that crept across her cheeks, and sounded stern and reproachful. 'I thought you had hurt your shoulder.'

His ribald gaze rippled over the contours of her face. 'What shoulder?'

As his lips descended once again, Moon Hawk lifted her head a little and met them with her own. So hot, and sweet, and full of power. She matched him in her ardour, showed how much she needed him, needed his touch, needed his love.

'Is this the Winter Man who was possessed by the spirits and fought the Piegan to a standstill?'

The voice, heavy with sarcasm, cut across Moon Hawk's rising passion. She opened her eyes to find Winter Man smiling down at her, but that smile, the quality it held . . . She knew his smile was no longer for her.

His arms released her, and he rolled on to his side to lift a hand in salute. 'And is this the Hillside who deliberately got himself shot so that he would not have to ride out in pursuit of them?'

The two men laughed in their bravado. Moon Hawk sat and wrapped her arms round her raised knees, trying hard to smile with them. They were Fox brothers, she merely a wife. There was no competition, not like a wife with a lover, and yet she felt there was. The two of them had exchanged oaths years before when she had still been a child. They had shared the fears and excitement of battle and the gaining of war honours. They were men; she a woman. Her place was alongside her husband, but not with him, not like Hillside.

Winter Man pointed to the strapping round Hillside's chest. 'You look well for carrying a ball!'

Hillside tossed his head nonchalantly. 'It passed straight through. It was nothing.'

Moon Hawk almost laughed. He would have said the same if he had been unable to walk. She wondered, momentarily, if his wife knew he *was* walking, but the silence between the two men was drawing out. It felt curiously odd, mystical even, as though the conversation was being carried on in thought alone so that no one else might overhear. Hillside was the one who broke the peace.

'Skins The Wolf is saying that it was his plan which saved the children. He is saying that he acted as a Good Man, that his men gave him their allegiance on his pipe.'

'I was not one of them.'

'I did not think you would have been. How was it?'

'Worse than you can imagine.'

Hillside puckered his lips and raised an eyebrow in speculation. 'I can imagine a good deal.'

'If Running Fisher had not arrived with his men, none of us would have returned.'

Moon Hawk shuddered. She saw Hillside glance at her, and she looked first at him and then, awkwardly, at Winter Man. He was gazing at her, too. It was not a conversation she should have overheard, she realised. She scrambled to her feet, wanting to be busy.

'Shall I bring you food?'

Winter Man nodded. Hoping to miss none of what was being said, she quickly made her way to where the saddle-bags had been lifted from the horses and laid on the ground.

'What happened?' she heard Hillside ask.

'Later. I shall tell you later.'

Moon Hawk looked back at them both. Neither was looking at her, yet she knew she was the reason Winter Man would not speak. Did he think he was sparing her unnecessary worry? Or was it something more basic . . . Did he have no faith in her, no trust? She bowed her head a little, her doubts searing into her heart. A husband was supposed to talk to his wife. Winter Man had not talked to her about his visits to Star Ghost, or about his fears for the power of his shoulder. She had learned about them from another.

By the first light of dawn the untidy line had reformed and was wending its way once again. Winter Man did not leave with the outriders but stayed with the column. As the day wore on, Moon Hawk noticed him repeatedly easing himself in his saddle. He was in more pain than he cared to admit to, she realized, and she vowed to make their lodge the most comfortable in the village so that he might rest his body and allow it to heal.

The site for the winter village was a feast for the eyes after the months of roaming so bland a landscape as the softly undulating, almost treeless grasslands. It was a steep-sided, tree-filled valley, angled perfectly to give the skin-covered tipis generous respite against the worst the weather could produce. A shallow creek meandered gently along its length, affording abundant pitching-places for the tipis. Pasture for the horse herd and wood for the fires were both in plentiful supply. Elk and antelope and big-horned sheep roamed the higher reaches, as well as cougar, beaver and bear. There would be no shortage of fresh meat, at least not until the heavy snows obliterated the land.

In the days following their arrival, the women worked with a will to get their lodges ready before the frosts came. Great armfuls of soft pine boughs were cut to lay on the floor to stop the cold striking up from the ground. Brush barricades as high as a woman were erected round each lodge as a last buffer for the coming gales. Some women even filled the gap between the inner skins and the outer covering of their tipis with dried grass to add to the insulation, but others considered that it stopped the draught needed to raise the smoke effortlessly through the flaps at the apex.

Winter Man mended quickly, Hillside also. The two spent a great deal of time together, and Moon Hawk came to look upon his wife, Jay, as kin, and not just as the clan-sister she was. When the men were out hunting the two women would visit one another, enjoying each other's company as they dyed porcupine-quills and sewed them decoratively to their possessions. There was always something to talk of, and occasionally they would laugh, remembering the celebration after the Shosone horse raid when they had turned Winter Man's ridicule upon himself.

The rains turned to sleet and finally to snow, and a piercing cold gripped the land, freezing the breath on the lips of animals and men alike. Of those wounded during the Piegan raid, only one more died, an ageing grandmother who had been thrown from her horse during the attack and had broken her hip. Storm, who had had a lung punctured by an arrow, steadfastly refused to let go of life. Mystics and healers continually sang their invocations for him, but although he did not die, he did not gain in strength.

'Has Skins The Wolf visited Storm's lodge?' Winter Man asked Hillside one evening as the two couples sat together in Hillside's tipi.

'Not that I know of.'

Moon Hawk watched the two men steadily, noting each change of expression and altering of tone as they spoke. Winter Man had been quiet for several days, almost moody. Something was on his mind. She knew the signs now, but as always, when asked, he laughed and refused to admit there was anything wrong. It was something to do with the Piegan raid or, to be more precise, the pursuit which followed it; she had gleaned that much. She had never heard what her husband had had to say to Hillside, and although she had questioned her brother as to what had taken place, he had merely enthused over Winter Man's bravery and she had found herself no wiser.

'Put it from your thoughts,' Hillside told him. 'There was nothing you could have done. Storm was not even riding with you.'

Winter Man sighed heavily and nodded at the same time, a peculiar set of actions which, to Moon Hawk's mind, seemed to cancel one another.

'It is the justice of the thing that eats at me. Skins The Wolf is strutting about the village as though he had led men in a venture that shone with success. He shows no thought for Storm and his family, nor for Bull Neck, who limps now and is liable to for the rest of his life. It is as though they are an embarrassment to him, detracting from his glory.'

'It would have been more of an embarrassment to him if they had both died,' Jay intoned. 'Or is that what you would have preferred?'

Moon Hawk drew breath and held it, mortified at the insult Jay was issuing to her husband. The two men also stared at her. Jay had the sense to look perturbed.

'Well,' she offered, shrugging her shoulders. 'It sounds like jealousy to me.'

'You have no knowledge of what we are talking about,' Hillside told her gently.

She shrugged again, her eyes flitting repeatedly to Winter Man. 'I know what I hear, and I hear that you have refused Running Fisher's invitation to the societies' celebration because Skins The Wolf will be there and he will easily out-call your war honours with his own.'

Moon Hawk gazed in surprise, first at her and then at Winter Man. The question came without thought. 'What invitation?'

Winter Man refused to turn and look at her.

'There,' Jay insisted, 'it is as I said.'

Moon Hawk could not believe that was the reason he had not mentioned the invitation to her. She reached out to touch his arm. 'Husband?'

Winter Man rounded on her with blazing eyes as if it had been she who had challenged his honour.

'I will not be questioned by you in another man's lodge!'

Without hesitation, and against all etiquette, he stood and pushed his way out of the tipi, dragging his buffalo robe behind him. Moon Hawk sat dumbfounded.

'Jay,' Hillside began in a measured tone, 'sometimes I could wish that you had been born mute!'

Jay tossed back her head in annoyance. 'It is what I hear.'

'It is not the truth.'

Moon Hawk turned abruptly to them both, her heart

beating plaintively with the need to know. 'What is the truth?'

Hillside could not hold her gaze for long. 'It is not for me to say,' he murmured.

'But Winter Man will not talk to me. He will not talk to me about *anything*. At times, it is as if I do not exist for him.'

'Except in his bed,' Jay added sourly.

Moon Hawk felt that remark like a quirt-thong across the face. Jay's expression softened immediately and she extended a hand in regret.

'Forgive me. My tongue knows no sense tonight. Moon Hawk . . .' But Moon Hawk was already collecting the bowls she and Winter Man had eaten from.

'No, I—I must go. It is late, and you are right; I must speak to my husband.'

She rose in a hurry, pulling her buffalo robe up on to her shoulders, trying to keep her face averted from the light of the fire so that neither of her companions would see the tears she could feel rising into her eyes.

'Moon Hawk . . .'

'It is well—truly. I shall see you in the morning.' She fumbled with the door-flap, almost dropping the bowls in her haste to be gone from the lodge.

After the heat of the tipi, the blast of icy air caught her unprepared, making her unshed tears prick her eyes like bees' stings. She blinked furiously, so that the tears fell, and, afraid that the rivulets of moisture might freeze on her cheeks, she faltered by the side of the tipi to wipe them away.

'Oh, Hillside,' she heard Jay say. 'What have I done?'

'Touched more truth than you realise, I think! Winter Man speaks of many things when we are alone together, but he never speaks of Moon Hawk.'

Moon Hawk ran, ran though her heart was breaking, across the trampled snow between the lodges, out towards the bare trees where the drifts began. There, she let herself fall into the soft, yielding blanket of white. All the fears and doubts she had collected and dismissed over the days erupted in choking misery. How often had she lain spent in Winter Man's arms and whispered words of love to him? Beyond counting. Beyond number. And how many times had he spoken of his love her for? The crushing pain of the reply refused to give voice in her thoughts, but she knew. She could hide the answer from herself no longer. Oh, he had showed her he loved her in his actions, in the way he took her in his arms —but how many had he showed before her? How many would he show again? Gifts had been exchanged between their families, they lived as man and wife, but what was she to him except another lover? How long could their marriage last when his lovers had been changed so often?

The cold was nipping at her toes and fingers, chilling the flesh of her body, frosting the tears she wiped on the edge of her robe. She could not stay there. She had no wish to face Winter Man, but she had to return to their lodge for the warmth it offered. She thought of going to her father's instead; she would not be turned away, yet the probing questions she knew she would meet would allow her no peace there. Besides, she was not a child to run back to her mother's protective arms at the first sign of disagreement. She was a woman now, a married woman. She should act with the responsibility of her years and talk to her husband, tell him of the way she felt. If Winter Man laughed at her she would know they had no future together, but if he cared . . . If he cared, they would sit and talk and right the wrongs between them.

She rose stiffly. How foolish to stay out in the cold so long! She had not worn her bulky fur-lined moccasins that evening, expecting to walk only from one tipi to another and back, and she had lost all feeling in the toes of her right foot. She stamped it heavily in the depth of the snow, but brought about no more than a mild tingling. She knew she would pay with pain when she sat before the fire again.

She stumbled back towards the gently glowing lodges. A snow-encrusted dog raised itself from the white pathway some distance in front of her and lowered its head in a menacing stance. It growled huskily, sending a cloud of silver vapour from its gaping jaws.

'Are you blind, dog? Have you lost your sense of smell? I am Apsaroke,' she hissed at it. 'I live here!'

Instead of calming the animal her words seemed to infuriate it, for she saw, quite plainly in the snow-light, its hackles rise. The ensuing growl left her in no doubt as to its intended actions should she step within reach of it. She changed her course and backed round a nearby tipi. The cold did strange things to some of the village dogs, and over the years she had seen more than one wound caused by their fangs. Thankfully, it made no attempt to follow her, and she took a more circuitous route, inspecting shadows and listening intently to the sounds of the night in case some other animal lurked unseen and attempted to jump out at her.

Horses stamped and snorted; an owl hooted further up the valley; the creek, so choked with ice now, gurgled to her right. In one lodge a woman was singing softly to a whimpering child; in another an old grandfather was snoring in his sleep.

The high-pitched giggle was so unexpected that Moon Hawk turned to gaze in surprise at the glowing lodge covering beside her. Lovers, she decided, locked happily in each other's arms. She ached for Winter Man's arms, and she bit her lip, regretting how easily she could be lulled by his smile and by his touch. The giggle came again, shorter this time, followed by words she could not catch in a voice she knew well—a man's voice. Moon Hawk turned back to the lodge and stared. It could not be.

She looked about her, at the position of the tipi among the others. It was. This was Swallow's lodge!

Her sharp intake of breath reached out from her lungs to chill her heart. No, he could not, not just because of some foolish question which had not even been meant as an argument!

She turned and ran, slipping and slithering over the beaten snow in her haste to return to her own tipi. She pulled herself up before it, and stood there, panting. Where the other lodges showed flickering firelight, hers stood a darkened shell, the cold cover glistened with frost.

She summoned her courage and stepped towards the doorway. The flap lifted easily, but after the reflected glare of the snow-bound land, it seemed almost as dark as a stormy night within. She had hoped to see a glimmer of a coal in the fire-pit, but there was nothing. She stood, her breath hanging round her head, waiting for her vision to penetrate the gloom. Bags, back-rests, firewood, the water-paunch, the sleeping robes, each slowly made itself visible to her. Finally she gazed down at the pine boughs spread thickly over the ground. They were brown, and crushed, but without the sign of a snowy imprint of a foot. Winter Man had not returned, and she knew, in her heart, that he would not that night. He was lying in another tipi. He was lying in another woman's arms.

CHAPTER FOURTEEN

IT WAS NOT the light that woke Moon Hawk, but a cold draught of air. She blinked open her sleep-filled eyes and looked across the tipi. Winter Man was standing there, gazing at her, his buffalo robe draped loosely over his shoulders. Unable to draw her wits from their drowsy torpor, she watched unconcerned as he turned back to the doorway. He was leaving. the thought flitted through her mind and took a hold. He was leaving!

She sat hurriedly and tried to call him back, to keep him there, but there was no need; he was only adjusting the flap across the opening. When he faced her again, the words she had sought so feverishly had gone from her mind.

He looked grim. His jaw was set tight and the skin across his brow was compressed into deep lines of concern. He was looking at her oddly, she thought. Did he know that she had stood outside Swallow's lodge? Was he daring her to accuse him of his infidelity? Was that what he was wanting? An excuse to argue? An excuse to tell her bluntly that he was tired of their marriage?

She watched him take wood from the pile by the doorway and place it in the fire-pit.

'You slept in your dress,' he said evenly.

Moon Hawk wanted him to look at her, for their eyes to meet and for them to exchange some unspoken response, but his attention was solely for the wood-shavings he had cut and the small, bow-shaped fire-drill in his hand. She swallowed down her agitation and clasped her hands together.

'I sat waiting for you to return. I—I must have fallen asleep without realising.' There; he had to say something as a retort to that.

She looked on as he applied pressure to the end of the

stick and ran the bow back and forth very fast across its centre. Smoke issued faintly from its base, becoming stronger as he worked. He laid aside the two pieces of the fire-drill and stooped to blow at the smouldering shavings. A small cloud of cold ash rose a handspan above the pit, and a tiny yellow flame crackled into life. Winter Man fed it, choosing larger sticks as the preceding wood took the light. With depressing certainty, Moon Hawk came to realise that he was not going to make any reply to what she had said.

'We shall be going to the societies' celebration,' he told her. 'I shall speak to Running Fisher after I have eaten.'

Moon Hawk stared at him, unsure that she had heard him correctly.

'What Jay said . . .' he added. 'It is not true.'

He stopped poking at the fire and raised his gaze to hers. What was it that she could see enshrouded in those dark eyes? Pleading? Was he pleading for understanding from her? For forgiveness?

'It is not jealousy of Skins The Wolf that I feel . . .'

The emphasis he gave to his words made them seem unfinished, but he did not add to them. He shrugged off his buffalo robe and held it before the fire to warm the woolly inner coat. The smoothly tanned outer surface, bearing the quilled decoration of his sex and the motifs of his honours, had a thin crusting of frost Moon Hawk had not noticed. She watched it melt, forming droplets of moisture which slowly ran in lines discolouring the skin.

'To explain would be to break an oath,' he said, his eyes still on the fire. 'I cannot do that.'

He draped the warmed robe across his shoulders again and huddled over the growing flames as if needing to feel each leap of heat they were throwing out into the tipi. He was cold, she realised. He shivered slightly as she watched him. Had he left Swallow's lodge and then found that his guilt would not allow him to walk into his own? Moon Hawk clung to that thought, to the belief that he felt remorse at what he had done. She would show him no tears, no inkling of the pain she felt. Let him think she was ignorant of the truth. Let his own conscience chastise him!

She threw off her bedding robe and reached for a beaded bag of toilet items that hung from a thong stretched between the tipi poles.

'If you are to see Running Fisher, I shall dress your hair. I cannot have his wife thinking that I do not know how to care for my husband!'

He glanced at her over his shoulder as she settled herself behind him, but she deliberately gave no indication that she had seen the movement. She took the great length of his hair in her hands and began to free each lock from the four untidy braids hanging down his back. His hair was slick with damp, even wet in places, and very cold. He had spent a good deal of time away from a fire. Moon Hawk took this as a sign that her assumption had been correct. It gave her courage and strengthened her resolve. Once his hair was free of all restraints, she applied a porcupine-tail to its length, beginning at the bottom to remove the tangles. She decided, in the silence, to drive her point hard so that he could not mistake it.

'Am I an able wife?' she asked. She was watching him closely, and noted the slight angling of his head. 'I know you do not complain,' she added, 'but you do not compliment, either. I wondered if, perhaps, you criticised me to others.'

Despite her having a tight hold of his hair, Winter Man turned to look at her, his expression a mixture of surprise and confusion.

'I do not criticise you to others,' he said, mild indignation rising in his voice. 'Who had been suggesting such a thing?' Moon Hawk averted her eyes and shrugged her shoulders. 'Do not listen to the gossip of old women,' he told her. 'They have nothing better to do than make mischief.'

'Then you think me an able wife?'

He looked at her again, more quizzically than ever, and turned his head so that she might continue to brush his hair.

'You are a good and able wife,' he murmured, 'and it

grieves me that I shouted at you in Hillside's lodge when here was no need. It was wrong of me not to tell you of he invitation we had received.'

The porcupine-tail hovered in Moon Hawk's hand as she contemplated the back of his head. He was sorry for shouting at her? What apology was that when he had left her side to seek solace with Swallow!

The change in his tone altered the course of the conversation irretrievably. 'Is there food?'

She brushed his hair one last time and resigned herself to carrying on as if nothing untoward had happened.

Winter Man left the lodge after he had eaten, ostensibly to see Running Fisher, but he did not return all that day, not until the stars were beginning to show through the darkening twilight. He said little, and immediately settled himself in his bedding robes. He did not reach for Moon Hawk, and Moon Hawk did not reach for him.

The following morning was fine and bright without a hint of wind, perfect for the celebration, which because of the attending numbers had to be held in the open.

As they had each day since it had begun to fall, children of all ages played in the snow. Some built high-walled circular shelters that the girls used as homes; others fought in groups from behind snow barricades, throwing balls of packed snow at each other with great accuracy. The frozen creek was a favourite place to slide. Older boys dared each other to walk from one bank to the other across a section the women broke daily to gain their water. Great cheers would echo among the trees each time the weakened ice gave way beneath one of them. Buffalo ribs lashed together with rawhide thonging made excellent sleds for coasting down the hills, and those children who did not possess one made do with a piece of old lodge cover. Four or five children liked to sit together on such a makeshift sled, their rides always ending in bursts of excited laughter and a confusion of flailing arms and legs.

Moon Hawk stood watching them, the food she had cooked for the feast in the kettle by her feet. Winter Man had left for his meeting with the Foxes some time before. He had brushed her hair and painted her face before he had gone, as a dutiful husband should, but there had still been an atmosphere between them, hanging heavily in the silence which had been punctuated only by the minimum of necessary conversation. She had brushed his hair—his Fox society colours would be applied at the meeting—but he had refused to have his arms ringed to denote the number of coups he had taken. He had also insisted on wearing an undecorated pair of elk-skin leggings instead of his scarlet trade-cloth pair, and absolutely no jewellery, not even his usual day-to-day earrings or a small bead and bone choker. She had not questioned his motives and he had not offered her an explanation, and so he had left and she had been glad that he had gone.

Antelope Dancer emerged from Bear On The Flat's tipi and tried to help their father out of the doorway with his crutch, but it was obvious from the way the older man waved his free arm in the air that he would not be treated like a cripple, no matter how serious his disability. Though Moon Hawk did not feel very happy, she smiled at them both and was nodded to in return. They were both wearing their Fox society regalia, their eagle feathers tied proudly into the back of their hair. Moon Hawk bit her lip as she saw the long black and white plumes. Winter Man was not wearing his. He had not even taken them in their painted rawhide case.

Little Face stepped out of the lodge, and Moon Hawk put thoughts of her husband to the back of her mind. She picked up the kettle by its handle and walked across to her mother. Turtle stood at her side, engulfed in a robe too large for her, her hand tightly clasping Bobtailed Cat's. Both the children scowled as she approached. Little Face looked harassed.

'Oh, Moon Hawk, it is good to see you! Could you carry this?' The bag she handed over was heavy and very hot. 'Stones to place inside your father's wearing robe,' she told her daughter. She shook her head and drew her lips into a thin line of exasperation. 'The argument we had over them . . . He has little feeling in his foot, Moon Hawk, none at all in his toes, and he thinks he can sit in the snow all day without harm to his leg!' She shook her head again and tutted to herself.

Moon Hawk directed her attention to the children. Their animosity towards each other was growing rapidly, she could see. Bobtailed Cat was trying to pull free of his sister's grasp, while Turtle was equally insistent that he was not going to succeed.

'I have no one to hold my hand,' she lamented, laying the bag of stones on the kettle lid. 'Can I not hold hands with someone?'

Both the children gazed at her. There was a pause for a moment's thought, then Bobtailed Cat snapped his little hand free of Turtle's and thrust it into Moon Hawk's, shooting Turtle a look of defiance for good measure. Moon Hawk was afraid that Turtle was going to do something spiteful in return, but managed to catch her attention to stop her. The young girl looked totally perplexed at first, but her eyes began to twinkle and a smug smile crossed her lips. She glanced slyly at her brother and went to help Little Face to carry extra buffalo robes. With both children believing they had out-witted the other, the walk to the celebration area was quiet and uneventful, for which Moon Hawk was extremely thankful.

Once the celebrations had started, Moon Hawk put her uneasy thoughts aside and enjoyed the spectacle. Each of the warrior societies made their entrance in turn, beginning with the Muddy Hands, singing the songs and performing the dances that were their right alone. Some songs were slow and high-pitched, accompanied only by deer-hoof rattles; others were loud and raucous, with drummers seeming to compete against each other. Everyone shouted and joined in the excitement, and some men fired their muskets into the air, creating clouds of acrid smoke and deafening all those close by them.

The Foxes danced into the area in a single, snaking line, their two living officers to the front. Four had been appointed at the first spring meeting, but two had been killed in skirmishes with enemies while protecting the backs of their companions, as their roles dictated.

Except for the officers, who bore staffs wrapped in otter-skin as symbols of their responsibility, all the men in the line wore the same regalia. To Moon Hawk's eyes, Winter Man looked half undressed without his body painted like the rest. The length of his raven hair seemed stark, too, swaying back and forth across his back without eagle feathers to flutter in the breeze he made. She kept expecting her mother to tilt her head towards her and comment on their lack, but either she did not notice, or she dismissed the observation without a thought. When the Foxes began to move aside, Little Face trilled for them as she had for each society before them.

'You see them?' she asked Bobtailed Cat perched high in her arms. 'You see how brave and proud they are, these Foxes?' The boy nodded without looking at her, spellbound by the scene. 'When you are old enough, I expect you to join the Foxes just as your father did, and your elder brother, and your brother-in-law, Winter Man. You watch them as you grow; you watch them carefully. They are brave men who protect us from our enemies, from the Piegan who tried to take your sister. When you grow into a man, you, too, will be a Fox and do brave deeds. When you gain war honours, the women will trill for you like this.'

Bobtailed Cat looked at his mother and smiled shyly. He said nothing, but from his expression the two women knew that his thoughts were already many years ahead.

Moon Hawk did not pay much attention to the Lumpwoods. Ever since she could remember, Winter Man and Hillside had danced one in front of the other in the line of Foxes during gatherings such as this. She had expected no change, and because of the uniformity of their facial decoration had not noticed that they were not together until the men were filing away. It meant nothing, she told herself as the group crowded to collect their warm robes, but she still stood on tiptoe trying to see over the heads of other spectators, hoping Winter Man and Hillside would stand together and watch the Lumpwood display.

The Foxes took an unduly long time to organise themselves so that they could watch the Lumpwood performance as a body. It was meant as a snub, she knew. The Foxes and Lumpwoods had been rival societies for many years, and it was a source of enjoyment for the people to see them pompously countering each other's claim to being the leading warrior society of the Apsaroke. For Moon Hawk, it was nothing but frustrating to see the Foxes milling constantly for no apparent reason. She kept losing Winter Man's position in the throng. If he stood still for more than a moment she eagerly sought Hillside, only to find that once she had sighted him Winter Man had moved. Finally, when the Foxes did become still, it was Hillside who stood to the fore of the group. Of Winter Man there was no sign. He might have been standing at the rear, hidden by equally tall men in front of him. He might, too, have slipped away, refusing to stand at all. It was an unbelievable thought, but she could not push it away.

When the Lumpwoods had finished and the women had stopped trilling for them, fires were built and the food reheated. Boys mimicked their elders and danced in snaking lines. Many of the women trilled for them, but when the boys began to sing a Lumpwood song, they found they had to escape from the wrath of that society's members.

Everyone ate heartily. Winter Man came and took a bowl from Moon Hawk, but he said little, either to her or to anyone else, and left as soon as he had eaten. She stood alone amid the noisy crowd, absently turning her horn spoon in her half-filled bowl. Her appetite, if she had ever had one, had gone. She tipped out her food for one of the slavering dogs and walked away in search of a little peace of mind.

The sound of high-pitched giggling jarred her hearing. Swallow! Indignation and resentment rose in Moon Hawk's chest. The woman had welcomed Winter Man the night before—there was nothing Moon Hawk could do to change that—but she was not going to stand quietly by and be laughed at!

She swung about, ready to oppose her rival, but she took no more than a single step forward. Swallow was sharing a man's robe. Moon Hawk's heart turned over.

No, surely not! The man raised his face, and relief flooded through her tensed body. From his paint, Moon Hawk could see that he was a Lumpwood. Horse In The Night—that was who it was. Swallow giggled at something he said, and Moon Hawk shuddered in disgust as she watched the woman hug him tightly to her. Horse In The Night also had a wife. Swallow seemed to be making a habit of stealing other women's husbands! Moon Hawk turned on her heel and walked away before she strode across to them and said something she would regret.

With the food eaten, challenges were issued. The first, as usual, came from Stone Eagle. He was shorter than any other Apsaroke man, shorter even than Moon Hawk. Some said that his parentage was not true Apsaroke, that his mother had come from some southern people who were all small, but it made no difference to his standing, within either the Apsaroke or the Muddy Hands, his society. Despite no longer being a young man, he had never been defeated in wrestling, and at each celebration issued bold challenges to members of the other societies.

'Are you all *women*?' he demanded when there was no enthusiastic acceptance. 'Are you just playing at being men? Are you fit only for singing songs and making love? Perhaps you are not even fit for making love! Perhaps I should entice your wives away and show them what a real man can do for them!'

There was a great uproar at this, as there always was, with men decrying him and women flirting with him to shame their husbands into action. It was almost part of the routine of the challenge for no man to offer himself until this part had been played.

In turn four young men either stepped forward of their own accord or were pushed forward by their society brothers. All of them fell to Stone Eagle. The women trilled for him, and he took their appreciation with much arrogant swaggering.

There was a foot-race, which the Foxes won easily, and a horse-race which, despite Winter Man not entering with either his grey racer or the long-legged roan, was also won by the Foxes. Almost in desperation, it seemed, the Lumpwoods challenged the other societies to a recounting of the coups gained that season. Though it was not said in truth, it was clearly understood that they were specifically challenging their rivals, the Foxes, for it was only the Foxes who came close to them in the number of war honours attained. The outcome was a foregone conclusion. Everyone knew who had gained what honours during the year, and if there was any person who had forgotten, there were plenty around to tell them. In fact, if the Lumpwoods had not been certain of victory in this instance, they would never have issued the challenge. It was not the receiving of admiration which was the driving force behind this defiance, but the shaming of the losers, the instilling in them, in all of the warrior societies, of the need to do better the following year and so absolve themselves. It was a slow process. Men who had taken their first war honour that season stood and recounted the taking of the coup. The people cheered them, the women trilled. Other men stood and recounted their coups. They, too, were cheered. The village Crier kept a strict tally, though it was hardly necessary.

'Am I welcome?'

Moon Hawk turned at the sound of the familiar voice and found Jay peering nervously at her.

'I have not seen you,' the young woman said. 'I was not sure if you had been avoiding me on purpose.'

Moon Hawk managed a smile for her. 'No, I have not been avoiding you. I am glad you are here.'

With some surprise, Moon Hawk realised that she was unaccountably glad. She had a need to unburden herself to someone, a need she had refused to acknowledge until that moment. Little Face would have been the ideal person with whom to share her doubts, but with Bear On The Flat's injuries and coping with two boisterous children, Moon Hawk felt that her mother had more than enough to contend with.

'How is it between you and Winter Man?' Jay asked.

Moon Hawk tried not to let her voice betray the depth of her feeling. 'Distant,' she murmured.

Jay stretched out her arm and laid a comforting hand on Moon Hawk's shoulder. 'I am sorry for what I said in my lodge, both to you and to Winter Man. It was unforgivable. I can only say that I have been so worried these last few days that I have hardly slept. I have snapped like a dog at everyone and everything. Even Hillside is losing patience with me.'

Moon Hawk wanted to tell her about Winter Man's visit to Swallow's lodge, but she could tell that the time was not right. Jay needed someone to listen to *her* problems. That was the reason she had sought her out, Moon Hawk realised, not to offer apologies for her behaviour. She stifled a prick of resentment. If she was sympathetic to Jay's worries, perhaps Jay might be sympathetic to hers. She looked expectantly at her friend and watched her anxiety bubble into a nervous excitement.

'Each morning for the last five days I have woken with the taste of sickness in my mouth and a queasy feeling in my stomach.' Her grin spread from ear to ear.

Moon Hawk blinked at her. 'A baby?'

'I think so.' Jay clasped her hands together. 'I *pray* so. I have been so frightened that the feeling might stop. This has happened before, more than once, and each time it has come to nothing. I have been waiting, hardly daring to believe, but I had to tell someone. I just had to.'

Jay was so agitated that she could not keep still. Moon Hawk could do little else but smile and feel happy for her. She and Hillside had waited so long for a child.

Moon Hawk wrinkled her brow as the full meaning of Jay's words came to her. 'Tell someone? Have you not told Hillside?'

Jay shook her head, her exuberance rapidly fading. 'I cannot, not until I am sure. He wants a son so much. You have not seen him speak of a son: the way his eyes light, the spring in his step. I have disappointed him so often. Before, when the sickness went and I was left with no child in my belly, he comforted me. He said it did not matter; but it does, I know it does. I can see it in his face, feel it in the air between us. He wears his sorrow like a robe. To build his hopes again and then cut them down like willow fronds . . .' A tear trickled down her cheek. 'Moon Hawk, he will take another woman for his wife, I know he will.'

Moon Hawk wrapped her arms about Jay's shoulders and hugged her tightly. This was not the time to speak of her own worries, she knew. They were so insignificant in comparison that burdening another with them could be counted as nothing less than a childish indulgence.

Jay raised her head and wiped her eyes. 'Thank you for listening,' she said. 'I shall be strong now, strong enough to face whatever awaits me. I had to tell someone, someone I could trust. You will not mention this, will you? I would not want Hillside to hear it from another.'

Moon Hawk shook her head. 'I shall say nothing, I swear. Come, let us go and see our husbands recount their coups.'

She steered Jay back to the front of the gathering, hoping that the excitement of the re-enactments would lighten her heart. It did Jay's, but not her own.

Hillside was already speaking. Winter Man stood a few paces behind him, waiting for his turn. He was taller than Hillside, broader in the shoulder, more powerful across the chest. Over the years she had stood so often looking at Winter Man like this, knowing that he was unaware of her observation. The sight of him had always stirred her blood and lifted her heart in a soft and dreamy evocation of what might be, but there was no lifting of her heart now. Even her blood ran slowly through her veins.

Hillside finished his recital with a flourish, and the women trilled for him. Moon Hawk tried to add her voice to the rest, but the power was not there to call upon. She took a deep, fortifying breath, the cold air filling her lungs and calming her unstable emotions. She dully watched Winter Man step forward and lift his arm to begin his oratory. His voice was strong, his tone measured and precise. Against her expectations, she felt her heart begin to swell with pride. As he spoke, Winter Man continually turned his head, his dark eyes seeming to seek out each person individually, to mark them, to ensure that they heard and understood what he was saying. Moon Hawk thought, at first, that she was mistaken in her belief, but the watching crowd grew hushed, more hushed than they had for any man before him.

How different he looked now—no—how much the same: tall, purposeful, elegant. This was the Winter Man she had fallen in love with so many years before. This was the Winter Man she had wanted as her husband, but this was not the Winter Man she had married.

Or was he?

She had loved Winter Man for so long, been his wife for so short a period. He had once asked her, during their stormy courtship, which she had wanted, the marriage ritual or the man. At the time, she had believed he had been merely taunting her, but, looking back, he could have been in earnest. Perhaps the question he should have asked was, 'Is it me you love, or what you think I am?'

Moon Hawk shuddered at the gravity of her own thought. She looked at Winter Man afresh, she hoped with a clearer eye. Had she married the man believing him to be the image she carried in her heart? Was their marriage failing because she expected too much? Was it all her fault?

The high-pitched ululations of the women snapped Moon Hawk from her reverie. She threw back her head and joined in the trilling. Men cheered and many fired their powder guns in salute. All for Winter Man, she thought. All for Winter Man, my husband.

When her breath had gone and she lowered her gaze from the cloudless sky, she saw Winter Man walking towards her. His face was bright and warm and open, so changed from earlier that she stared at him in disbelief as he approached. Before she found the wit to react, he stepped up to take her firmly by the shoulders and hold her at arm's length.

'Ah, wife!' He paused to smile down at her from his towering height. 'Did I speak well, or did I speak well?'

Moon Hawk closed her gaping mouth and fought for a suitable answer. 'You spoke well,' she said, though, to her embarrassment, she could not recollect a single word of what he had said.

Hillside stepped up behind him and slapped him playfully on the back. 'He did not offer a murmur, did he?'

The broad smile on Winter Man's face lost its glowing edge as a shadow flitted momentarily across his eyes. He inclined his head slightly, so that he could see Hillside at his shoulder. 'I was sure he would.'

Hillside shook his head, his smug expression full of bravado. 'After the reaction you gained from the people? He did not dare!'

Moon Hawk looked from one to the other. 'Who did not dare to do what?'

Both men turned their gaze to her; neither spoke. It was happening again, she thought. Nothing has changed at all.

'You must tell me, Winter Man. You must include me in your life. I am your wife!'

He frowned at her and a quirky chuckle escaped his lips. 'I know you are,' he said. 'I do not exclude you from my life. I . . .' He shrugged. 'I do not wish to cause you worry.'

'But I do worry.'

She watched him glance either side of him to see whose ears were listening. Hillside turned away, drawing Jay with him. Winter Man and Moon Hawk stood alone in the cold, whispering urgently to each other.

'Sometimes there is a rivalry between men of similar prowess, as there is between warrior societies.' Winter Man indicated behind him. 'As with the societies, this rivalry is not always good-natured, or in the best interests of the people.'

Moon Hawk gazed up into his face, into those dark eyes which sought her understanding, and tried to grasp what he did not wish to put openly into words.

'I would speak his name,' he added, 'but I do not wish to fan the flames of a wild-fire.'

'Skins The Wolf,' she breathed.

Winter Man sighed in resignation. 'Yes, Skins The Wolf. Jay speaks her mind—Jay and others.'

But it had not been Jay's remembered accusation that sprang into Moon Hawk's mind. In the distance, over her husband's shoulder, she could see Skins The Wolf standing apart from the other Lumpwoods, his captured Piegan honour bonnet caught loosely in his hand.

'Is he looking at us?'

Her gaze returned to Winter Man, to the taut skin round his eyes. 'Yes.'

His arm slipped about her shoulders, and he turned her around and began to guide her away. 'Do not look at him. It is over.'

Moon Hawk did as Winter Man asked her and did not look back, but her restless mind was fraught with doubts. If Skins The Wolf was seeking to discredit her husband it could be for only one reason, because she had rejected him. Whatever Winter Man believed, Moon Hawk knew with fearful certainty that it was not over, not as easily as that.

CHAPTER FIFTEEN

WINTER MAN HEARD a movement outside the tipi and raised his eyes, hoping that Moon Hawk would enter. The good weather enjoyed on the day of the celebration had not lasted long, and for the past four days icy winds had howled down the valley, forcing everyone to retreat inside their tipis. Stored fuel had dwindled steadily, but during the night the wind had abated, and that morning women from every lodge had taken the opportunity to collect wood and replenish their stocks. To Winter Man's knowledge, Moon Hawk had made six journeys up the timbered slopes of the valley, each time returning with her tumpline straining beneath the load she carried. The fruits of her labour were piled outside the brushwood barricade that protected the tipi from the drifting snow.

'Moon Hawk?'

He listened, waiting for a reply which would mean she had heard him and had not left to continue her work. He had news he wanted to share with her, news that would bring light back into her eyes and a smile to her lips. She seemed so passive of late, almost submissive, with hardly a word for him which he did not have to coax from her. Each night, when they lay together, she did not resist when he drew her to him, but there had been times when he had felt he was holding a woman of wood in his arms, such had been his difficulty in arousing her. He wondered if he was losing the art, or was it, more likely, that he was losing his desirability? However he acted, Moon Hawk did not reach for him first, not any longer.

He laid down his paint-stick and rose from the spread wearing robe on which he was painting his war honours. She was taking too long to enter the lodge, he reasoned, she had not heard his call, but as he moved round the fire-pit the door-flap was lifted aside and a large bundle of sticks was fed through the opening. A moment later

the top of Moon Hawk's snow-dusted head appeared
and she entered, pulling the flap closed behind her. Her
face was pinched with cold, her lips thin and dark. She
looked decidedly tired. Winter Man stepped forward
and drew the heavy robe from her bent shoulders,
shaking off the fine, powdery snow.

'You have been outside too long,' he said. 'You
should have made Turtle help you collect the wood.'

'Little Face has more need of her than I.'

The quickness of her reply made him look at her
again. Had he made his voice sound that harsh? He had
not meant his words as a rebuke. He watched her draw
her mittens from her hands and hold her painful fingers
to the warmth of the fire. He crouched opposite her,
hoping she would raise her eyes and see his smile, but
her gaze was only for her hands, and for the flames.

'Hillside came while you were away,' he began. 'He is
going to be a father at last!'

He waited for her reaction, for her to show surprise,
for her to laugh, for them to laugh together, but she only
nodded her bowed head.

'Yes,' she said. 'I know.'

You knew? The words formed on his lips, but no
sound breathed life into the thought. He felt his good
humour crushed, and quickly shook the feeling from
him. Of course. Women talked of such things. Of course
she would know.

'He has asked us to eat with him and Jay this evening. I
said we would go.'

Another nod of her head was all response he received.
What was wrong with her? He would have expected her
to be so happy for Jay. The woman had believed herself
barren.

Barren. Was that it? Was that the thought which
weighed so heavily upon Moon Hawk's shoulders? Four
times she had gone to the women's lodge since they had
shared their bedding robes. Did Moon Hawk believe
herself unable to conceive a child?

Winter Man moved round the fire-pit to kneel next to
his wife, and he slipped a comforting arm over her
shoulders.

'Do not fret. You, too, will suckle a child. I have no fear of it.' He hugged her playfully. 'I want a son, mind, whom I can teach to hold a lance. I know nothing of quilling robes!'

She raised her head and looked at him in astonishment. 'You want a child?'

Her question stunned him. 'Why would I not?'

She turned her face back to the fire. 'Oh,' was all she said.

There was fresh elk-meat at Hillside's lodge, roasted turnips and parched maize. Where he and Jay had acquired it, neither of them would say, but it tasted delicious and was enjoyed by all. Winter Man had never seen Hillside so exuberant and cheerfully encouraged his extravagant statements.

'The first thing I shall do,' Hillside told them, 'is to teach him to ride my buffalo-horses.'

'Before he can walk?' Winter Man asked.

'Of course before he can walk! He will be bringing down his first calf before he sees five snows!'

'And what if you find you have a daughter?' Moon Hawk asked, her face aglow. 'What then?'

Hillside did not even hesitate. 'Then she will kill the calf *and* dress the skin!'

Everyone laughed. Winter Man glanced across at Moon Hawk. It was good to see her laugh again. It seemed to him that it had been so long, since . . . Since they had last sat in Hillside's lodge.

'A tongue-twister! I have a new tongue-twister,' Hillside interjected. 'Listen: buzzing bees, bellowing buffalo, brightly blooming blues, dance before the dappled dogs dozing in the dew.'

Moon Hawk pushed him in the arm and laughed scornfully. 'That is not a tongue-twister! I shall give you a tongue-twister!'

Her voice took on a distant quality to Winter Man's ears. Her face was so animated, her eyes so bright as she repeated the verse for Hillside, and it was for Hillside that she spoke, not for himself, or for Jay. Her gaze never moved from his face, and his, Winter Man noticed, never left hers.

At the end of the recitation, Jay clapped her lips with her hand in her delight, bringing Winter Man forcefully from his thoughts.

'I am not even going to attempt that one,' Hillside snorted, waving his arm demonstratively in the air in front of him.

'Winter Man will do it,' Jay insisted. 'He is good with tongue-twisters!'

Despite hearing the verse only a few moments before, Winter Man could not call it to mind. He tried to cover his embarrassment by pulling a face and making the others laugh.

'Moon Hawk has beaten us all!' Hillside announced, and to Winter Man's surprise he leaned over Jay and took Moon Hawk purposefully by the hands. 'Not only is she pretty in face and figure, but she has an agile mind as well!'

Moon Hawk blushed from her chin to her hair-roots and pushed him away, making ambiguous noises beneath her breath. Jay roared with laughter, but Winter Man found he could hardly force a smile. Almost in the same breath Hillside changed the subject.

'I heard today that Skins The Wolf has left the village with a few bored youngsters, ostensibly to trade with the hairy-faces.' He raised his eyebrows and shrugged. 'In this weather? I ask you! I shall tell you what it is: he feels he lost face during the celebrations, that is what it is. He let it be known that he was going to challenge you to stand against his coups—discredit you, more like—and then he lost his nerve.'

'I do not know why he acts as he does. I see no sense in it. When did he leave?'

'Several days ago, I hear; just as the blizzard began. Some say he laughed at the building clouds, defied them to do their worst. He was not afraid. There is talk of him having Weather Medicine, but it is the first I have heard of it.'

Jay began to fidget uncomfortably. 'Let us not speak of him. This is a good day. Let us not bring bad memories into it. Winter Man, Hillside has said he will gain a fine pelt for our child's cradleboard. I will worry if he goes alone in the snow. Will you hunt with him?'

It was a strange request, one which almost spoke of doubts as to her husband's competence. Winter Man chanced a glance in Hillside's direction and found him staring speechless at Jay.

'I would like you to be there at the killing,' she continued. 'It would be right. You saved my husband's life during the horse-raid on the Shoshone village. I have not forgotten. I would like you to be the one to name our child.'

Winter Man's mouth dropped open. Good Men named children, mystics, ageing grandfathers whose Life Medicine was strong. He looked again to Hillside, to sense his feelings on this.

Hillside was smiling now, and nodding his head in affirmation. 'If that is what you both wish.'

'Yes,' Hillside insisted.

'Then I will be honoured.'

'Ah, good. Now, how about a song to accompany a stick game?'

The evening wore on with singing and frivolous banter as Hillside and Jay repeatedly beat Winter Man and Moon Hawk at the stick game.

'This is embarrassing,' Hillside offered. 'The only way you two are going to win is if we change partners!'

Winter Man's lightness of spirit evaporated in that single phrase. He wanted to look at Hillside, to give some witty retort, but he could not bring himself to raise his eyes from the yellow flames licking at the edge of the fire-pit. To look at Hillside would be to look at Moon Hawk, and he did not want to see her expression. If her gaze was for Hillside, if she was smiling, happy with his suggestion . . .

'I do not think so,' Winter Man offered. 'The stars are bright. It is time we left you. Jay will be getting tired. You must look after her, you know.'

Hillside hugged his wife to him and growled lasciviously. 'Of course I shall look after her!'

Winter Man reached for his robe and rose to his feet. Moon Hawk followed his lead and they offered their goodbyes. They left arm in arm and made their way through the lightly falling snow back to their own lodge.

'It was an enjoyable evening,' Winter Man murmured. 'You laughed a lot.'

Moon Hawk nodded. 'Yes,' she said, 'I did. Hillside was so funny.'

In their bedding robes, Moon Hawk snuggled unbidden into her husband's arms, but for Winter Man there was little pleasure. He could not cast aside the thought that he was not the one she made believe she touched.

Despite the changeability of the weather, Hillside was eager to hunt, and visited Winter Man's tipi each morning to try to persuade him that the time was right to leave. Sometimes Jay would accompany him, but often he visited alone, and on two occasions Winter Man entered the lodge to find him in whispered conversation with Moon Hawk, a conversation which was cut short with his appearance.

It was a new experience for Winter Man. He had had many lovers in his life, some other men's wives, most not, but in every instance he had been open in his dealings with them. There had never been any need for furtive meetings or stolen kisses. Not one had been more than a passing dalliance, discarded with gifts when he had grown tired of them. He had been discarded himself, on more than one occasion, but he had accepted it with good heart, and could, perhaps with the exception of two, say that he was on amicable terms with all his old loves. Four of them had even allowed him to take them back from their Lumpwood husbands during the wife-stealing ritual in the spring. So what was this bitter rancour that swelled within him? It was not as if he had expected his marriage to last. He had expected it to last longer than this, it was true, but . . . But. There was no denying it, no matter how he tried. He had expected himself to grow bored with Moon Hawk, not for Moon Hawk to grow bored with him. It hurt.

Six days after Jay had first asked him, he and Hillside packed their horses and walked out of the village.

Winter Man held a vague notion that while on the hunt he would tackle Hillside about his relationship with Moon Hawk, but a hunt in bad weather, when one man's life might depend on the other, was best undertaken without acrimony. Besides, Hillside was a brother-friend. If he were to tackle anyone, Winter Man felt it should be Moon Hawk.

The brightness of the dawn did not continue past mid-day. They took shelter in the depths of an ash thicket and heated a broth of dried buffalo meat and snow while a blizzard raged around them. The following morning was better, with a sky the palest blue of an abalone shell. In the crisp white landscape tracks were few, mostly of coyote and wolf, but later in the day Hillside spotted what he was after, the tell-tale prints of a bighorn sheep, driven off the high peaks by the weather. It was while they were trailing it that Winter Man realised they were, themselves, being followed.

If Hillside had asked him, Winter Man would have said his Medicine had warned him, but Hillside had witnessed this phenomenon before and both men believed implicitly in its infallibility. They picketed their horses in the shadow of a rocky outcrop and, keeping as low as they were able, encircled their own tracks. Sounds drifted over the stillness of the white expanse: the puffing of tired horses ridden long, the crunching of the frosted snow beneath their hooves, snatches of conversation.

'They are speaking Apsaroke!' Hillside hissed. 'Who could it be out so . . .?' He groaned. 'Skins The Wolf. That man haunts us!'

'We had better get back to our horses and meet them straight on,' Winter Man whispered. 'Otherwise, they might make an attack on us at dusk when the light is at its worst, believing we are Shoshone or Bannock.'

Hillside grudgingly agreed that it was their best course and they made their way to their mounts. They retraced their path out of the rocks into the open in sight of the Apsaroke. There was a moment when the group reined in their horses in their surprise, but Winter Man stood in his stirrups and waved his arm above his head, calling to them so that they should make no mistake over who it was. Their lead horseman waved in return, and the group continued towards them.

'That will be Skins The Wolf in front,' Hillside observed. 'Never a one to be led. What is he wearing on his head? I can hardly see his face for the dazzle.'

Winter Man had been contemplating a similar thought. A head-covering of mirrors, by the way the sunlight was reflected. He watched Skins The Wolf unburden himself of his buffalo robe and lay it over his horse's back behind the saddle. As he neared, and the dazzling effect of his headgear waned, Winter Man realised why. He was wearing a stiff shirt of vivid scarlet festooned with loops of bright yellow rope. It was slit down the front from neck to hem, with rows of brass buttons ranged down each side. Twisted yellow fringing danced from thick pads on his shoulders, making him seem much broader than he was. His head-covering, which had flashed so brightly in the sunlight, was far smaller than Winter Man had imagined. It was square, scarlet like the shirt, with loops of the same yellow rope adorning it. Skins The Wolf wore its short, black peak pulled down over his eyes in the manner of the hairy-faces. It was covered, all round it seemed, with many shiny discs in brass and silver.

Skins The Wolf drew his horse up in front of them, the young men with him reining theirs close at his back. None of them spoke, not even Skins The Wolf, who sat astride his mount with the proud and haughty air of one who had single-handedly run off an enemy's entire herd of horses.

Hillside guffawed. He nudged his horse so that it walked closer to that of Skins The Wolf, and looked him up and down with exaggerated distaste. 'Did you sell your body for that?'

To Winter Man's surprise it was not Skins The Wolf who reacted to the baiting, but one of the young horse-men waiting patiently at his back. If the snow had not been so deep and his mount so tired, his lunging attack with the long-barrelled powder gun would have opened Hillside's head. The vicious blow was so unexpected that

Hillside stared at the youth in stunned incomprehension, allowing Skins The Wolf time to calm the assailant with a growl and a fierce gesture of his hand. The young man hunched himself back into his buffalo robe like a dog lying at his owner's command. Winter Man let his gaze sweep over the others who hung a pace behind. What, he wondered uneasily, would have happened if Skins The Wolf had given the opposite command?

'The cold gets to them like dogs. They have no sense of humour!' Skins The Wolf chuckled amiably. 'Not like us Men!'

Winter Man latched on to the implication, and against his better judgment felt his ire begin to rise. *Men*: a blanket title which identified him and Hillside as Good Young Men and himself as a Good Man, which he was not. Skins The Wolf did not hold the necessary honours. And yet the people seemed content to act as though he was one.

'Your eyes are large, Winter Man, but you say little. Are you daunted by the Medicine Jacket?'

Winter Man raised his eyes from the bright clothing and gazed into his expectant face. 'Why should I be daunted? I have seen such clothing before. A Yellow Leg man wore one. I saw him on a visit to the Earth Lodge people two summers ago.'

Skins The Wolf nodded. 'I was there, too. I saw him. He was a powerful man, a strong leader; strong because of his Medicine Jacket.'

It was easy to see what was running through Skins The Wolf's mind. If he wore the trader's shirt long enough, continually referred to it as his Medicine Jacket, the people would associate him with it until its name became his own—and with it its alleged power. Winter Man affected indifference and looked beyond his shoulder to the men at his back. Each carried a long-barrelled musket, bright with newness. They were young, these men, none of them from prestigious families, none of them with the material possessions to trade for guns.

'You show interest in the weapons.' Skins The Wolf turned to those behind him and called for a musket. No sooner did he hold the gun than he tossed the weight of it towards Winter Man. 'Try it. It is a fine weapon.'

Winter Man lifted it to his shoulder and glanced down the sights. With the length of the barrel still intact, it felt far heavier than his own, and awkward for it, but it had a sturdy firing mechanism and overall the balance was good. There was nothing he could say against it.

'What did it cost?'

Skins The Wolf grinned. 'Nothing.'

Winter Man looked sceptical. The hairy-faced traders did not make gifts of guns. He had exchanged a good horse for his. However, the Apsaroke also paid heavily for cloth, mirrors and for beads. Considering the casual way the traders gave large amounts of these to their own women, Winter Man was inclined to believe that it was not the traders who were so wealthy, as they always maintained, but that the goods they bartered were worth less than the price they demanded.

'The hairy-faces do not give powder guns as gifts,' Hillside countered vehemently. 'They give needles, tobacco, vermilion sometimes, but they do not give powder guns.'

Skins The Wolf threw back his head and laughed. 'Not to such as you, no! But to a Good Man . . .'

'You are not a Good Man.'

Skins The Wolf narrowed his eyes, but chose to ignore the remark. 'The leader of the traders was a man I had not seen before. He spoke a little Apsaroke, but not much. He kept lapsing into Shoshone. It seemed that he did not know the difference.' Skins The Wolf looked back at his men and laughed at the joke. They smiled and nodded in return.

'We smoked together,' he continued. 'I told him I had many coups, many followers, that these were only a few. He kept calling me . . .' he thought for a moment, '*cheef*. It meant much to him.' He glanced slyly at his men. 'It meant he gave me guns!' The young men roared with laughter and lifted their new possessions high into the air in triumph.

Winter Man swallowed the sickly taste filling his mouth. It needed no effort to imagine what had happened. Skins The Wolf had said he was a Good Man.

He had recounted his coups, exaggerated his standing among the orators of his people. He had lied about his followers. Lied! *Again*. Was he totally without shame?

Winter Man threw the heavy musket back to him. 'You have returned with guns. It is a change from coups, at least.'

Skins The Wolf tossed the weapon back to its owner and smugly eyed Winter Man. 'There were a few Piegan there with their women, but they saw we were Apsaroke and they trembled at the sight of us. They would not stand and fight. Have you managed to gain any coups since I have been away?'

The question was loaded with sarcasm, and Winter Man wondered what sort of a trap he would be entering by making an answer to it. 'The village has been at peace,' he said. 'There has been no opportunity.'

Skins The Wolf shook his head in a deprecating manner. 'If you wait until coups present themselves to you, you will be blind and toothless before you have gained the honours needed to elevate you to a Good Man!'

Winter Man's reticence finally snapped. 'I shall become a Good Man in the next season. Men will follow me, not because I give them gifts of guns or wear a trader's jacket, but because my Medicine is strong, and I shall ensure that all those who ride out with me shall ride back with me *unharmed*!'

'Brave words, but it is deeds that gain followers, the counting of coups.'

'Coups! If it is coups you want to see, I shall give you coups, come the spring! When the Foxes elect their officers, I shall not shrink back if the pipe comes to me. You shall see me bring so many coups back to the village that your eyes will stare from your head in disbelief!'

With a sharp slap of his quirt, Winter Man forced his roan to pull away from the group. Hillside followed him. Across the clear air, Skins The Wolf insisted on having the last word.

'I shall be waiting to see it, Winter Man! We shall all be waiting to see it!'

'Then you will not be disappointed,' Winter Man muttered beneath his breath.

Hillside rode by his friend without attempting any conversation. He could tell that Winter Man was still seething with anger and resentment; he knew the signs. Unlike himself, such emotions were slow to rise in Winter Man, but also unlike himself, they were equally slow to dissipate. He tried to pick his moment.

'Did you mean what you said about accepting an officership in the spring?'

Winter Man glared at him in response.

'I was not calling you a liar,' Hillside added quickly. 'Being an officer is a great responsibility: covering a retreat, standing alone before the enemy. We lost two of our officers this season. Their wives cut their hair and wailed their grief.'

'That is as it should be.'

Hillside looked steadily at him. 'You have not been married long. I would not want Moon Hawk to have to do the same.'

'Why not? You would be clear to take her as your second wife.'

Hillside snorted derisively. 'That is spite for Skins The Wolf that I hear! Do not use it on me. You know very well my feelings on taking a second wife. Moon Hawk enjoys Jay's company, not mine. If you and Moon Hawk are not sitting well together, look to yourself for the reason.'

Winter Man turned to look pointedly at him.

'Yes, you,' Hillside retorted sharply. 'Not married a season, and already you are taking lovers.'

'Who told . . .'

'I have eyes! And with Swallow, too.'

'It was by chance. I was angry. She was out in the snow. Horse In The Night had said he would meet her and then he had not come. She was cold.'

'And you warmed her!' Hillside shook his head in exasperation.

'It was the once.'

'Once! How many others have there been?'

Winter Man set his jaw. 'What is this? I am not like

you, Hillside. I have no intention of being such a fool. You are laughed at for staying so close to Jay. A blinded bull with broken legs, you are called.'

'They can laugh all they like. I can stand any amount of ridicule; but when the summer ceremonies come around, whose tipi will the mystics call on when they want someone to take up the sacred duties? They will not call upon those who have acted like rutting elk!'

Winter Man made no reply, and the two men returned to tracking the bighorn sheep in a discordant silence.

They came upon the animal at the foot of some ice-hung cliffs. It tried to escape when it caught their scent, but Hillside brought it down with an arrow and finished it with his knife. Winter Man stood by while he spoke quietly to the animal's spirit.

'Do not be angry that I have done this, Bighorn. You were chosen because your pelt is thick and fleecy. My son will be born during the cold nights of the spring and needs the warmth your coat will provide. Be proud that I have chosen you for this.'

He tied a little tobacco to one of the bushes the bighorn had been feeding from, and he and Winter Man lifted the carcass over the pommel of Hillside's saddle.

The kill lifted Hillside's humour, and as they turned their horses back towards the Apsaroke village he spoke easily of where he was going to cut the wood for the base of the cradleboard and what design Jay had decided would decorate it. Winter Man made interested noises, but his mind was set on Moon Hawk, on his own infidelity and on the cutting accusations levelled at him by Hillside earlier.

His relationship with Swallow had always been an on-off affair without any shadow of permanence attached to it. She liked to call on a string of lovers and changed her favourite on a whim. Sometimes it was him, sometimes it was Strikes The Drum, sometimes it was some other man. Horse In The Night was new; she was still running him down—the wolf and the antelope—but he had eluded her that evening, and instead she had come across himself.

Even now Winter Man could not say why he had gone

with Swallow to her lodge that night. It was not as if Moon Hawk did not satisfy him—she did—he had just not given any thought to the consequences. A man took lovers if and where he could. It was expected. What had not been expected was the guilt which had accompanied it. He had felt it as soon as he had laid back on the warm bedding robes and looked up at the sides of the tipi. It was not his tipi, its decoration not the decoration painted by Moon Hawk's hand. He had left then, to Swallow's annoyance, but he had been unable to enter his own lodge, unable to enter and look Moon Hawk in the eye.

'She never said anything.'

Hillside turned in his saddle and looked at him quizzically.

'Moon Hawk,' Winter Man told him. 'She never gave any indication that she knew about Swallow.'

Hillside tossed back his head and grunted. 'Of course she did; not in words, perhaps, but she did. She has been so unhappy of late that I am surprised you have not been visited by her brothers wanting to know the reason why.'

'You think a lot of her,' Winter Man said evenly.

'Yes; and of you, too. Treat her well, and she will be a good wife to you. Ignore her, and it will be your loss. She is young, like a flower whose petals are shaped but not yet open. When she blossoms, many men will cast their eyes at her, and there will be some who will try to entice her from you.'

Winter Man shook his head. 'I still cannot understand why she kept silent when she knew.'

'You are a fool! You have had so many women that they have run one into another. You have not looked at any of them and seen what was there. What was she supposed to say to you that would stand against the wiles of Swallow? It would be like pitting a child in a cradleboard against a mesmerising night spirit.' Hillside suddenly laughed. 'Like pitting *you* against a night spirit! She has you mesmerised, Swallow does. You have not seen it yet, have you?'

'Seen what?'

'Horse In The Night.'

Winter Man shrugged. 'His wife found out about his

relationship with Swallow and threw his possessions out of their lodge. It caused much amusement. He has moved into Swallow's tipi.'

'Yes, the first man ever to, permanently. And still you cannot see it, can you?'

'See what?'

'Horse In The Night is a Lumpwood. She has, more or less, married him. You were her lover—and you are a Fox.'

A cold chill rippled down Winter Man's spine as the consequence of this made itself apparent to him. As her ex-lover, he would have every right to attempt to steal her from her Lumpwood husband come the spring wife-stealing ritual. And Swallow, knowing Swallow, would put no obstacle in his path!

'She could not be so devious,' he said.

Hil!side laughed uproariously. 'If you believe that, you will believe anything!'

And for this, Winter Man reflected bitterly, he had put his marriage in jeopardy!

In the half-gloom of twilight, they came across a small group of antelope. Winter Man managed to bring one down before the animals fled. When the two of them reached the village the following day, he presented the stiff and snow-frosted carcass to Moon Hawk with a flourish.

'Fresh meat!'

She smiled at him, a little wanly, he thought, and she set to tending to his horse. He watched her for a moment, wondering if he should offer to help her and chance the derision of those who stood close by. He decided not to; it would not help him if he inadvertently offended her, and he turned to enter their lodge.

It was warm inside, suffocatingly warm after the intense cold of the trail. It made him feel light-headed. He looked about him at the familiar furnishings and at the decorations painted on the lining skins. They seemed dull, lacking their initial lustre, like Moon Hawk, a mere shadow of their former selves.

He dropped his robe by the doorway and walked

round the fire to sit at his place at the back of the lodge. A kettle stood over the gentle flames, its contents bubbling softly, forcing a tantalising smell of permeate the tipi. Winter Man had chewed on dried meat and pemmican during the hunt. He had looked forward to the good meal he knew would meet his return, but now he sat there, he had no appetite for it.

Moon Hawk entered with his saddle and weapons, and pulled the door-flap closed behind her. She let slip her own buffalo robe and reached above the fire for a warmed pair of Winter Man's moccasins. Without a word she bent to his feet and began to remove his wet ones.

Winter Man reached out a hand and smoothed back her dark hair. 'I missed you,' he said. He held his breath as she glanced up at him, held it and listened to the drumming of his heart.

She smiled a little. 'Did you?'

'Yes, Hillside has such an ugly face.'

She smiled again and chuckled faintly. He chuckled with her, then she turned back to her work and he wished he had not said anything so frivolous.

'Did you miss me?'

There was a pause before she raised her eyes to him; a long, torment-laden pause when he thought she was going to ignore him.

'Yes,' she said simply. 'Of course I did.'

'I wondered if you were glad to see me go, if you were sorry to see me back.'

Moon Hawk sat upright on her heels and stared at him. She shook her head very, very slowly. 'No.'

His gaze ran over her questioning expression, the touch of vermilion she wore to enhance her cheekbones, her small mouth, her thin nose. Finally he took his courage and looked her in the eye. She was pleading with him, he could see, silently pleading with him to speak his thoughts.

'You were the only one in my mind, Moon Hawk.'

'The only one?'

He nodded. 'The only one.'

Her gaze held his a moment longer, hoping for what

he could not give, then it slipped in regret, taking a piece of his heart with it.

'It is enough,' he heard her whisper, but it was not, he realised. It was not nearly enough.

He reached out to smooth her hair again, but he changed his mind, and instead offered her his open palm. She looked at it, gazed at it, wishing it was more, and finally she placed her hand in his. He leaned forwards and slipped his other arm about her shoulders to draw her back into his chest. They sat nestled into one another, their warmth coming more from the fire than from themselves.

He turned his face and kissed her lightly on the cheek. She inclined her head towards his lips, her quiet murmur of response almost lost in her throat. She would not draw away, he knew, when he kissed her again, when he pulled her to him to show her how much he cared; but that was not what she wanted, not what she yearned for. Why could he not tell her that he loved her? Such small words, such unimportant words that he had spoken without count during his life. They had meant so little to the giver, so much to those who had received them. Why could he not speak them to Moon Hawk? It was all that she wanted, all that would be needed to brighten her eyes and make her reach for him. Why could he not say them?

CHAPTER SIXTEEN

MOON HAWK'S SPIRITS rose as the winter wore on. Perhaps it was the remarkable change in Jay. Everywhere she went she seemed to take a stream of summer sunshine with her, so happy was she at having a child growing within her. Moon Hawk sought her company at every opportunity, helping with the carrying of water and firewood, anything to share in the glow of peace and goodwill she exuded. By Jay's side, she found it difficult to allow any melancholy thought to dwell in her own mind.

Winter Man, too, seemed to change before her eyes, becoming more attentive than he had ever been since they had married. It put Moon Hawk on her guard at first, wondering at his motive, fretting in case it meant that he had visited Swallow again, but his thoughtfulness remained steadfast. He brought her small gifts of shells or elk-teeth so that she could adorn herself or decorate her clothing. On one occasion, after winning a game of dice, he presented her with a beautiful necklace of painted bird-quills. In return she made him a double choker of blue and white beads, each coil as thick as two of her fingers. His uncontrolled expression of delight at receiving the gift surprised her, and she felt slightly embarrassed at the way he kept drawing people's attention to it and praising her skill.

They received invitations to gatherings at other lodges, where they sang heartily and made a good show at the games played. Winter Man encouraged her to recite the numerous tongue-twisters she knew, and the lip-clapping applause she received helped to add to her growing self-confidence. On one occasion she found that Horse In The Night and Swallow had also been invited. She wondered what looks would be exchanged, and carefully watched for them, but Winter Man ignored Swallow's every gesture, each subtle altering of her tone as she spoke. His eyes and his arms were locked about Moon Hawk, and it seemed to her that no one else existed for him. It was a warming feeling, which finally broke the barrier of ice she had let freeze round her heart. Their nights together took on the heady passions of the first days of their marriage, and Moon Hawk knew nothing but happiness.

When Winter Man went to see to the welfare of his horses, she would accompany him. Like children they slid on the frozen creek, and even shared a robe down a frosted hillside, tumbling one over the other and shrieking their laughter. Sometimes, on fine days, they would climb the wooded valley slopes to sit arm in arm looking down over the straggling expanse of the village, over its herd of horses and the movement of its people.

'I have something to tell you,' he said one day. 'I should have told you long ago, when I first decided, but I did not want you to worry.'

'Worry about what?'

'I am hoping to become an officer of the Fox society.'

Moon Hawk stared out at the blurring scene below her, knowing that she should give no sign of the scream of anguish that had rent her soul. She raised her chin, trying to be proud for him, but could not.

'It would be a great honour for our lodge to hold an officer's staff. There is much prestige attached to the position.' Her voice began to shake. 'I—I had hoped you would wait a while, another season . . .'

His arm encircled her shoulders and she felt herself being drawn into his body.

'Not every officer dies, Moon Hawk. Two died last season, it is true, but the season before all returned their staffs to the society lodge. A man can die by falling off his horse. It is the way. Better to die courageously, saving a fellow Fox, than by coughing blood into my lungs, or being struck down by the spotting sickness.'

'I know,' she nodded, and wiped away an errant tear. 'I know.'

'And hear me, Moon Hawk, I have no intention of dying! My mind is set on my becoming a Good Man, as the mentors of my youth would have me. As a Fox officer, there will be many opportunities for me to gain the coups I need to elevate me to that position. Do you not want me to be a war-band leader? Think of the booty I shall bring back for you from my raids!'

She smiled. 'It is a role I always knew you would fulfil. Even before I married you, I knew you would become a Good Man.' Her smile faded, and she became more serious. 'Tell me,' she said. 'Your decision, has it anything to do with Medicine Jacket?'

Winter Man frowned at her. 'His name is Skins The Wolf.'

'It is a name that is losing favour.'

'It is still his name.'

'Has it anything to do with him?'

His hesitation told her what she wished to know, and her heart sank.

'To say "Yes" is to speak only a half-truth, as is to say "No".'

'He goads you because of me, Winter Man. Twice he tried to make me his wife. I would not go to him.'

His fingers gently lifted her chin and she looked up into his face. His dark eyes seemed unusually bright, unusually deep.

'I am pleased you threw the turnip at me and not at him,' he said.

A kernel of warmth burst in Moon Hawk's heart. It sent a glowing heat down her every fibre, making her whole being pulsate with her love for him. It lit her eyes, and it lit her smile. It made her want to sing, to run down the hill and feel the wind in her hair. It made her want . . .

She slipped her hands inside his robe and curled them about his neck, drawing his head down to hers as she fed her fingers through his hair. Their kiss was the sweetest she had ever known, but its delicacy made her hunger for more. She rose to her knees so that her mouth was level with his, and she flicked her tongue across his lips. His arms tightened about her, threatening to crush the breath from her body, but her blood was up and she would not yield. It was Winter Man who drew his mouth away.

He tilted back his head to see her face more clearly, and arched an eyebrow. 'Here?'

'Here!'

'In the snow?'

'In the snow.'

A grin spread across his face, showing a perfect set of teeth. As he untied the neck-thongs of her robe, an irrepressible light simmered in his eyes. 'I might get to like this,' he murmured.

She stretched back her head and gave her weight to his strong, supporting arms, luxuriating in the fiery arousal his merest touch could evoke.

'I already have,' she whispered back to him. 'I already have.'

The wind blew cold, the snowfalls continued, but each day the sun climbed a little higher in the vastness of the blue-grey sky and slowly, so very slowly, the land began to thaw. Flocks of geese honked noisily as they winged their way north to their breeding-grounds. Buffalo, which had wintered in the sheltered valleys, made their first tentative forays out on to the grasslands ready to bear their calves. In the Apsaroke village the warrior societies called their men together.

Moon Hawk laid down the moccasin top she had been decorating with porcupine-quills; she had made too many mistakes already. Her mind kept wandering to the Fox lodge, to the rituals she could only guess at, where a pipe was passed from man to man until one brave enough to carry the responsibility, strong enough to accept the taboos, to endure the penalties, took the stem and bowl in his hands and drew on the sacred smoke in a vow and in a prayer. There were many Fox warriors, only four officer positions, yet it was said that even the strong-hearted shrank back when the pipe was offered to them. Winter Man was strong-hearted, and Moon Hawk knew that he would not shrink back.

Oh, that he would! That she could have persuaded him to give her one year of marriage without the worry, without the gnawing fear, of his loss! But how could she? How could she have wept and begged him to forget all that he was, all that she loved him for? He would have despised her. She would have despised herself.

She wished, now, that she had gone with Jay to listen outside the lodge to the singing of the society songs. Jay had begged her to go, but she had been afraid. She had wanted to distance herself from the choosing, as if, by being out of earshot, she would somehow undermine Winter Man's determination, somehow make him think again. Foolishness! Stupidity! When he emerged from the lodge holding the symbol of his officership he would expect to see her. He would expect her to be the first to press forward with her congratulations.

She rose quickly, spilling porcupine-quills right and left over the furs which had made comfortable her seat. She reached for her wearing robe as she hastened to the doorway. How could she think of disappointing him? She was his wife.

Many people were gathered outside the Fox lodge, some sitting, some standing. Children played catch with a soft hair-filled ball, shouting directions and encouragement to each other as they ran about; but the adults were strangely quiet, strangely hushed in their meagre conversation. Moon Hawk sighted Jay and made her way through the throng to stand at her side. She was large with her child now, and stood with her hands resting comfortably on her swollen abdomen.

'Ah! You decided to come. I am glad.' She inclined her head towards the Fox lodge. 'They stopped singing some time ago. Everyone is waiting now.'

There was a sudden movement among the crowd. The children stopped playing and stood to watch as the door-flap to the Fox lodge was thrown back and the leaders emerged. Moon Hawk drew her breath and held it, clasping her hands in front of her in her anxiety. Winter Man was first out of the lodge behind the leaders. Standing tall and proud, he raised aloft for all to see a model emblem of his new office.

A hooked stick! He held a hooked stick! Her husband had become a hooked-staff bearer. He would carry it at important gatherings, when the village moved, during raids on their enemies. If the men were threatened, he would be the one to dismount and stand alone against their foes.

She felt an arm slip about her shoulder and gazed up into Jay's smiling face.

'Do not look like that! You should be happy for him. Listen to the people salute him. Be proud!'

And proud she was as she looked about at the jostling crowd and listened to the trilling and the lip-clapping adulation Winter Man and the other chosen officers were receiving. They deserved it. They were strong-hearts. They were Fox men.

Moon Hawk pulled herself free from Jay and ran across to where Winter Man stood to fling her arms round his neck. He looked bemused and a little embarrassed.

'I have not done anything yet!' he reproved.

'But you will, I know you will. I am so happy for you.'

Hillside came and struck him playfully in the shoulder. 'I may not be the first, but I congratulate you all the same.'

Moon Hawk smiled at him. For two whose lives were so strongly entwined, it seemed odd that he had not sought to become a bearer. 'Are you to be the one who will cut the true staff with him?' she asked.

Hillside shook his head. 'He has honoured Bear On The Flat.'

'My father?' She looked at him incredulously and saw a sadness flicker across Hillside's guarded eyes.

'He gave an impassioned speech inside the Fox lodge. He filled every man's heart with power. He knows he can be a Fox no longer. He can hardly walk, even with the help of a crutch, and it pains him to ride. He is an old one before his time, but Winter Man has honoured him, and I am proud that he has.'

She turned back to her husband, but he had already left her side. He was walking back towards the Fox lodge, to help Bear On The Flat over the threshold. She watched them move away together, Winter Man respectfully taking her father's pace. Was it her imagination, or had he changed from that indignant Good Young Man she had thrown the turnip at? She decided that he had, and she smiled a little, contented.

Jay was sitting at the edge of the fast-flowing creek, dabbling her feet in the water, waiting for the swelling in her ankles to subside. An old woman skilled in childbirth preparations had given her a medication for the complaint which was attacking her regularly now, but Jay said it tasted foul, and dabbling her feet in the cold creek worked just as well. Moon Hawk filled the water-paunches and watched Jay wince with her pain. If she could have helped her in any way, she would have done so.

There was a crashing through the bushes, and two young girls almost fell down the bank into the water. Both dragged wearing robes behind them, and one had a bundle under her arm.

'The Lumpwoods are wife-stealing!' she cried.

Jay and Moon Hawk looked at each other and burst out laughing.

'It is not funny!' the other girl scolded. 'Flyer promised me that he would not steal me from my husband, then he comes and starts singing outside our lodge! I only managed to escape by squeezing under the back of the cover!'

'It is your own fault,' Jay admonished. 'Everyone has known that the wife-stealing was about to start. Why did you not leave when the other women did? You *want* to be stolen!'

'No! No!'

Strains of the wife-stealing song drifted towards them over the water.

'Well, you will be,' Jay told her, 'unless you move fast!'

The two young women lifted their dresses and waded across the deep creek.

'If they come, do not tell them we went this way.'

'I shall!' Jay shouted back. She turned her head towards the source of the singing. 'Here, Lumpwoods! They are here!'

Moon Hawk rapped her sharply on the arm. 'Do not do that.'

'Why not? She wants to be stolen. It is fun to be stolen.'

'And what of her husband? I do not think they have been married long.'

Jay snorted derisively. 'Him? Ha! If he shows how he feels, he will be ridiculed from here to the next snows! Think of the presents she will get if she allows herself to be stolen. The elk-tooth dress alone will be worth three good horses.'

Moon Hawk turned away, not wishing to continue the conversation.

'What is the matter with you? You are not eligible to be stolen. You have never been the lover of a Lumpwood.' Jay faltered. 'Oh,' she said. 'It is not you, is it? It is Winter Man. You are afraid that he will steal back one of his lovers and bring her to your lodge.' Jay considered the matter a moment. 'He will not do that. Hillside stole back one of his lovers last year, but he did not bring her to our tipi. She lived in his father's lodge for a few days, and then he presented her with a horse and told her to leave.'

Moon Hawk looked pointedly at her. 'And how did you feel?'

'When she left?' Jay shrugged. 'Relieved. But Hillside is a Fox. It is his right. I knew it when I married him. If he had not tried to steal back one of his lovers, the other Foxes would have laughed at him.'

She picked up her moccasins and pushed her feet into them, fastening the ties across her ankles. Moon Hawk watched her, her heart empty and flat. Winter Man was not Hillside. If Winter Man stole back one of his lovers, he would bring her to their lodge and expect Moon Hawk to welcome her.

Jay stood and picked up one of the water-paunches. 'I have to admit, though, that I would be worried if I were you. Have you seen the way Swallow has been dressing lately? And you know which society Horse In The Night belongs to. If ever there was a woman waiting to be stolen, it is Swallow.'

Moon Hawk shuddered.

They walked back towards the lodges, through the knots of watching people. Snatches of the wife-stealing song could be heard quite clearly. The hunting Lumpwoods were riding through the village, showing off their finery. There was a lull in the singing, and then male voices raised as if in the striking of a coup. Jay caught hold of Moon Hawk and made her stop and listen. Sure enough, when the singing started again, the song was one of triumph and derision.

'They have taken a woman!' Jay grinned. 'I wonder who it is?'

Moon Hawk did not want to know who it was. The two warrior societies tried to out-score each other in the stealing of one another's wives. If the Lumpwoods had gained a Fox's wife so easily, Winter Man would surely steal Swallow. What would she do when he brought her to their lodge? What could she do?

The Lumpwood men came close and the people pressed forward to see who they had taken. There were six Lumpwoods, dressed in their brightest clothing, their faces painted in their society colours, their arms marked with their war honours. Skins The Wolf rode at the front of their rank, his scarlet Medicine Jacket flapping open at his chest as his painted horse pranced left and right as though it was dancing to the song they sang.

'I notice *he* did not become a staff bearer when the Lumpwoods elected their officers,' Jay muttered in disdain.

'Did you expect him to?'

'Hillside did. Evidently Winter Man and Medicine Jacket had a big argument, which ended in Winter Man vowing he would become a Fox staff bearer. Hillside was sure Medicine Jacket would have become one, too, so as not to lose face. Did Winter Man not speak of the argument?'

Moon Hawk shook her head, watching the Lumpwood men as they passed with their stolen woman sitting behind her captor. The women in the crowd trilled for them, the men and boys shouted encouragement and clapped their lips. She had done so herself on previous occasions, but she had not the heart for it now.

Winter Man was sitting at the back of their lodge, his full-sized society staff lying across his thighs. He was tying red ribbon streamers to the otter-skin wrapping, and did not look up as Moon Hawk entered and pulled the door-flap behind her. She regarded his bent head a moment before stepping to one side to hang the water-paunch on its peg above the wood pile.

'There,' he said. 'It is done.'

Moon Hawk turned and looked at him. He was still sitting, but he had pushed the sharpened end of the staff into the ground beside the fire-pit and was admiring his workmanship. He raised his hand and flicked the eagle feathers he had attached to the curved head, one feather for each of his coups. She had to admit that it was a most awesome banner of his courage.

'When I dismount to jab this into the ground and stand before it singing my Medicine song, our enemies will think twice before trying to cut *me* down!'

She smiled at him, though he did not see her. He was proud that he was a Fox staff bearer, and she was proud of him, too. If only . . . She took a deep breath to steady herself.

'The Lumpwoods have started their wife-stealing.'

'I know,' he said. He chuckled, but his mind was still on the otter-skin wrapping of the staff he was fingering. 'We took more wives than they did last year. Running Fisher let it be known that we would give them a day's start.' He looked up at her, his eyes alight with mischief. 'A better taunt I could not have thought of myself!'

'They have already stolen one woman.'

He nodded, unconcerned. 'I heard the singing. We shall still get more.'

'Are—are *you* going wife-stealing?'

'I shall be riding with them, yes.' Moon Hawk felt her world fold in on her. She watched him raise his face again. This time his eyes held a softer light. 'But I shall not be stealing any lovers.'

Moon Hawk knew her eyes were widening, but, try as she might, she could not stop her own reaction. Winter Man shook his head and laughed.

'Did you think I would?' He rose and stepped across to her, holding her tenderly by the shoulders. 'Moon Hawk, I have a wife. What would I want with another, even for such a short time as a stolen wife would be kept?'

Moon Hawk felt slightly giddy. Her blood was surging through her veins and she did not know whether to laugh or cry in her relief. Was he truly doing this for her?

'There—there is prestige to be gained in stealing back a lover . . .' she began.

He took her chin with the tips of his fingers and raised her face so that he could look into her eyes. 'And what is there to be lost?'

He reached down and kissed her on the lips, slipping his arms behind her back to give power to the embrace. She leaned against his chest and let her eyelids close upon the world.

Outside, growing louder as the riders drew near, the Lumpwood wife-stealing song rose to a crescendo.

The lodge shook beneath a blow from a riding quirt.

'Come out, Moon Hawk! I know you are in there! Medicine Jacket is claiming you!'

Moon Hawk twisted in Winter Man's arms and stared in horror at the doorway. This could not be happening! A man could not call out a woman who had not been his. It was a dream. A nightmare!

CHAPTER SEVENTEEN

'COME OUT, Moon Hawk! Come out to Medicine Jacket!'

The tipi covering began to blur before Moon Hawk's staring eyes.

'He lies,' she breathed. 'He lies!'

In her panic, her blood began to surge through her veins. She turned back to Winter Man, her eyes frantically searching his face for a reason she could understand. 'Why is he *lying*?'

Winter Man's face had turned ashen. His lips moved to speak, but no sound came out, and his hands slipped down her arms until they hung limply by his sides. He shook his bowed head and gazed at the ground. 'I have been a fool.'

Moon Hawk stared at him. 'Fool? What are you saying?' She pointed out beyond the lodge covering. 'A man cannot claim a woman who has not been his lover! He is *lying*!'

He backed a pace and looked at her. 'It makes no difference. He has called you out. I can do nothing . . .'

'*Nothing?*' Moon Hawk's voice reached almost a shriek. 'He is lying!'

'I know.'

She stared at him, at the man she called 'husband', at the man who had just told her that he cared more for her than for the prestige to be gained in stealing back a lover.

'Lies!' She jumped forward and beat her fist on his chest. Winter Man did not flinch. 'It is all lies. All your words, all your actions, our marriage—*everything!* You do not love me! You have never loved me!'

'I do, Moon Hawk.'

'No! Tell me nothing, Winter Man! I know what you will do. You will sit here hiding in this lodge with your heavy heart until the Foxes ride for the Lumpwood wives—and then you will go and steal Swallow!'

She lifted her hand for another blow, but he caught

her wrists and held her from him, lowering his head until their faces were level. Moon Hawk could hardly see him for the tears bubbling from her eyes.

'I will have you believe many things, Moon Hawk, but I will not have you believe that! I have no intention of stealing Swallow. I do not love Swallow. Swallow is not the only Lumpwood wife I can call out. Three are eligible this year, but I shall not be stealing any of them. I do not love any of them. I have *never* loved any of them.' The fierceness of his tirade melted away.

'I did not realise it, but I only ever loved myself before I married you.' He paused again. 'It was you I learned to love, Moon Hawk, and though I shall never be able to look at you again . . .'

Moon Hawk jerked her arms, trying to break free of his grasp. She knew what he was going to say. She did not want to hear it, did not want to believe the finality of its truth, but Winter Man would not let her go.

'*Listen*, Moon Hawk, *understand*. If a Fox man weeps for his stolen wife, he is jeered by the people, shunned by his friends, children sing songs about him—not for a day, not for a month, perhaps for a year, perhaps for the rest of his life. I am not just a Fox man; I am a staff bearer, an officer of the society. When I smoked that pipe and took the hooked stick into my hands, I did not just take it for myself, I took it for all the younger men, the inexperienced men, for all the people of this village. I gave my oath. I gave my pledge. I vowed that I would act honourably in every thought, that I would bring no dishonour to the society. I cannot stand against Skins The Wolf, Moon Hawk. I *cannot*.'

He let slip her wrists and stood to his full height, his hardening gaze fastened somewhere above her head. 'And Skins The Wolf knows it!'

Moon Hawk rubbed her burning wrists. She was trembling, her legs threatening to give way beneath her. It had been planned. Skins The Wolf had planned this from the start, to hold her husband to ridicule, to get her for himself although she had rebuffed him so often. There would be no fine gifts to accompany her back to her father's lodge, Moon Hawk realised. Skins The Wolf intended keeping her. She would not be allowed to leave. He would beat her if she tried—beat her like a dog!

'Moon Hawk! Medicine Jacket speaks for all to hear! If you do not come out to me, I shall come into that lodge and take you! Ask Winter Man if he wants to see you dragged out before his eyes!'

Winter Man drew a deep, steadying breath. 'He will do it,' he murmured.

Moon Hawk nodded. She knew he would, too. She looked up at her husband, drinking in the sight of him, impressing every contour, every outline of his face into her mind to sustain her through her empty life. Slowly, so very slowly, his eyes lifted to hers. Their gaze was long and lingering, full of what they had shared together, of what they might have shared.

'I love you, Winter Man.'

He turned away, his voice breaking. 'Do not make it worse. Just go to him.'

'Go to him?' Her eyes traced the curve of Winter Man's bent shoulders, the fall of his dark, unbound hair. Somehow, somewhere, she felt a burgeoning of courage. 'I am not going to Skins The Wolf,' she said. 'I shall face him and I shall call him what he is: a liar.'

Winter Man turned back to her. 'No! Listen to me, Moon Hawk; you are a woman he is calling out. He is a respected warrior with coups to his name. Whatever you say, you will not be believed. Try to shame Skins The Wolf, and his revenge will be beyond imagining. Moon Hawk . . . !'

But Moon Hawk was decided. Before Winter Man could pull her back, she stepped out of the lodge and closed the door-flap behind her.

'Ai-ee!'

The cry of triumph which issued from the mouths of the waiting Lumpwood men was so shrill that Moon Hawk hesitated. There were six, sitting astride their horses in a semi-circle a few paces from the doorway. Skins The Wolf was a little in front of the others, the sun glinting off the bright discs on his scarlet Medicine Jacket. Behind them, pressing forward with laughing, eager faces, were people from nearby lodges who had come to watch. They were so many, and she a woman alone. The truth of Winter Man's last words came winging back to her.

Skins The Wolf thrust his quirt up into the sky. 'A Fox's wife has come out to a Lumpwood man! Moon Hawk has come to Medicine Jacket!'

Moon Hawk drew breath to cast her denunciation at his feet, but her voice was drowned in the noise that rose and met her. There was trilling from the watching women, lip-clapping from the men. The Lumpwoods were singing their victory song. She could not be heard. Skins The Wolf walked his horse towards her, expecting her to climb up behind his saddle. She was trapped between him and her own tipi and the edge of the jubilant crowd.

There was nothing else she could do. She balled her fist and brought it sharply down on the horse's nose. It reared back, startled, and Skins The Wolf had to fight to keep it within his control. He bared his teeth in his anger and brandished his quirt in her face. The cheering of the crowd began to subside.

'You *lie*!' she spat at him. 'I have never been yours. You have no right to stand before my lodge and call me out! Name yourself Skins The Wolf or Medicine Jacket, it makes no difference. You are worse than a Shoshone dog of a man. You have no honour! You are a *liar*!'

The gasp that swept round the waiting crowd sounded like an autumn wind whistling through dead leaves. Moon Hawk blinked; stunned, herself, by what she had said. Even the Lumpwood men were sitting open-mouthed on their horses in front of her.

The stony expression of Skins The Wolf broke into a smile and then into a grin. He laughed. He laughed long and loudly, and turned to embrace in his raillery all those who watched. The people shuffled, undecided. It was an offence against First Maker to call out a woman who was not eligible. He leaned over the pommel of his saddle and peered down at her, his lips curling into a sneer. His eyes seemed so bright, so very large: Moon Hawk had to force herself to stand straight and unflinching before him.

'Try to discredit me, would you?' He sat upright in his saddle and pointed at her with his quirt. 'It is this woman who is the liar! She was my lover. I courted her with a flute and she shared my buffalo robe. This was near the bend in the creek of the last village site, the place of the marsh.'

Moon Hawk gasped. She knew the place. She had fled from him there! But she had told no one of their confrontation, and had no witnesses she could call to her defence.

'You lie!' she cried.

Skins The Wolf chuckled as one might at the antics of a child. 'I have proof,' he said simply. 'I can prove you are the liar.' He turned to the man beside him. 'Owl, do you remember the day I met you along the creek and spoke of my seduction of Moon Hawk?'

The Lumpwood nodded. 'It had been raining. The creek was full, and ran brown with silt. You showed me your robe. The blood of her maidenhood was fresh on its wool.'

Moon Hawk rocked back on her heels. Owl, too, was lying! How could he?

But Owl was not lying, she realised. She saw disquiet in his eyes, not malice. He could not understand why she stood against Skins The Wolf. Skins The Wolf had lied to him, too. And so long ago. Had it been just for this moment? Had he planned it from the first?

'It is lies,' she repeated, weakly. 'All lies. I have never been his.'

Owl frowned. It was plain that he was not at all easy with what was happening. He extended his hand to her. 'Moon Hawk, there is no dishonour in being called . . .'

Skins The Wolf slapped the thonging of his quirt down on the man's arm. 'Do not appeal to her! Take her by force!'

In the moment of doubt, when the Lumpwood men looked to each other for support, Moon Hawk backed towards the tipi, hoping for a chance to escape. Her only refuge lay in gaining her father's lodge, though what help Bear On The Flat could be she did not know. Little Face would help her. The two of them would fight with knives and awls, but could two women, an old grandmother, perhaps, keep six men at bay for long? What clan-sisters could she call upon? Practically none. How could anyone believe what she said against the proof Skins The Wolf had proclaimed? Jay would help her if she could, but the fight that would ensue would be without mercy, and Jay, so close with her child, might lose it with an injury.

All round her, hands were being raised to open mouths in a show of stunned astonishment. Even the Lumpwood men were staring in awe at something beyond Moon Hawk's shoulder. She dared to turn and look behind her.

Winter Man was standing there, his expressionless face painted in his Fox society colours, his eagle-feathers hanging from the back of his unbound hair. He wore the coup shirt he had gained when he had taken a gun from a Lakota, the one with the hair-lock pendants ranged along the sleeves. In his left hand he gripped the beaded shaft of a battle-axe. In his right he held his hooked staff, the emblem of his rank in the Fox society.

The sight of him confounded Moon Hawk. He could not stand against Skin the Wolf—he had explained that, and she understood—but with a weapon in his hand? Was he going to call Skins The Wolf to fight? How *could* he? Did he not realise what it would mean? His family, his clan, would be disgraced. If he killed Skins The Wolf, everything he owned would be forfeit, perhaps even his own life. He would be driven from the village, naked and beaten, to live as a wanderer, despised and derided by every Apsaroke who came across him. Was he doing this, courting this fate, in protection of *her*?

She lifted a hand to him, but he swept past her without acknowledgment, to stand tall and proud before Skins The Wolf.

'Ha!' the liar scoffed. 'Winter Man comes to take back his wife! His heart is soft like a young pup's. It squeals in anguish at the thought of his loss! And such an unworthy dog as he would be a Good Young Man, even stand as an officer of the Fox!'

He laughed contemptuously, turning in his saddle to seek derision from the growing crowd, but hardly a one offered him the support of a smile. It was right to scorn a man who could not accept the stealing of his wife with an unaffected air, but what man ever stood before the captors as Winter Man was doing?

Moon Hawk desperately searched the many faces for an orator who would step into the space between her husband and the Lumpwood men to offer counsel before harm was done, but she could see no man who would offer himself for the role. Every member of the village seemed to have assembled in front of her tipi. They were peering over each other's shoulders to gain a better view of what was happening—or about to happen. She felt sick with fear. Was there no one to help?

Winter Man jerked his head, sending a succession of ripples snaking down the length of his unbound hair. His eagle feathers lifted like graceful wings to hover a moment before settling back on his blue-black hair. The movement was slight; it took no time at all, but it was enough to focus the people's attention, to quell the rumbling of their spoken thoughts. It was enough to fill every heart with awe.

'Not only do you lie when you call this woman out, Skins The Wolf, and lie when you speak before these witnesses, but you lie to your brother Lumpwoods, to the men who would ride by your side and die willingly in the protection of your life! As I stand in the shadow of First Maker, hear this: the woman, Moon Hawk, knew no man before the exchange of marriage gifts. She held her maidenhood sacred until she gave it up to me, willingly, when she became my wife.'

A rush of horrified murmurings engulfed the crowd. The Lumpwood men sat as still as stone upon their horses, their jaws slack, their eyes large in their astonishment. Moon Hawk thought she could almost see them blench beneath their society colours. Skins The Wolf was staring down at Winter Man, just staring as if his life had stopped for him, as if all power to think or move had been wrenched from his grasp.

'Malicious spirits have devoured your heart, Skins The Wolf. You are the festering sore which slowly grows and kills a man. You are the enemy within. I hold the hooked staff of the Fox . . .' Winter Man shook it gently, making its ribbon streamers and white coup feathers dance upon its otter-skin wrapping. 'I pledged to stand alone before the enemy and not retreat. I do so now.'

He raised the staff in the air and plunged its sharpened end into the ground by his side. While the force of the blow still shuddered up its length, Winter Man calmly passed his battle-axe from his left hand to his right and slipped his wrist through the strap. Cradling the weight of the weapon in his hands, he took a single step forward, and balanced himself ready for attack or defence.

The crowd fell back, aghast. Moon Hawk clasped her hands to her mouth to stifle a cry. Every instinct told her to call him back, to run the three paces that separated them and drag Winter Man away from this suicidal confrontation. She was not worth this: not to him, not to anyone!

There was a movement in the Lumpwood ranks. Owl was pulling his horse back, out of the middle of the group. As though they had been waiting for his signal, the other Lumpwood men began to drag on their mounts' jaw-thongs, wishing to be gone. Skins The Wolf stood in his stirrups and roared like a whirlwind, thrashing left and right at his men, catching them cruelly with the long thonging of his riding quirt.

'Heartless fools!' he spat at them. 'He stands before you, and you run like women! Look at him! It is Winter Man you see, the seducer of maidens and other men's wives! I, Medicine Jacket, am the coup taker, the leader of men, the one who is blessed with Weather Medicine! I speak with the rain and the wind and the snow. I fly with the Thunderbird. And you are afraid of *him*?'

Moon Hawk watched the Lumpwoods falter and closed her eyes in her anguish. They did not know whom to believe, and Skins The Wolf was going to talk them round. He was going to make them face Winter Man!

There was a hubbub among the crowd as a man forced himself through. Moon Hawk heard the noise and prayed it was a mystic, carrying a pipe and a sacred bundle, coming to call a halt to the encounter before blow countered blow. When she opened her eyes she saw it was not a mystic, but her own father hobbling awkwardly towards them on his crutch. He positioned himself slightly behind Winter Man's left shoulder and lifted his arm to call for silence so that he could be heard.

'Know me! I am Bear On The Flat. Think not that I am this man's father-in-law. Think not that I am a fellow Fox. Nor am I this man's clan-brother, for we are of different clans. I stand here because I am Apsaroke. My legs are buckled and weak, but my heart is strong. Rather I die here today than live the rest of my life as a lie the way Medicine Jacket lives his!'

Again the people gasped as one. The Lumpwoods moved restlessly on their horses, still undecided.

Another forced himself through the crowd—Hillside —wearing his coup feathers, a club in his hand. He stood to the right of Bear On The Flat, a little behind Winter Man. He made no speech, but every man and woman present knew what was in his heart. The Lumpwoods knew what was in his heart, and their shoulders sagged with the weight of their decision. Another came— Antelope Dancer—Moon Hawk's elder brother. Her heart began to fill with hope as she watched him take his place behind Winter Man.

Frost! And Running Fisher! A Good Man come to stand behind her husband! She could not believe it, dared not believe it. Tears were blurring her vision, streaming down her cheeks, but her anxiety was gone now. They were tears of happiness, of relief. She brushed them aside. Who came now? Runs His Horse? The sight of her second brother entering the widening space in front of her tipi brought to her the full implications of what was happening. Never had she expected Runs His Horse to stand behind Winter Man! He was a Lumpwood, and he stood as a Lumpwood, in his society regalia. He had with him a short robe, such as a child might wear. He did not speak, but cast his gaze over his fellow Lumpwoods, before bowing his face and placing the robe over his head, so that no one might see the shame standing in his eyes.

The Lumpwood men broke away. Skins The Wolf turned first to one and then another, trying to rally them, but it was no use. They had decided who was lying. They had decided it was he.

Astride his horse, Skins The Wolf sat alone, alone against Winter Man, alone against the whole of the Apsaroke village. Moon Hawk could see the desolation in his eyes. Why did he not turn his horse aside? Why did he not give an indication of his defeat, that the confrontation was over? She willed him to submit, but he just sat there, his cold, empty gaze fixed on Winter Man.

His jaw tightened, the muscles bulged in his arm. She drew breath to shout a warning, but Skins The Wolf moved so fast that there was no time to cry out. His mount plunged forward at his command and he raised his quirt to strike at Winter Man—but Winter Man had seen the action. Side-stepping the horse, he raised his axe to block the blow. Moon Hawk held her breath, expecting him to turn and follow through with the blade, to cut Skins The Wolf across the back, but Winter Man only turned to watch his assailant kick at his horse's belly and gallop away through a gap opening in the crowd.

It was over.

The people began to murmur, then to talk. There was trilling and lip-clapping, and men pressed forward to congratulate Winter Man on his courage. Moon Hawk fought her way through it all.

'Winter Man! Oh, Winter Man!'

He saw her, and he smiled a little, and she ran into his welcoming arms. He held her tightly, lifted her off her feet and crushed her to him as if they had been parted a life-time. Her heart swelled with love for him, for she knew that to him a life-time had passed while he had stood against Skins The Wolf.

'I was so afraid,' she whispered.

He set her back on the ground and looked into her eyes. 'So was I,' he said. 'Afraid of losing you to another man, afraid of the ridicule I would bring upon myself for fighting for you; and then I heard you speak, and the sound pierced my heart. I could not let you stand alone.'

She smiled up at him. 'It was not just for me that you stood against him.'

He looked down, and a heavy breath whistled uneasily through his parted lips. 'No,' he admitted.

'It was for the people,' she told him. 'You stood for the people. It made me very proud.' She lifted her hand to touch his cheek and he raised his eyes to look into hers.

'I would have stood against him, just for you. I would have fought him, him and the others, if they had forced me.' He sighed. 'It makes my heart shudder to think of this, but I would have killed him, Moon Hawk. I would have shamed myself for all time and killed him, rather than watch him take you to his tipi.'

She nodded. 'I know. If you had, and his clan-relatives had let you live and had driven you out of the village, I would have followed you, even into the wastelands.' She watched him frown, watched his surprise steal his words.

'You would?'

She laughed, and flattened her hand against his chest. 'Can you not feel it? Feel it, here? I am Moon Hawk! I am your wife!'

He smiled and placed his hand on top of hers. 'Yes,' he said. 'You are my wife, and you will be for as long as it takes the mountains to crumble and the sun to die. I love you, Moon Hawk.'

She bit her lip to stop herself from crying out in her delight. He loved her! He was so sure of it now that he told her in front of everyone. He loved her!

'I love you, too,' she murmured, and she hugged him all the tighter.

Moon Hawk felt a prod, and turned to find her father gazing happily at her. 'You have a brave husband, daughter. Take good care of him. He will become a Good Man. He will become an orator of his people. I know it.' He looked Winter Man in the eye and nodded. 'I have always known it.'

'Yes, at the very least an orator,' Hillside added. He

winked at Moon Hawk. 'You chose well when you threw that turnip at him!'

Moon Hawk chuckled at the memory, and turned back to Winter Man with a scurrilous look in her eyes. She pursed her lips.

'Yes,' she said, self-satisfied. 'I did.'

Winter Man merely laughed and pulled her to him.

EPILOGUE

THERE WAS JOY for many that day, but not for all. Skins
The Wolf left the village in disgrace, but his family—his
aunts and uncles, his brothers and sisters—remained to
face the shame he had brought upon them. It was a
shame, they felt, that was too deep to bear. To repair the
damage their kinsman had done, they offered gifts of
horses and robes to Winter Man, which he accepted
quietly, without recrimination, and gave to the needy.
The dishonoured relatives pulled down their lodges and
packed their belongings. Wearing their poorest clothing, as if in mourning, they left the village to seek shelter
with the Apsaroke who lived to the east.

Of Skins The Wolf no more was heard directly. Later
that spring, a family group of Hidatsa visited relatives
among the Apsaroke and told of how they had seen a
man in a scarlet shirt which had dazzled their eyes.

'There was a storm,' the teller said. 'We sought shelter
in a stand of trees, but the man would not join us. He
rode back and forth in the rain and the wind, laughing
and shouting abuse at us. One moment he was there, the
next the Thunderbird opened its great beak and flashed
its huge eyes, and the land turned white and shuddered.
Then the man was gone. When the storm was over, we
looked for him. He was dead. The Thunderbird had
pierced him with its light.'

Winter Man knew the place the Hidatsa spoke of, and
he and Hillside rode out to it. They found the man's
remains, his horse's too, but the scavenging animals had
done their work well and not enough was left to be
certain of identifying him, even of identifying the scarlet
shirt which dazzled.

Late during a fine, crisp spring afternoon, Jay bore
Hillside a healthy daughter. On the fourth day of her

life, Winter Man sang prayers over the child and gave her the name Sunset.

During the season in which Winter Man held his office as hooked-staff bearer, he brought prestige to the Fox society and to himself. In the first encounter with an enemy raiding party he counted a grand coup, the war honour he needed to raise himself to the status of Good Man. When the Crier called the names of men he wanted to take on a horse-raid against the Lakota, the men came willingly to smoke his pipe. The raid was successful. No man was lost, no man was injured, and the stolen horses numbered more than one hundred and fifty. In the three days it took to mount the raid, Winter Man had become more wealthy than he had ever dreamed. He held a feast, and promptly gave all the horses away. There would be other times. There were other times. Winter Man's Medicine was strong, and the people knew it. He became a leader of his people, and Moon Hawk stayed his one and only wife.

A SIREN'S LURE

An international jewel thief called 'Le Chat Noir.'
A former intelligence officer suspected of being a Russian spy, gone to ground in Capri.
A young woman anxious to find her father.
The lives of these characters are cleverly interwoven in this intriguing, contemporary story of love, drama and betrayal from Andrea Davidson, author of THE GOLDEN CAGE.

Available in September, Price £2.50.

WORLDWIDE

Available from Boots, Martins, John Menzies, W. H. Smith, Woolworths and other paperback stockists.

NOW ON VIDEO

Two great Romances
available on video . . .
from leading
video retailers
for just
£9·99
R.R.P.

The love you find in Dreams.

From Autumn 1987

MASQUERADE

YOU'RE INVITED TO ACCEPT
2 MASQUERADE ROMANCES
AND A DIAMOND ZIRCONIA NECKLACE
FREE!

Acceptance card

A BATTLE OF PASSION AND DENIAL

Freed from her tedious existence in England, Catrina sets sail for Gibraltar and her long lost family. She finds herself caught up in the tensions within the home and the onset of war with Spain.

Catrina falls hopelessly in love with the captain with the silvery eyes – the one man forbidden to her.

Can the secret of their illicit love remain hidden in an unforgiving society?

A colourful and stirring romance from Christina Laffeaty.

Available October Price £2.95

W●RLDWIDE

Available from Boots, Martins, John Menzies, W H Smith, Woolworths and other paperback stockists.